finessed

play chess or get check'd

LOWKEE

EEE NOTE
PUBLISHING

dedication | discipline | determination

eezy ..
this one is yours.
thank you.
for all of it.
-kee.

kee note.

WHILE THE CHARACTERS and events of this book are fiction, they are not impossible. In some way or another, you may very well relate to at least one character &/or event. In fact, I hope that you do.

More importantly, I hope that this story encourages you to take a deeper look into your past. I encourage you to take a look into your childhood trauma(s). After reading this story, I encourage you to seek therapy. I encourage you to seek a safe space where you can share your story, speak your heart, live in your truth and work towards becoming the healthiest, happiest, most healed version of yourself.

one
abuelita.

EVERY NIGHT BEFORE BED, I put my earbuds into my ears and listen to *"Back Door" by Pop Smoke*. When I was younger, whichever artist was my favorite at the time would blast through my speakers so loud that I could feel the bass rattle through my body. It was therapy. It was a shelter. Music has gotten me through some of the most horrific times in my life. It seems like the only thing that can silence the noise enough for me to fall asleep at night, is music.

As a child, I would hide in a little nook between my bed and my nightstand, covering my ears with my hands and humming as loud as I could in order to block out the sound of my father beating my mother up and down the hallway of our two bedroom apartment.

Whenever my mom would yell out, "Lexy close your door, Baby!"

I knew that regardless of her sweet tone, it was going to be a bad night. After about a year of the same ol' bullshit from my dad, Ma purchased my first set of headphones. You would think she would pack our shit and leave his ass, but no, she bought headphones to block out the sound, instead. I can't lie, some part of me was grateful for that because the sound of my fathers bare fist hitting her skin while she screamed for him to stop was painful for me to listen to. On the other hand, I was old enough to know that even though the sound of her cries were muted by the music, she was still crying.

Lucky for me, Daddy isolated his domestic violence behaviors to my mother and my mother only. Even though some part of me hated him for hurting her, I was still daddy's little girl. Every morning after a big fight, Daddy would be gone when I woke up and I would find my mom in the bathroom nursing her wounds. That was always the time my resentment would kick in.

"Ma, we have to go to the doctor." I would always say.

Her reply was always the same. "Lexy, Mama is fine. I'm just clumsy, that's all."

Being clumsy and being beaten are vastly different, but she'd cake some makeup on, slap some sunglasses across her face and then go outside and act like nothing had ever happened. I had no choice but to follow her lead; she was not only my mother, she was my best friend. I guess it was some sort of apology to me, but we would spend the day doing girly shit like shopping or getting our nails done and she would talk to people about my dad like he was some fucking saint. We'd be in the car and she'd talk on the phone to whoever the fuck would listen and act like her and Daddy were *Bonnie & Clyde* or some shit. Meanwhile, they were really *Ike & Tina*. I hated that for her. I hated it for us, really. But once Daddy got back home, all of my resentment would melt away and I was daddy's little girl again.

He would walk through the front door saying, "Lady-bug, where you at?!"

And I'd come running from my room to jump into his arms and retrieve whatever toy he had brought back for me. My daddy bought my forgiveness and my mommy bought my ignorance. It was a very sick cycle that happened way too often. First he'd beat my mom up, next he'd disappear for the day, then he'd come back with a stack of cash for my mom and a toy for me. It worked every time, so I guess it makes sense that nothing ever changed. Not until I was seventeen years old, anyway. That was the year my life changed forever.

The entire day had been weird from the moment I had woken up. My mood was sour as fuck for no reason at all. No bullshit, I had a stank ass attitude and I knew that it was not the day for anybody to try me because I was ready to pop off for whatever, no matter who it was. My mom and dad were both on some other shit that morning, too, which made matters worse. They were being sneaky. I'm not sure if sneaky is the proper term to use but they were just moving around the house a lot differently than they normally would and it was noticeable. I couldn't put my finger on what was sneaky about their behavior, but I knew the shit was off because other than the nights Daddy would beat on Ma, we lived a pretty routine life. It was a good life. I mean, we didn't have everything, but Daddy always made sure we didn't want for nothin'.

Any other day, my mom would drop me off at school and I'd catch a ride home with my best friend Sydney. But on this particular day, along with her already sneaky behavior, Ma told me that I would have to figure out how to get to school on my own that morning. It made shit even more weird and made my attitude even worse. First of all, my mom loved taking me to school. It was like our bonding time. The fact that she was so casually choosing to miss out on that time, really blew my mind. Secondly, my dad wouldn't usually go for no shit like that. My daddy thought I was too pretty to do anything even remotely strenuous so walking to school should have been completely out of pocket and I genuinely expected him to come to my defense. But that morning, he co-signed my mom's declaration. You know what, I'm lying. It wasn't actually that weird. See, when my dad wasn't beating my mom's ass, they were two peas in a damn pod. They were best friends; very, very childish best friends. But Ma was really Daddy's ace boon. On good terms, the two of them together were as annoying as being the only sober person around a bunch of drunk people. On good terms, their love was pure and passionate. It's very unfortunate that on bad terms, their love was poison.

It's hard to believe that this is just a memory because as I recall that day from four years ago, it feels like I'm still presently in the moment. I guess that's what a memory that lasts a lifetime feels like. The emotion it sends through my body makes me feel like I'm still experiencing this memory and I guess in some ways, I am. Anyway, as I was saying, I had to hit the two-ten to school that morning. Two feet, ten fucking toes. I couldn't believe I was walking to school. The only upside to walking was that I could listen to music as loudly as I wanted to. Since my morning was already thrown off I just hit shuffle on my playlist instead of choosing a specific song. I was hoping that whatever song that played would change my mood.

Mask Off by Future began to vibrate through my ears as thoughts of confusion and betrayal swam through my mind. Alright, look, that sounds dramatic as hell, but I'm an only child and my parents spoiled the fuck out of me. What do you expect? On my way to school I kept thinking about how I was going to run away from home because it was obvious that my parents didn't love me anymore. Granted, I was just going to go to my abuelita's house, but my broken heart kept telling me that my parents needed to feel my absence since they had my ass walking to school.

School was probably the only thing that felt normal that day, thank God. After my last class, Sydney and I met in the quad area like we always did after school. She wanted me to braid her hair that day and usually, we'd go to my house, but I was obviously beefing with my parents, so I told her that we'd go to Abuelita's instead. To add insult to injury, I hadn't heard from my mother that entire day. I didn't always agree with the decisions she made but Ma was really my dawg.. We'd usually text each other throughout the day, but that day, I chose not to say anything to her because I was still salty that she had me walking to school. The gag was that she hadn't said anything to me either, which was weird seeing as though she shouldn't have had any beef with ME! But the audacity to not even check in with me to see if I had made it to school safely, really sent me. Like, what the fuck, MOM?! You know?

Abuelita is the sweetest and purest person I have ever known. I'm ready to raise hell behind her any time, anywhere, and for any reason. She's my maternal grandmother and when I was first born, my daddy had gone to jail for a few months on some drug charges so my abuelita basically moved in and helped my mom take care of me until Daddy came home. We've been damn near inseparable since then. Unfortunately, as she gets older, her health declines more and more. She doesn't move around the house like she used to. More specifically, she doesn't get down in the kitchen like she used to and that's what I miss the most about her younger years and mine. Because of that, by the time I was sixteen, I started to make it a point to spend weekends at her house so that I could just help her with little chores and errands and keep her company. Her house was also closer to my job than my house was, so it worked out well. Anyway, being that I was feeling some type of way about my mom and dad making me walk to school, I was planning on spending the whole week at Abuelita's.

Now, Abuelita was always happy to have me at the house, hell, I have my own room at her house too. But whenever I would bring Syd with me, she was over the moon with excitement. Honestly, I loved that for her. I loved seeing her heart be filled with so much joy because her joy was infectious. My relationship with God, my ability to pour into myself the way that I do and my ability to do anything even remotely domesticated is all because of my abuelita. There is truly no love like hers.

"Abuelita! Hola, Mami!" I yelled out as Syd and I walked through the front door.

I understand Spanish very well, but don't speak it well at all. Abuelita always spoke to me in Spanish when I was growing up and I always replied in English. My mom is one hundred percent Puerto Rican and doesn't speak a lick of Spanish either, so outside of Abuelita, I didn't really stand a chance because Daddy was Black and grew up in New York. That nigga barely spoke English properly but he spoke money fluently and made sure I did, too

Abuelita stands at all of about four foot, eleven inches. Watching her rush from the kitchen to greet me at the front door, brought peace to my mind after a day full of chaos. Even though Ma and I were really close, Abuelita was my emotional sanctuary; she still is today. That's yet another reason why I love her so deeply.

She squealed, "Oh, Mija!" once she realized I wasn't alone.

She embraced Sydney's face into both of her hands.

"Hey Abuelita, girl!" Syd replied with more energy than Abuelita.

They embraced one another for a hug.

I walked past Abuelita and Syd and said, "Mami! I'm about to braid Syd's hair and then I'll help you clean the kitchen, okay?"

"¿Tienen hambre chicas?" Abuelita replied.

"¡Mucho!" I said as I walked back to give her a kiss on her forehead.

Sydney knows less Spanish than I do, but she's spent enough time with Abuelita to catch a few things here and there. Kinda.

"I heard "hambre", does that mean hamburger? Because sí!" That was Syd's way of saying that she was hungry, too.

Abuelita headed right to the kitchen. Although she wasn't able to throw down in the kitchen like she used to, she always made sure there was a hot meal for me and whoever was with me.

The way Abuelita's house was set up was so that you could walk through the kitchen to get to any room in the house. Syd followed behind me as I headed to my bedroom. As soon as she got into my room, she began to comb her hair out while I removed packages of braiding hair from a box underneath my bed. That was typical for us. I had a job at a local sneaker store, but my real passion was braiding hair. Lucky for Syd, she was my best friend, so she was always my guinea pig when I wanted to try new styles or products.

Syd was sitting down in the chair and going through her

phone while I chose a playlist to be the soundtrack to our gossip about high school shit. As soon as I started separating the braiding hair, Abuelita burst into my room. She was crying hysterically. Sydney and I were both shocked and I dropped the hair and paused the music

Abuelita had never come into my room that way before and I'm not sure I had ever seen her cry in my entire life. It seems like everything happened so fast because the next thing I remember was her speaking Spanish to me quicker than I had ever heard words come off of her tongue. Between the tears, the Puerto Rican dialect, and the trimmers in her voice, I couldn't make out what she was trying to tell me.

"English, Mamí! English!" I kept yelling.

As Abuelita tried her best to gather herself, I was checking her body for blood. The way that she was crying, I just knew that she had to be hurt. There was no other explanation in my mind.

"Tu Mamá." She said with pain in her voice as tears rolled down her cheeks.

My heart stopped.

Abuelita was finally able to control her emotions enough to find the English words she was searching for. "Your mother! Your mother is in jail!" She screamed.

At that moment, my mind had too many thoughts for me to feel any emotions. *Jail is better than death*, I thought to myself. But I was worried that if my abuelita didn't calm down, she'd be the one that was dead. I had always been pretty mature for my age but that was the day I had really become an adult because Abuelita was in no condition to be that for me. It was a good thing my daddy was a street nigga because he always taught me how to stand ten toes down in the midst of chaos and confusion.

"Don't ever let a nigga see that they got you pressured up!" He always told me.

There had never been a moment in my life where I had to exercise my understanding of any street lessons he ever taught me but they were never lost on me.. Whatever pressure Daddy was referring to, had never found its way to me. But with Abuelita in shambles, Sydney crying and finding out that my mother was in jail, pressure had finally found me.

There was no time for me to get the details about why Ma was in jail or where my father was because I had to make sure that Abuelita survived the chaos. The issue was that Sydney was almost doing just as bad as Abuelita was and I think that it was making everything worse.

I looked Sydney directly in her eyes and said, "Syd. Take a deep breath!" as I wrapped my arms around Abuelita.

"Breathe." I said calmly to Sydney. "I need you to go get Abuelita a glass of water."

I knew that if I gave Sydney a task, she would be able to snap out of her trance of emotion. Syd and I had experienced lots of tricky situations together in school because we weren't necessarily the most liked amongst the girls because we were most liked amongst the boys This particular situation was trickier than anything we had ever experienced though, because it was family and not a situation we could fight our way out of. Instead, there was absolute chaos behind it because Abuelita was losing her shit and we didn't really have any details about WHY my mother was in jail.

Daddy had always taught that when shit gets tricky, I need to move like I'm an OG. That basically meant that I needed to take control of the situation. Sydney's father had come from the streets just like mine, but we were raised differently. Syd can hold her own but she gone cry while she does it.. She's just emotional. Seeing somebody that she loves cry, makes her cry. Hell, seeing somebody cry that she doesn't even know will make her cry. She's like a sensitive ass thug but I time for that. While she rushed to the kitchen to grab a glass of water, I sat Abuelita down on my bed and guided her through a breathing exercise. I don't even know where I learned that type of shit from, I just knew that if my grandma didn't catch her breath, she might have had a heart attack or some shit.

Syd finally made it back with a glass of water and Abuelita was finally able to catch her breath. I, on the other hand, was losing my shit on the inside, trying my best not to show that I felt pressured up and praying to God that Abuelita was able to pull through.

"Abuelita, you scared me. You have to stay calm. Keep breathing in your nose and out of your mouth. Everything will be fine. I know it will." My tone was calm, but my heart was beating a million times per second.

Sydney and I sat on either side of Abuelta as she continued to catch her breath and find some peace.

"Stay with her. Please. I gotta call my dad." I told Sydney as I began to walk out of the bedroom.

I definitely needed to catch my breath but calling my dad was the only thing I knew to do. Abuelita didn't mention anything about Daddy and it made no sense at all that Ma was in jail. Now that I think about it, I don't even know where Abuelita received her information from.

Anyway, as you could imagine, I was nervous. I was confused. And the guilt of not having spoken to my mom the whole day started to take over my emotions.. I sat on the couch in the living room and took a long deep breath before going to Daddy's contact in my phone. Some part of me was afraid he wouldn't answer. Each time the phone rang with no answer on the other end, my heart sank deeper into my chest and it became harder to breathe.

"Hey, Ladybug." He finally answered with a somber tone to his voice as if shit was sweet

I caught my breath. "Daddy!" My eyes swelled up with tears. "Where's Ma? What happened? Where are you?"

My dad's voice was calm. Almost soothing. "Everything is fine, baby. We got pulled over and the police searched the car and found a gun. Your mom said it was hers, so they arrested her. She'll be out soon. Stay at Abuelita's and let me take care of this. We'll pick you up when she gets out."

"But, Daddy.." For some reason, rage came over me.

Still very calm, Daddy said, "Lexington Rae. Not today. Please. Let me take care of this. I love you. I'll see you soon. We will see you soon." He assured me.

Tears rushed down my face. So much for not letting niggas see that they had me pressured up. "I love you too, Daddy." I tried my best not to let my voice crack, but I'm sure Daddy heard the pain in my voice.

That was the end of the phone call. There was nothing for me to do and no more information for me to gather.

Syd and Abuelita must have come out of the bedroom during my brief and less than informative conversation with Daddy, because they were sitting at the kitchen table. As I walked toward them, they both looked at me as if they expected for me to have some answers. Unfortunately, I didn't. I didn't say a word to them as I sat down to join them at the table. There was nothing for me to say and nothing any of us could do but wait.

Even though Daddy was calm and he did his best to reassure me that every thing was going to be fine, I was still shook that my mom had been arrested. And on a gun charge at that.

two
jimmy.

"LEXY, MAMA IS FINE." My mother said to me in the same sweet tone I remembered from my childhood..

She wasn't fine. She wasn't fine when she was nursing her wounds and she wasn't fine on the other end of that phone. I wasn't fine either. The fact that I was talking to my own mother while she sat in jail really fucked my head up. It had been three days and she was still in jail. Come to find out, the gun she claimed to be hers, was Daddy's gun. I'm not sure why Abuelita and I were pretending to be shocked by that news because like I told you, Ma thought that her and Daddy were somebody's fucking *Bonnie & Clyde*. What I couldn't understand was why my daddy would allow my mother, his best friend and partner, to take a charge for him. Daddy had priors, yes, and I'm assuming that had the police known that it was his gun, he would've gone away for a very long time but even then, I felt like letting Ma take the charge was trash. I couldn't figure out what part of the streets that was and I couldn't recall a time Daddy ever taught it to me. As much as I loved him, I knew that he was a coward for that.

Ma ended our phone calls with that same line for three days. I don't know, maybe some part of her really felt like everything would be fine. Maybe some part of her knew it wouldn't but wanted me to believe it would, the same way she wanted me to believe that she was fine after Daddy beat her up. I was angry with her. Angry that she made me walk to school that day which caused us to miss out on our morning bonding time. Angry because had she taken me to school, she wouldn't have been in jail. Angry because she took a charge for my daddy, the man who beat her ass on a regular basis. Don't get me wrong, Daddy was good to her. He was good to us. But no matter how good he was to either of us or how much I loved him, I knew at a very early age that he was no good for either of us. The pressure of my mother being in jail paired with only hearing from him once, maybe twice after he told me he'd take care of everything, made it even more clear that Daddy was no good and nothing was fine.

Abuelita was more stressed than I had ever seen her before and I was beginning to worry about her because she wasn't healthy enough to endure that level of stress. And her only child being in jail because of a man that she wasn't even particularly fond of seemed like it would have sent her straight to heaven. My heart ached for my abuelita. My heart ached for me.

For three days, we were on auto-pilot. I'd sleep in a chair next to Abuelita's bed each night just to make sure she was okay. There wasn't a chance in hell that I was going to school for those three days because not only did I not feel comfortable leaving Abuelita alone for that extended period of time, but I also couldn't focus for shit. Sydney would stop by to bring us food each day, but we were barely able to stomach anything. We fed our spirits with prayer as

Abuelita would say and that was the only thing keeping us going.

On night four, as Abuelita slept, I placed one earbud into my right ear and allowed myself to listen to *R & B* music. I hadn't listened to music in three days but for some reason, on the fourth day, I was under more pressure than I had been the days before and decided that I needed to finally attempt to decompress. I think the pressure was beginning to cave in on me. The weight of Abuelita's pain combined with the thought of my mother having to suffer through the jail system and my father not only allowing it but also not really showing up for me the way that I needed him to was becoming too much to bear.

My playlist had probably gone through three songs before I was finally able to doze off. My soul was tired, my heart was heavy and my mind was in overdrive so I thought I was dreaming when I heard the sound of the doorbell.

"Mija. Mija, wake up." Abuelita said softly as she tapped my knee to get my attention.

Realizing I wasn't dreaming, I quickly removed the earbud from my ear and said, "What's wrong, Mami?"

Abuelita slowly began to rise from her bed using my knee as a crutch. "Somebody's at the door, Mija. Maybe it's Isabela and Jimmy. Come on."

It was the first time in four days I had seen hope in Abuelita's eyes and felt peace in her spirit. Someone was at the door and Abuelita assumed that it was my mother and father. Abuelita's hope gave me hope. Her peace gave me peace. The truth was that there wasn't anybody else it could've been other than Daddy and Ma. Sydney wouldn't have come that late and it wasn't like me and Abuelita had sneaky links pulling up in the midst of chaos or at all for that matter.

As Abuelita opened the front door, we quickly learned

that chaos was exactly what stood on the other side. Two police officers stood with notepads in their hands as hope and peace escaped me.

The female officer said, "Hi, ma'am. We're looking for the guardian of Lexington Williams, is that you?"

Abuelita looked up at me with pain and confusion in her eyes. Shit, I looked at her just the same. I hadn't done anything wrong. The police being at the house to see me or my guardian was just as confusing to me as it was to Abuelita.

Placing her hand over her chest, Abuelita replied, "Si. Yes. That's me. I'm her grandmother." You could hear the pain in her voice.

I didn't have time for introductions or small talk so I quickly interrupted. "I'm Lex. What's up? Why are you here to see me? Or my guardian or whatever?"

The female officer shook her head and greeted me. "Hi, Lex." Her tone was soft. Sentimental, almost.

The male officer cut in. "Ma'am, can we come inside?" He looked down at Abuelita with compassion and sincerity in his voice.

Abuelita began to step aside to let the officers in but I quickly remembered my daddy telling me to never let a police officer come inside of your house or look inside of your property without a warrant. I gently placed my hand onto the center of Abuelita's back, preventing her from moving any further.

"No. You can tell us what you want right here." I said with an attitude.

The male officer took a deep breath and said, "We're here about James Williams." He took a moment to look both of us in our eyes before he looked down at his notepad again.

"That's my daddy. What about him?" My defenses were up.

Abuelita grabbed my forearm as if she were bracing herself.

"Sweetheart, I'm sorry. Your daddy was involved in a fatal collision." The female officer said.

The space between my ears became empty as my ability to hear completely disappeared. My heart became too heavy for my chest as the weight of the officer's words anchored atop of that already broken heart. Those same words acted as a tornado whose strong gust of wind caused Abuelita to lose strength in her legs. Her body crashing against mine like waves, both of us lost in a sea of tears.

Tuh. So much for that warrant because the next thing I remember is sitting on Abuelita's couch as the officer's sat across from us explaining that daddy had gotten into a police chase and crashed into a building causing him to die on impact. There were no words for me to say. No thoughts for me to think. I could only feel.

Finally, "Why was he running?" Not sure the answer really mattered because Daddy was dead, but it was the first and only sequence of words I was able to put together.

Abuelita's body was cradled into mine as we sat next to each other sharing the same pain.

Both of the officers took a deep breath and looked at one another before the female officer began to speak. "Lexington, we believe the gun that your mother was in possession of, was used in a double homicide. We attempted to make contact with your father as a part of our investigation and that's when the pursuit ensued."

I almost threw up. All the pain, all the pressure, all the anger I felt, tried to escape my body. As quickly as I could manage, I gathered myself. "Get out! LEAVE! You don't have a right to be here! Get out of my house right now!" I was yelling. Screaming, even.

The nerve of that bitch. They came to my Abuelita's house to tell me that my father died and then attempted to imply that my mother was in possession of a gun that killed two people. A double homicide? They had to be fucking kidding me. Abuelita was on her hands and knees praying-- crying her heart out to God.

My rage transitioned into complete grief. As I tried to stand up to show the dickhead officers out of Abuelita's living room, I realized I didn't have the strength. My body collapsed to the floor and there I was cradled next to Abuelita, in shambles. I was crying for my daddy. Crying for my mommy. Crying for myself. Over the course of four days life as I knew it, no longer existed.

After about twenty minutes of doing their best to console us through a series of the most tragic events we had ever experienced, the officers asked us if they could call anyone to be with us. We were all we had left. I had Abuelita and she had me. That's it. The officers left their business cards on the living room table in case we had any other questions. Of course we had questions, tons of them. But we would never have the answers. The answers we needed would have to be laid to rest with the only person that could truly answer them, my daddy. James "Jimmy" Williams. My first love and as of that day, my first heartbreak.

Abuelita and I sat in stillness for a while after the offi- cers left. The only sound that filled the room was the sound of both of us sniffling to prevent being snot faced. We sat there hand in hand as Abuelita rocked back and forth. My mind was so empty that I could hear the sound of my heart beating between my ears.

Neither of us got any sleep that night. Neither of us said

a word either. The next morning, the phone rang and some part of me hoped it was my daddy telling me that he *finessed* the officers and was on the run. Wishful thinking, I know. Instead, I had a collect call from Isabel Colón.

My eyes swelled up with tears at the thought of having to tell my mother that her best friend, the man she took a gun charge for, was dead.

"Hello?" She said, anxiously waiting for the response on my side of the phone.

I tried to be as strong as I could be in the moment. "Ma." There was so much pain in my voice.

There was no way to build up to sharing the tragic news. There was no way to console her as she stood at a jail phone all alone and that made things worse for me. At least Abuelita and I had each other. Ma was all alone.

As soon as I attempted to give her the news, "Oh, Lexy. Baby." My mom began to cry hysterically over the phone.

She couldn't even finish whatever it was she was going to say but it was obvious that she had already known what I was going to share.

The sound of pain in her voice made it hard for me to stay strong. My mother had always stayed so strong throughout my childhood. She never once allowed me to see that she was under pressure, even in the worst times. I just wanted to be that same source of strength for her at that moment, but I couldn't. I had no strength to give. Sadly, we didn't have time to discuss whether or not she knew about the potential charges she was facing. Hell, knowing that my daddy had died was probably enough torture for one day, anyway.

The next three months were the hardest for Abueltia and I. We planned and attended my fathers funeral while my mother sat in jail. In fact, we learned that she'd be sitting in jail for the foreseeable future because they pinned the deaths of two individuals I had never heard of, onto my mother. With Daddy dead and Ma trying to stand her ground on claiming the gun but not killing anybody, she didn't stand much of a chance at getting off. Shit, you know 12 don't give a fuck who takes the charge as long as their arrest stats are up. Plus, we didn't have the money it required to retain a lawyer long enough to fight the case properly and the public defender they assigned her was trash.

From the bottom of my heart, I do not believe my mother killed anyone. I don't even believe her when she says that the gun was hers, but for some reason, she was standing on that and sitting in jail. My heart ached for her because she sat in jail for a man that would beat her ass whenever he was upset with her. She sat in jail for a man that didn't protect her the way he should've. If he had done his job, she wouldn't have been in jail in the first place. Shame on my mother for being so loyal to a man, that she forgot to be loyal to herself.

Essentially, I lost both of my parents over the course of three months; Daddy in a grave and Ma in the system. Luckily I still had Abuelita. There was no question of where I would live or who would be my guardian for the few months it'd take me to turn eighteen because Abuelita wouldn't have tolerated anything other than me living at her house with her being my legal guardian. Honestly, I needed her just as much as she needed me. Sydney was a great help in keeping my thoughts out of the dark, but there was only so much that she could do. She could only understand the pain Abuelita and I felt to a certain extent and so in some ways, it caused me to disconnect from her a little bit.

After we laid my daddy to rest, I never stepped foot at his gravesite again and I never picked up the phone when my mother called. Of course she and Abuelita spoke often, but at that point in my life, I carried a lot of resentment toward my mother. It wasn't her fault that Daddy had died, but somehow I held her accountable.

three
dré.

EVENTUALLY, I had to get back to life -- or start my new life. My job allowed me to take as much time as I needed to heal; my position was secure. It wasn't like I was working at some top notch-reputable company, I was working at a shoe store so I didn't really care whether or not my position was secure but I did appreciate it. My high school was decent enough to allow me to homeschool through a majority of the chaos. Sydney would bring my school work to me each week and then turn it in to my teachers for me when I completed it.

At some point I had decided that I wanted to get back to a sense of normalcy. Three or four months was really no time at all to heal through everything that I had experienced but I figured the only way I'd get over everything was by going back to school and work. Plus, Daddy always said not to let niggas see that they had me pressured up, remember?

Getting back to school was really for the birds, but such is life. As you would imagine, I graduated and turned eighteen years old without my parents being present. My mom sent a letter and made it a point to call me for both of those milestones, but I wasn't really trying to hear from her. Abuelita passed the message along and that was really enough for me. Abuelita had enough love and encouragement to share with the entire graduating class, but there was still a sense of emptiness inside of me without my parents being present to share that love with me. I'd come to accept that the emptiness would always be there. Even today, as I look back to share this story with you, there's a piece of me missing. I'm not sure there's ever really a way to fill the void of losing both of your parents the way that I did. Anyway, going back to work was actually a life changing event for me as well. Who would have thought?

When I went back to work, I decided to take an opening shift because I figured there would be fewer customers and it would give me a chance to ease back into the groove of working again. My first morning back at the store, a young boy came in eyeing a pair of *Yeezy's*. After I greeted him, I noticed that he had to be all of sixteen years old, no drip, his line up didn't exist and the kicks he was wearing were trash. Basically, I knew there was no way he was going to be able to purchase a pair of *Yeezy's* on his own so I was thinking he was probably going to ask to try on a pair and then run off. Listen, I'm from Detroit, niggas get got every single day so it wasn't anything new to me but for whatever reason, I was contemplating whether or not I cared if he stole them. As soon as I came to the conclusion that I didn't care, another nigga walked into the store.

"Yeah, grab them." He said to the young boy.

It was obvious that this man was either the boys big brother or big homie; he wasn't old enough to be his father. Either way, it was clear that he was the one that would be paying for the *Yeezy's* the boy had his eye on.

The boy turned to me and said, "You got these in a ten?"

Looking at him and then his big homie, or whoever he was, I said, "Yeah, I got you." I was almost looking for the big homie's permission.

While I was in the backroom grabbing the shoes, I took a quick look at myself in the mirror. My hair was in a high messy bun and I had on a uniform polo, but Sydney made sure that my lashes and brows were always on point, so I didn't look too crazy. See, whoever the big homie was, he was fine as fuck and from the looks of it, he had a bag. Granted, he wasn't wearing anything but basketball shorts and a pair of 1's but he was also wearing a *Rolex* on his wrist and a buss down cuban around his neck. It was a light flex but it was enough to let you know that he had money and didn't particularly care about flashing it. My daddy had always taught me that *Rolex* was an investment piece.

He'd always say, "A nigga with a buss down Roley is doing it for the bitches, not for his family. Choose the nigga that's doing it for his family."

Basically, Daddy always believed that if a nigga bussed his Roley down, he didn't truly understand the value of money.

The man who I thought to be the big homie was covered in tattoos and his line up was crispy as fuck. His waves were dip'nn too and his hair was almost silky which led me to believe that he was Black with a touch of some other race. At the time, my guess was that he was about six foot one, maybe six foot two and weighed about two hundred pounds. I hadn't necessarily found my angle to shoot my shot yet, but taking the shoes out so that the boy could try them on was obviously a start. As I walked back onto the floor, the boy already had his shoes off, eager to try on what I'm willing to bet were his first pair of *Yeezy's*.

"Oh, you READY ready, huh?" I said with a smile as I handed him the shoes.

The boy laughed.

"Don't do the lil homie like that." Fine Ass, said.

We all laughed.

I remember thinking to myself that I wasn't even going to have to do much work to pull him because I already had him laughing. Anyway, while the young boy tried on the shoes, I asked Fine Ass if he wanted to try anything on but he respectfully declined.

"What up doe? What's yo name?" He asked, leaning against the cashier counter as he waited for the young boy to make a decision.

I'm sure there was a sparkle in my eye when I replied, "I'm Lex. Who are you?"

He could've *finessed* me out of my panties right then and there. "Ok, Lux Lex. I'm Dré. What yo pretty ass doing working here? Yo nigga must not be doing his job."

You know I was flattered by the nickname; Lux Lex had a nice ring to it, but I had to keep my cool. "First of all, ain't no nigga. But even if there was, I do what I want to do." I said.

The young boy brought the shoes over to the counter and then walked back over to his seat. It must have been a rule for him to stay out of the way or something. You know, sort of like the whole stay in a child's place type thing. Naturally, I checked the box to ensure that the shoes were the correct size and a matching pair before I rang up their purchase.

Dré didn't miss a beat. "Shit, that all sounds good but what is it that you ACTUALLY want to do?" He looked me dead in the eyes when he asked that question.

His gaze had me feeling pressured up. I thought I was running game on him but somehow, the tables turned and he was running game on me. Hoping that he couldn't tell that I felt the pressure, I said, "I braid hair, why? You trying to put some money on my salon or something?"

Dré reached around the register and grabbed a pen from behind the counter. I watched as he pressed the receipt machine so that it dispersed clean receipt paper.

"You play your cards right and I'll buy the whole salon." He said as he wrote on the receipt paper.

With a smirk on my face, I handed him the bag of shoes and said, "Niggas always want to promise the world."

He smiled, took the bag that held the young boys shoes and simultaneously handed me the receipt he had written on. "Here. Tap in. I like yo fake ass attitude."

I snatched the receipt paper from him and rolled my eyes as if I didn't care. I'm sure he knew just as well as I did that I was hype.

As he and the young boy made their way out of the store, Dré looked back and said, "You pretty as fuck, too!"

After that, we were damn near inseparable.

In the beginning, Dré and I being together was a little harder than necessary because I refused to tell Abuelita about him. You see, with him being twenty-three years old and me just turning eighteen, I knew she wouldn't approve of our relationship. Granted, I was technically an adult but I still lived under her roof and I had no desire to add any extra stress to her life. Dré was a really great man who came from a well put together family. The issue was that he was very different from his family. In fact, he was almost exactly like my daddy which gave me even more reason to believe, or know, that Abuelita wouldn't subscribe to our relationship under any circumstance.

With that being said, as far as Abuelita knew, I was spending more time with Sydney's family, picking up more hours at work and braiding hair more often. I mean, none of those things were really blatant lies except the part where I wasn't actually spending more hours at work. After our first six months of being together, Dré had me quit my job. Remember he told me that my nigga must not have been doing his job when he first met me? Well, when he became my nigga, he felt like his job was to take care of me and teach me how to get money. The way he saw it was that if I knew everything he knew, then if shit ever went bad, I could hold us down until he was back up. He also really believed in my vision of owning a braiding salon and creating my own luxurious braiding hair. He felt as though in order to achieve those things, I needed to learn the art of hustling.

"You can't be an owner without understanding hustle, Lux. Ain't no hustle in selling shoes unless you sellin' them out the trunk." He would always say.

Deandré Lamont Givens is Dré's government name. Eventually, I learned that he comes from a Black father who happens to be a highly decorated Veteran turned Software Engineer and a White mother who runs a successful home based business. Truth be told, no matter how much Dré has shared with me about his parents, I still have no clue what type of business his mother had. Dré's father had always been the tough love type of guy, while his mother had always been the unconditional love and support type of woman. A really good balance, if you ask me. I'm not sure where the disconnect first started because Dré was never really one to go into the details of it, but he has an older brother who he never really got along with at all. Trévon and Dré were polar opposites as far as I knew. Tré followed in their fathers footsteps and became a Software Engineer, married his high school sweetheart and had two children; a boy and a girl.

Obviously the boys grew up in the same household, received the same parenting and education; a private-school education, yet, they took completely different paths in life. By middle school, Dré had ditched all of his private school classmates and made friends with a few of the boys from the public school up the street. In turn, he also made friends with all of the girls from that same public school. The boys always followed his lead and the girls couldn't get enough of him. Regardless of his choice in friend groups, Dré always maintained a 3.8 or above grade point average, but he was also selling drugs in his free time. Trévon knew about Dré's extracurricular activities because Dré tried his best to recruit his older brother into the crew. When I say crew, I don't mean gang. If it makes any difference at all in how you view Dré, he had no gang affiliations whatsoever. In fact, he literally got along with everyone. The people's champ, if you will.

Unfortunately, along with the tough love that his father provided, came a power struggle. Now, there's no way for me to know whether or not Dré's father knew what his son was into as a school-aged boy, but I'm willing to bet my life that he knew by the time Dré was on his own.

Dré graduated high school and didn't even consider college while Trévon applied to every prestigious college there is. Dré never punched a clock or earned a legal dollar in his life while Trévon worked two jobs and did tutoring on the side to earn his money. Same environment, different hustles. Dré was the black sheep of his family and the only person it really took a toll on was his mother. She practically begged Dré to show up at family functions and tried her best to encourage a better relationship between him, his father and his brother, but it just never worked out that way. Sadly, the only way she'd get to communicate with him was if she reached out--he never initiated contact.

Dré would always tell me that he felt as though his brother felt entitled but didn't understand where the sense of entitlement stemmed from. He also felt as though Trévon judged him for his lifestyle. Dré was doing better financially than Trévon was but that never created a sense of entitlement or superiority in Dré's mind and he felt as though it shouldn't have created it in Trévon's mind either. He would never say this out of his own mouth, but Dré felt as though his father and brother were jealous of him and as much as he loved his family, he knew that there was no room for jealousy in any part of his life.

I came to the conclusion that he believed his dad and brother were jealous of him one day when he and I were talking about something Sydney had said to me that didn't sit well with me.

Dré said, *"Jealousy will get you killed out here, Lux. I don't care if it's Sydney, or somebody else, if you think a bitch is jealous of you, she's out. We don't play that jealous shit over here. Niggas got the same twenty-four hours I got. How are you jealous I used mine to elevate? And if you can't be happy from your heart to see other people elevate, how you think you gone elevate?"*

That was the day that brought everything full circle for me. It was the day that I realized that although the issues he shared with his brother and father from childhood had carried over into adulthood, in Dré's mind, they posed too much of a threat to his livelihood to try mending those relationships.

About a year into our relationship, I told Dré that he needed to introduce me to his mother regardless of the beef he had with the rest of his family. You can imagine how happy she was when he reached out to invite her to dinner with us. For her, it was the opportunity to hug her son, hear his voice and have a peek into a small portion of his life. For him, it was the opportunity to introduce us to one another so that he wouldn't have to deal with her as often. The way he saw it, well, the way that it was, was that I was an extension of him. Therefore, she could communicate with me instead of, or more often than she did with him. She and I both knew that she'd get more compassion from me and more detailed updates about his life than she would ever be able to get from him. It didn't take long before she and I were talking on the phone at least once a week so that she could update me on her life and feel like she was in the loop on Dré's life. I'm not going to lie, at that point in time, I hadn't seen or spoken to my own mother in almost two years, so for me, having a relationship with Dré's mom filled some empty parts of my spirit. It was a win for all of us.

In some ways, Dré and I shared a trauma bond as it related to our family dynamic. The same way I felt as though he should, at the very least, communicate with his mother, is the same way he felt I should communicate with mine. My argument was always the same, he wasn't there the morning my mom made me walk to school and he wasn't there the day the police told me that my daddy was dead. On the other side of that, Dré's rebuttal was always the same, I had no clue what his childhood was like so if he was able to take his mom to dinner for me, I should be able to visit my mom in jail for him. At some point, I gave in and promised that once he taught me enough of the game for me to start making real money, I would start visiting my mom and putting money on her books.

**four
ma.**

OVER THE COURSE of our relationship, Dré had taught me everything he knew about the streets and what it meant to be a hustler. They say the realest nigga on your team is your girl and that quickly began to ring true for us. That's not to say that the rest of the crew wasn't full of real niggas, but I was Dré's right hand man. He didn't make a decision without involving me, even if he felt like it was too dangerous for me to be physically present. He would always tell me that there was something special about me; he believed that I was directly connected to some *other worldly powers*, as he'd put it, and because of that, I was his good luck charm. As far as I was concerned, I was protected by my abuelita's prayers and my daddy's spirit so if that was what Dré meant by other worldly powers, then he was right.

Remember the young boy from my old job? The one that was with Dré when he and I first met? They call him Blanco. It's funny because the complexion of his skin mimics rich dark chocolate; smooth and milky, nothing "blanco" about it. They called him Blanco for two reasons;

the first one was because that was how he came into the game and it took him no time at all to catch on and cash the fuck out. He very quickly became one of Dré's key players. The second reason was because he only fucked with white girls; the blonde hair, blue eyed kind. None of us understood it, but we didn't knock him for it. There was just one rule: don't let no white girl fuck up the bag or compromise the crew. Blanco was my right hand man, my security guard, my chauffeur and my personal DJ. Whatever I needed, Blanco got it done. He was like a brother to me. Well, the truth is that Dré wouldn't ever allow me to be alone so he assigned Blanco as my protector. There really was no other option except to embrace the ridiculous amounts of time Blanco spent in my space.

When Dré decided that I was officially his girlfriend, he turned to Blanco and said, "Lux Lex is worth more than your entire life, Blanc, so you protect her as if your life depends on it--because it does."

Dré wasn't a killer, but he meant what he said. I know that because Blanco took his position in my life very seriously. If I chose to sleep at Abuelita's house for any amount of time, Blanco was always parked right in front with the burner on his lap. If I chose to have a girls night with Sydney and just go out for drinks, or a movie or whatever it was, Blanco was always in my line of sight. The only time Blanco wasn't there was if Dré was and even then, whether we were on a date or just outside in general, somebody from the crew was ducked off somewhere paying attention to the things Dré couldn't.

You know, it sounds crazy to compare the worth of one person's life to that of another, but somehow, every nigga in our crew valued my life more than they did their own. It was like they had some sort of secret law of loyalty and royalty and it was some shit that must have been put in place well before I became part of the crew. I respected it, of course, just as much as I respected and valued each of them. Dré wasn't an uptight boss, or big homie, but he was definitely about his business. He was very particular about the ebb and flow of his business and his relationships. It didn't matter if it was street business or something legit, he had always believed in leading his crew with tough love but making sure that he also provided a place for them to call home. To be clear, when I say place, I mean that both physically and mentally.

Truthfully, I think that he ran the crew the way that he wished his father had run their household. I also believe that it was the reason why the crew valued me so much; because they valued him. He made sure that every nigga in the crew knew how to get money with or without him. He made sure they all knew how to clean their money, too. Besides money though, he made sure he taught them how to feed their minds. So the crew was really a family and truth be told, any of them could have left the crew and did their own thing but they all saw the value in being under Dré's command. Between me and you, as I look back on that portion of my life, I realize now that as much money as the crew made together, they were each way more valuable than they allowed themselves to believe. They actually allowed themselves to stay in a box working under Dré's command, but I guess that's how the game goes.

Being that Abuelita was under the impression that I was still working full-time at the shoe spot and part-time braiding hair, I was able to spend most of my nights at Dré's penthouse. She always assumed that Sydney was driving me from my job to whatever location I needed to be at to braid hair and that I was sleeping over Syd's house. The truth was that even though Dré had gotten me a Range Rover, Blanco was taking me wherever I needed to be. Now, when the crew would go out and do nigga shit, I would sit up in the penthouse and write out my goals and create vision boards or use that time to chill with Abuelita. Dré had really changed my life. Besides taking care of me entirely, he had also put me in a position to make some real money.

Abuelita didn't know this, but he was taking care of her, too. I'd give her money every month to cover whatever she needed and she always assumed that I was just working hard. And I guess I was, but not in a way she could iagine. In addition to all of that, my dream of owning a braiding salon and developing luxurious braiding hair was beginning to feel like it was actually possible because of Dré. He was willing, able and ready to keep his word from the day we met and buy the whole salon for me, but twenty-one years old was right around the corner for me and I wanted to gift myself with a salon. With all I had been through with losing my parents and Abuelita's health steadily declining, I wanted to feel like I had taken charge of my own life. Dré would never take back anything he gifted anybody, but I wanted to have something I felt like no one could take away from me, even if it took a little longer than I hoped.

One night after the crew had been out doing whatever it is they do, Dré walked into the bedroom just as I was adding a new possible hair manufacturer to my list of resources. He'd never been much of a drinker, but I could tell that he had some drinks that night. His eyes were low and his speech was much slower than usual. Whenever he would drink, he would speak slowly because he wanted to make sure that he chose his words wisely. Another lesson Dré always taught us was that, as soon as the words come out of your mouth, they become bond to whoever heard them -- make sure your words always work *for you* and *never* against you.

"Words are powerful, make sure yours are profitable." He would always say.

That night, Aa he watched me write the manufacturer name on the list he slowly said, "I'm proud of you, Mama. This shit gone change yo life. You special and I love that shit."

With a partial smile on my face I said, "Thank you, Baby. You changed my life. I wouldn't be writing this shit down if it wasn't for you." My cheeks were warm. Even after two and a half years, Dré could still make me blush.

He sat down on the edge of the bed. "Look, ain't no rush, but you need to write visiting your mother on that list, too. That needs to happen in the next month or less. You said teach you the game and I did. Shit, you *are* the game, now. Go see your mother."

Still sitting on the floor, I looked up at him and said, "I know, Babe. It's hard. I'm not ready."

Choosing his words wisely but with more assertion in his voice, Dré said, "There is no 'ready'. You don't get 'ready' for shit like this, you just handle your business. By the time you're 'ready', it might be too late. Handle your business, Lux. You got a month. Max." He looked me dead in the eye to let me know that he meant business.

He was right. I knew that he was right and he knew that I knew that he was right. It didn't change the fact that I didn't feel like I was ready, though. I hadn't spoken to my mother in almost three years. I hadn't sent a letter or even put a dime on her books, either. I'm sure that with the money I was giving Abuelita each month, Ma was being taken care of, but I was never directly doing any of those things. It had been almost three years later and I still hadn't let go of the day that she had forced me to walk to school. In my mind, had she just taken me to school that day, she wouldn't be in jail and my daddy wouldn't be dead. I carried so much pain and resentment toward both of my parents but my mom was obviously receiving the worst of it. Hell, my daddy was dead. He couldn't receive it at all. His spirit still lived within me though and even then, I still never visited his grave. When Dré practically ordered me to go visit my mother, it forced all of my feelings to resurface.

My resentment toward Daddy was rooted in a different space than my resentment toward Ma. With Daddy, my attitude was almost like *niggas will be niggas*. Like, yeah, he fucked up. He fucked Ma over, he fucked me over and he fucked himself over, too, but what did we expect? Daddy had a record before he even met Ma and then went right back to jail pretty much immediately after I was born and came out doing the same shit that got him locked up in the first place. That nigga didn't learn his lesson for shit so we knew who the fuck he was.

My daddy wasn't a perfect man, but he was a present father and that almost trumps all of his shortcomings. Do I condone domestic violence? Not at all. Truth be told, dead or alive, I don't know that I could ever forgive him for putting his hands on my mom but at the end of the day, he was still my daddy. Up until the day my mom made me walk to school, which I'm sure was under his direction, he protected me, provided for me, taught me life lessons, loved me unconditionally, taught me to love unconditionally and supported every single dream I've ever had. Daddy was a pillar of strength in my life. I am strong because he was strong but at the same time, I was angry with him because he was selfish, careless and irresponsible.

Dré didn't know this, but my thoughts kept me up that

entire night and somehow, I concluded that I needed to visit my fathers grave before I visited my mothers cell.

The next morning I was showered and dressed at least two hours before Dré had even opened his eyes. When he had finally woken up, he was shocked to see me dressed already. He grabbed his phone off of the side table to check the time and then looked over at me with sleep and confusion in his eyes. Without saying a word, he raised his eyebrows, tilted his head and lifted his hands in confusion. His actions asked me what I was doing or where I thought I was going. My heart was heavy that morning. My emotions were all over the place and my thoughts were racing through my mind.

Looking away from Dré and down at my phone I said, "Take me to see Daddy." My tone was stern and dry.

Dré and I were best friends. He knew when to switch hats between being my man, my best friend and the man that taught me the game. That morning, I needed my best friend and I think that between my demand, my demeanor and the tone in my voice, he knew that and showed up as such. He didn't even reply to what I had said to him, he just placed his phone back onto the side table, headed right to the bathroom to wash himself up and then threw on the first pair of sweats he could find. As he quickly shuffled around the room to gather himself, I sat on the edge of the bed, never looking up from my phone. The heaviness of my heart anchored down any words I may have been able to speak. My mind was blank but full of thoughts at the same time. Almost like I could see that the words were there, but I didn't hold the capacity to read them.

Dré kneeled down in front of me, wrapped his arms around my waist, and kissed my thigh through my jeans. "I'm proud of you. I'm right here with you every step of this journey."

Tears rushed down my cheeks onto the sleeve of his hoodie. I didn't even know I still had tears to cry. I wrapped my arms around his and closed my eyes as a river of tears continued to flow. He stood up and wiped my tears with his bare hands, kissed my lips and just held me for a moment.

Now, when we first met, we had moments just like that one where I cried and shared different stories about my parents with him but that particular moment was different. It must have been different because I wasn't sharing any moments with him; I had already shared them all. This was a new moment. It was a moment of grief but a new level of healing. It was also a moment of gratitude because I knew that Dré meant what he said about being with me every step of the journey. He was bonded to that statement by his words, yeah, but his actions told me everything I needed to hear.

As Dré and I walked out of our bedroom, Blanco was resting on the couch watching reruns of *'Martin'*. He paused the episode as soon as he realized we were fully dressed and preparing to leave the penthouse.

"My bad, D. I ain't know y'all was finna leave. Just give me like five minutes." He said as he walked toward his bedroom.

"Nah, you good, Blanc. We got some shit to handle. Locations on. Hold us down from here." Dré said as he walked over to Blanco to dap him up.

With a smile on my face, I said, "My dawg. Always love, Blanco." I made a silly face at him just to assure him that everything was fine.

Truthfully, that was more for me than it was for him. Blanco knew he had no reason to worry.

"Alright, Boss. Y'all be easy then." Blanco said to me with a head nod.

Then he looked at Dré, "Say the word, D." He said.

That was Blanco's way of acknowledging that one, he understood that whatever mission Dré and I were about to embark on was none of his business, but two, if Dré needed him for any reason, he was trained and ready to go. Blanco really did hold a special place in my heart. He was a little brother, with big brother energy and a sniper mentality. Sometimes I find myself laughing about that now because I never would have imagined him to be any of the things I know him to be today, by just looking at the young boy who walked into my store for a pair of *Yeezy's*.

The drive to my father's grave site was fairly quiet. Dré placed his hand between my thighs while both of my hands rested on top of his. *Nipsey Hussle* blasted through the speakers as I gazed out of the passenger window and watched the trees disappear as we rode past them. The music was loud, but I could hear the sound of my daddy's voice from the last time I had spoken to him, playing on a loop. I kept hearing Lexington *Rae. Not today.* It was playing over and over and over again until we finally arrived at the cemetery where he was buried. I hadn't even realized that we had gotten there because I was stuck in the loop of his voice.

Dré rubbed my thigh and snapped me out of the loop. "Come on, Lux. You got this."

I sat for a moment, not saying a word.

Then, "Baby." I looked over at him, "Can you just stay in the car for a second. I just.." I paused and a tear rolled down my cheek. "I just need a second with him by myself first."

Dré placed his hand on the back of my neck and pulled me closer to him, kissing my temple. "You got all the time in the world. I'm not going nowhere." He reassured me.

A deep breath in my nose and a long, slow breath out of my mouth was my version of a pep talk before I made my way out of the car. Even though Dré had parked fairly close to Daddy's grave, it felt like it took me hours to walk there. My heart was pounding so hard, I could hear it. My body felt cold, but my pits were sweating and my palms were clammy. For some reason, I was nervous. It was like I had immediately felt guilty for not going to visit him all that time. Some part of me felt like I was justified in my choice while the other part of me felt like Daddy was disappointed in me.

Finally, I was there. Standing face to stone with my daddy. Suddenly all of my nerves; my anger; my confusion; the resentment I carried, all of it was gone. The feeling that came over me mimicked what I felt when Daddy would come home with a new toy or some other gift the day after he beat the shit out of Ma. At that moment, I was just daddy's little girl again

"Hi, Daddy." I said through tears and a shaky voice. My heart smiled. "I've missed you so much." Naturally, my body led me to sit down in front of my father's grave stone with my legs crossed Indian style, like I would as a child.

"I know you've been watching over me. I feel your energy every single day. I'm strong like you. Street smart. Just like you were. Lucky for me, I'm book smart like Mommy. No offense. Imagine that. You and Mommy gave me the best parts of both of you. I know you would prob- ably tell me that makes me a dangerous woman." The tears began to flow again. "Why did you have to leave me, Daddy? Why didn't you just fix it like you said you would? Look at our family. We're broken. I'm broken, Daddy. I'm trying my best to be strong 'cus I know you wouldn't want me to let these niggas see that I'm pressured up, but it's hard, Daddy. Maybe that's why I haven't come see you. I'm sorry. I haven't seen Mommy either." I cried out.

I took a moment to wipe my tears away and breathe in

my nose and out of my mouth again. "Abuelita is doing okay. I mean, she's as stable as she can be, but I think she'll keep thug'nn through a little bit longer. I hope so. She's all I have left. Well, not all I have left. I have Dré. Abuelita doesn't know about him yet, but I think you'd really like Dré."

Telling my father that he'd like my boyfriend was a wild moment for me.

"He actually reminds me of you. A lot. He teaches me things. He loves me unconditionally. He's gentle with me. I didn't think I'd ever feel protected again after you left, but Dré makes sure I feel safe no matter what. Not just physically, Daddy. Emotionally, too." It felt like I was talking directly to my father. It was like he could hear me and I could hear him.

"I'm going to be twenty-one soon. Can you believe that? Your little princess, a grown woman. Time has been moving slow and fast at the same time without you and Ma around. It's weird. I wish it wasn't this way because I'm probably going to be opening up my own braiding salon soon and selling braiding hair, too, and I wish that you and Ma could be there with me when I sign those papers and open those doors. Remember you used to tell me that when I finally opened my own business you would buy me a chain with the name of my business on it? *Luxurious Cabello*. That's the name of my shit. You know I couldn't leave Mommy's crazy non-Spanish speaking ass out of it." I laughed through my tears as I wiped them away.

"The ticket on a buss down with all them letters would have been heavy! Don't worry, I would've settled for *Luxurious*. Maybe now it can say *Lux Lex*. That's what Dré calls me. He always tells me that I have a multimillion dollar mind and that it makes me luxurious no matter what I'm doing." That was the moment where I felt like Dré and Daddy were ready to meet face to stone.

Taking another deep breath into my nose and out of my mouth, I said, "Daddy, I want you to meet Dré.I wish you could've met him face to face but face to stone will have to do."

As I turned my head to motion for Dré to come out of the car, I noticed that he was already out, leaning against the passenger door. It made me laugh a little because even at a cemetery where we were seemingly the only two people present, Dré couldn't just chill for a moment. With my head, I motioned for him to join me and he smiled and made his way over to Daddy and I. He positioned himself right behind me. My legs were folded like a pretzel while his long, praying mantis legs formed triangles next to my body.

He hugged me from behind and kissed my neck. "I'm proud of you. I'm gone *Prada* you after this." He said, insinuating that he was going to buy me a *Prada* bag

Leaning back into Dré's body, I took a moment to embrace his touch and absorb his energy. There was nothing to protect me from as we sat in front of my father's grave, but Dré's presence always provided an extra layer of comfort and I had appreciated that layer more in that moment than ever before.

"Told Daddy that you reminded me of him. I think he would have loved you. He was a real nigga though, so he would have made sure that you knew my life was worth more than your life, but I think he would have fucked with you." My voice was soft and even though I was talking to Dré like he was just one of the big homies, my energy was very feminine and confident.

Dré pulled me in closer, as if that was possible. He chuckled, "Why you think I made sure the whole crew knew that your life was worth more than theirs? Pops raised a trill one. I knew that off top. Hopefully I'm living up to his expectations." He paused and rubbed his finger from the back of my ear, down the side of my neck. "Thank you for sharing this piece of you, with me. I'm honored."

I'm not sure why those words penetrated my heart so deeply, but tears began to roll down my cheeks.

While he wiped my tears away he said, "I ain't gone let you down, Pops. She's in good hands. I promise you that."

We probably sat with my daddy for an hour while I shared any memory I hadn't already shared about him with Dré. It was a bittersweet moment for me because it really felt like I had introduced my man to my father and they were getting along great. The other side of that was reality; Daddy was dead. At least half of the stories I shared with Dré included my mom in some way or another and that was yet again a brand new level of both grief and healing that I was going to have to embark on. The difference was that it wasn't going to be face to stone like it was with Daddy. And Dré wouldn't be there to protect me.

When we made it back to the penthouse, there were two dozen long stem roses and a *Prada* box sitting on the dining room table. Dré really never missed a beat. When he told me at Daddy's grave that he was going to *Prada* me afterwards, I heard him but I didn't think much of it. I guess I just thought he was being silly -- trying to make me laugh at the moment. The joke was on me though because he had Blanco make sure that the flowers and gift were at the penthouse before we returned. Little things like that always meant so much to me. The only other person in my life that had gifted me things was Daddy and those gifts were always apology gifts. Dré had always paid attention to the things I'd share with him about my parents and one of the things he always did was get me "just because" gifts. It was his way of rectifying a piece of my childhood that I felt had tainted me. Of course he always made it clear that Daddy sounded like a good father but he wanted to undo the idea of mine that gifts were apologies.

"Gifts aren't apologies, Lux. Apologies are AA Meetings; accountability met with action. You take accountability for what you fucked up and then you meet that accountability with action to make it right. We don't cut corners for AA Meetings. We grown. We handle all of our bullshit like adults." He would always say.

As you would imagine, seeing the roses and putting my new *Prada* bag into the closet had me crying all over again. It was less about grief and more about gratitude, though. Even though Daddy hadn't ever met Dré in the flesh, having them meet face to stone lifted my spirits a little. Visiting Daddy's grave in and of itself was fulfilling for me. Truth is, I didn't know how much I needed that. It was the ending of the chapter of death and the beginning of a chapter that included acceptance and healing.

Dré stayed home with me that entire day. He wanted to make sure that I was okay. I felt fine staying alone and honestly, I sort of preferred it. Plus, I knew he had tons of business to handle but he was a family first type of guy so I knew he wasn't going anywhere. Any business he needed to handle immediately was delegated to Blanco or someone else in the crew and everything else was postponed until the next day. It actually worked out in my favor because I knew that I wanted to be with Abuelita the next day and Dré certainly wouldn't have been going with me.

∼

The next morning, I had my road dawg take me to Abuelita's. Even though he was compensated very well for each of his roles, sometimes I felt bad for Blanco. Yeah, he was able to have time to himself to spend time with his girl or whatever he chose to do in his free time but it seemed like his life was dedicated to making my life easier and I was never able to find the reciprocity in that. Granted, he and I were able to build a relationship like siblings where I would give him girl advice or talk shit about his choice in women and he'd share pieces of his childhood with me; the things that made him who he was before he became Blanco, but I always felt like he deserved more than sitting outside of my abuelita's house for hours at a time while I spent time with her.

Anyway, Abuelita was very happy to see me. It had been about a week since I had seen her last, which is much longer than usual. When I walked into the house, I could smell the aroma of black beans and it reminded me not to go a week without seeing her again.

"Mami! I'm home." I yelled out as I closed the door behind me.

I could hear the excitement in her voice when she called out, "Cocina, Mija!"

She sat at the kitchen table working on her *Sudoku* puzzle that I had gotten her to keep her brain healthy. It was a simple activity but she really enjoyed it and always felt so accomplished when she completed them.

Abuelita motioned for me to sit down. "I'm almost done. I've missed you, Mija, where've you been?" She asked without looking up from her puzzle.

I sat down and cradled my chin into my hands propped up by my elbows on top of the kitchen table. "Lo siento, Mami. It was a busy week. It won't happen again. How are you? What have you been doing all week?"

Abuelita looked up from her puzzle. "Lexington? What's wrong?"

Abuelita's health wasn't always on point but her mind was still sharp. She knew me like she birthed me herself. It was silly of me to think that I could spend the whole day crying and then pop up on her the next day like everything was fine. Other than my mom and dad, Abuelita had always been my best friend. We shared such a different relationship than I did with my parents. As far as I was concerned, Abuelita's life was worth more than mine and I was willing to protect her life at all costs. That included being honest with her when she asked questions. It was rare that she asked them, but when she did, I wouldn't dare lie. It was obvious that she picked up on the day that I had experienced and I knew that if I didn't tell her the truth, she would stress about it. Stress is a silent killer and Abuelita had enough of that.

Tears began to rush down my cheeks. I was sick of crying but it was like I had no control over it for the span of forty-eight hours. "Abuelita. There's so much I need to tell you."

She immediately began to speak in Spanish quicker than my brain could translate it. The same way she did when we learned about Ma being locked up and Daddy dying. Whatever she said, it must have included directions to leave the kitchen and migrate to the living room because that's what she was guiding me to do.

As we sat down on the couch, her tiny body embraced mine as if she could protect me from any harm coming my way. She couldn't, by a long shot. But her embrace was assuring.

Tears continued to stream down my cheeks as I began to speak. "I don't want you to be mad, Abuelita. I'm sorry. I'm so sorry. I lied to you. I haven't worked at the shoe store in like two years. I've only been braiding hair but I'm doing so well. I'm about to open a salon in a few months, Mami. But it's because I have a boyfriend. He's been taking care of me. He's good to me, Abuelita. If you give him a chance, I know you'll love him." The words rushed out of my mouth like a river up a stream.

She laughed. "Oh, Mija. You think I don't know that? You are your mother's child. I'm only mad that you thought.."

Before she could finish, I continued, "He made me go see Daddy. I saw Daddy yesterday. Face to stone, I saw Daddy."

Abuelita began to cry. "Oh, Baby. I'm so proud of you. I can't believe it. I can't believe you did it. Tell me you'll go see your mother, Mija. Please. She misses you so much. She needs you, Mija. She needs you."

The sound of Abuelita's voice echoed through my mind. The irony of my mother needing me while she sat in a jail cell that she probably wouldn't have been sitting in had she been there for me the morning I needed her, filled me up with anger. My abuelita didn't mean any harm but her statement triggered me. Regardless, I had already planned on going to see my mother--Dré didn't really leave me any other choice. I'm not sure why visiting her didn't sit with me the same way that visiting my dad did because realistically, she was in jail because of him. My anger should have been directed toward his inability to stay out of trouble, the influence it had over my mother and the literal grave conse- quence it had over our family. As a man, my father's role was to be the leader of our household. He was supposed to protect and provide. Protecting and providing was not limited to physical protection and financial providing, it also included protecting us mentally, spiritually and emotionally. It also included providing stability and leadership but he failed us in every aspect. He failed me. I was the one left alone in the world while my mother sat in a jail cell and my father lay dead in a grave. So, yes, I am fully aware now that my animosity never should have been toward Ma. Truth be told, it probably would have done me some good not to have animosity toward either of my parents but somebody had to take the blame for it all and I guess it belonged to the only living parent.

That night, I slept in my bed at Abuelita's house. It was always very nostalgic staying there. It was a feeling I couldn't ever describe in words but could always feel deep down in my spirit. She and I had laughed all night. We talked about my relationship with Dré and I gave her all of the tea on *Luxurious Cabello*. She loved the idea of me owning my own business. My grandfather, whom I never had the opportunity to meet because he had died before I was ever even conceived, owned a restaurant back in the day, according to Abuelita.

Poor Blanco stayed in the car the entire night, but I made sure he had warm food, plenty of snacks and a blanket in case he fell asleep. Of course, falling asleep was out of the question, but it made me feel better to give him a blanket.

Blanco doesn't do jail runs. Nobody in the crew does, for obvious reasons. So, after running it by Dré I had arranged for Sydney to meet me at Abuelita's house to take me to visit my mother the next morning. Dré didn't love that I'd be outside without at least one pair of eyes from the crew on me, but my location was turned on and I'm sure he was tracking my every move. He was more concerned than I was. Honestly, even though it wasn't considered a girls night out, I was sort of looking forward to being outside with Sydney without "security" because it took me back to the old days -- before I was practically an orphan.

Syd and I had been best friends for as long as I could remember. We had done and been through all types of shit together. If I had a nigga, she had his boy. If she had beef with a bitch from the block, I had beef with that bitch and her whole crew, too. Syd was my ace and I was willing to ride with her through whatever, forever. I'll admit, things switched up a little bit after I had met Dré but only because she wasn't really trying to make money with me. As we grew older, we grew different in a lot of ways. After high school, Syd went right to college, got herself an uptight college nigga and had her a regualr nine to five type job. Her relationship didn't last long but she was doing well for herself and I was always going to support her through whatever choices she made, even if they were different from mine. It sucks that while she drove me to see my mother, I learned about how much she didn't support my lifestyle, my relationship or my dream to braid and sell hair.

Besides learning that my best friend might have been a little bit of a hater, the car ride to go see my mother left me empty. It seemed as though my brain wasn't able to fully process what was going to happen and my heart didn't hold the capacity to feel any emotion behind it. It was almost a surreal feeling to know that I was on my way to go see the woman I hadn't spoken to in so many years. It was surreal to know that I'd be visiting my own mother in jail. What would her hair look like? Would she look different? Smell different? Weigh more or less than she did the last time I saw her? Today, all of those thoughts sound irrelevant, but at the time, it was all I could think of. My mother was gorgeous. Like, supermodel gorgeous. Even when she wore pounds of makeup to cover up the damage Daddy had done to her face, she was still the most beautiful woman I had ever seen. She was always very well put together; never a hair out of place, always smelled like a million bucks and even on her "bummy" days, she still looked like she belonged on the cover of a magazine. The idea that she wouldn't look or smell like Ma, was fucking my head up.

"Ok, girl. This is it. This is the day Abuelita and I have been praying for." Sydney said as we approached the visitors parking lot.

Her voice interrupted my irrelevant thoughts. I looked over at her and took a deep breath. "I wish you could come inside with me. This shit is going to be so awkward." I looked down at my hands as tears filled my eyes.

"Lex, this is your mother. You can pretend that you don't need her. You can be mad at her all you want, but she's still your mother. She lost your father the same day you did. She's paying for her mistakes." Syd's tone was empathetic.

"Yeah, well, I'm paying for her mistakes, too." A tear dropped from my eye, onto my hand.

Sydney reached over and hugged me. "Be strong, Lex. And go easy on her. She misses you, I'm sure of it. I'll be right here waiting for you." She released her grip around my body, and used her hand to place my hair behind my ear.

Quickly wiping my tears away, I sent a quick text to Dré letting him know that I made it and was going to head inside. He told me that he was proud of me and that he loved me. I placed my phone into my purse and placed it on the floor of the passenger seat.

"Love you for life, Syd." I said as I exited the car.

. . .

Going through the whole sign in process to enter the visitors area was a lot in and of itself. It was probably more mental than anything but fuck, it was a lot. As I sat waiting for my mother to come out, thoughts of the last time I saw her played in my mind like a movie. It was a weird morning, but she was so happy. She was so sure that walking to school for once wouldn't kill me. It did though. It killed me. It killed her. It even killed my dad. Just as I began to think about my dad, Ma was being escorted to my table by a guard. I didn't know whether to stand in her presence or just stay seated while she approached. Ultimately, I decided to stay seated. Tears rushed down her cheeks the moment she saw that I was the visitor she would be with. It was obvious that Abuelita hadn't told her I'd be coming.

As the guard unlocked her front cuffs, she was already beginning to sit down across from me, obviously eager and excited. For me, there was no eagerness or excitement. The only emotion I felt was shock. She was still the most beautiful woman I had ever seen, but she was different. The spark in her eyes that I was so used to seeing, was nowhere to be found. The confidence that she normally embodied had disappeared. Her hair was thrown in a messy bun and it looked like it had been the same bun for at least a week. There was a scar above her lip that I had never seen before. She was the same, but she was different. She just sat there as if she was allowing me to examine her.

My stare was glued to her lip, I said, "What happened to your lip?"

Without so much as a flinch as the tears continued to roll down her cheeks, she said, "I got in a fight. She cut my lip, but you should've seen her throat."

Ma didn't say that with pride. No, she wasn't being

boastful at all. It was obvious that she was telling the truth, almost deliberately being honest so that we could start off on the right foot. Even still, it was unsettling for me. My eyebrows frowned in confusion.

"It's not as bad as it looks, Baby." She said, finally wiping the tears from her face.

Looking directly in her eyes I replied, "Don't call me Baby."

Shaking her head in agreement, Ma said, "I'm sorry."

Sydney's voice rang between my ears, reminding me to go easy on my mother. I closed my eyes and shook my head from left to right. Taking a deep breath I said, "No. It's fine."

We both sat there in silence for a moment. My eyes were looking beyond my mother but not at anything or anyone in particular. I could feel her eyes watching me. She was probably taking in how much I had grown. Gold chains layered on my neck, gold rings on six out of ten of my fingers, and a gold *Lady-Date* on my wrist. I wasn't the same seventeen year old Lexington Rae Williams that she remembered. Lux Lex sat in front of her and she knew nothing about Lux Lex.

Ma cleared her throat, "You look beautiful, Lex." She said with a small sniffle.

My eyes shifted from looking beyond her, to directly at her. "Thanks, Ma."

We just stared at one another. Both of us were uncomfortable for different reasons, or maybe the same, I don't know.

"What's it like in here?" Honestly, I didn't know what else to ask, but I wanted to break the silence.

Ma smiled a little and looked away from me. "It's hell, Lex." She shrugged her shoulders and looked back at me. "It's like a living hell."

I could feel myself beginning to have the urge to cry. I swallowed the lump that formed in the back of my throat and said, "You didn't have to be here, you know? You didn't have to lie for him."

Ma leaned back in her chair and rubbed the top of her thighs with her hands. She glanced over at the guard and then placed her hands back on top of the table in front of her. "I know, Lex. I know." She looked down at her hands. "I'm sorry. Believe me. I'm sorry." She looked me in my eyes.

Completely disregarding her apology, I said, "I saw Daddy yesterday."

Ma's face showed confusion.

"Face to stone, I mean. I went to his grave. It was the first time since we put him there that I've seen him. I always feel his spirit but sitting there with him, sitting there with him felt different. It was like he was right there with me." I couldn't even look at her as I said that.

You could tell that there was some form of relief in my mother's energy. "How do you feel now?"

My voice was dry. "He's dead. Does it really matter?"

"I miss you so much, Lexington." Ma said as she attempted to touch my hands.

With a smirk on my face I said, "But you didn't have to be here, you do understand that, right?" My tone was sarcastic.

I should've known there was only so much disrespect my mother would tolerate. She was a real bitch before she sat down in that fucking jail cell and the cut on her lip plus whatever damage the bitch that cut her had, told me that Ma was still a real bitch on the inside of that cell, too.

"Did you come here to punish me, or visit me? You don't think I punish myself enough every single day? You don't think sitting in a fucking jail cell is enough punishment for me? What about missing your father's funeral? You don't think that's enough? How about missing my daughter's graduation or not knowing what the fuck is going on in her life? You don't think that shit punishes me every day?" Ma was hurting. She was fighting through tears and barely opening her mouth to talk.

Ma was right, but for some reason, I couldn't let go of all of my resentment. I just stared at her.

"I'm sorry, Lex. I'm sorry that I left you. I'm sorry that Daddy died. I'm sorry that Mami is not doing well. You feel abandoned, Baby. I get it. Believe me, I get it. I know that I'm responsible for that." Ma began to cry again.

My eyes began to carry a pool of tears waiting to rush down my cheeks.

"If I could go back in time, I would. I swear to God I would. But I can't, Lex. I'm probably going to be here for the rest of my life but I don't want to go another day knowing that you hate me. Forgive me. I know it's going to take time, but let's start now. Please."

The pool of tears started to overflow. "I don't hate you, Mama. I don't…. I gotta go. I'm sorry. I'll come back. I just….I gotta go." I rushed out of the visitor center and quickly ran outside.

I just needed fresh air. I needed to breathe. I was beginning to feel suffocated by my emotions inside of there. I hated seeing my mother cry. I hated knowing that she felt as though I hated her. It was too much. Seeing Daddy was easier than seeing Ma. I just needed to get away. My mouth filled with saliva as I ran back to Sydney's car. The wind against my face dried my tears where they fell. When I finally arrived at Syd's car, my body plopped against the passenger door with a loud thump. It scared Syd right out of her nap. She was in a frenzy trying to unlock the door quickly because she wasn't sure what was happening.

"Lex! What happened? What's wrong?" She yelled.

Poor Sydney, she was always around for the most traumatic moments in my life and it always seemed like way more than she bargained for as a friend.

You would've thought someone was chasing me by the way I hopped into the car and slammed the door. "Syd!" I cried out. "Syd, I couldn't do it. She thinks I hate her, Sydney. My mother thinks I hate her. She looks the same but she's different. You can tell she's different just by looking at her." I began to cry uncontrollably.

Sydney grabbed my body and nestled me into hers with a bear hug. "Sis, you already did it. The hardest part is done." She rocked our bodies back and forth. "You can't give up on her. Not now. You need EACH OTHER!"

Sydney and I sat in her car for another fifteen minutes while I cried silently. She didn't say anything else for the entire ride home and neither did I. The silence was necessary for me and I think that somehow she knew that. I craved silence so desperately that I didn't even want to call Dré because I knew he'd ask me more questions than I was ready to answer if we were on the phone. Instead, I sent him a text that read, *going to A's* and he replied with, *Blanc otw*. Dré knew me well enough to know that I was struggling with my emotions. As much as he loved me and kept me safe in so many ways, he knew that going to Abuelita's house was my ultimate safe space. When he and I first met and I would have nights where I struggled with Daddy's death or Ma's incarceration, I'd go to Abuelita's house, so he knew what my text meant. He knew that it meant that I needed space.

When I got to Abuelita's house, I literally didn't do

anything but sleep. The next morning, Abuelita had made breakfast and as usual, I snuck a plate out to Blanco while he sat guard in the car. To this day, I don't know what Dré and Blanco thought they were protecting me from and I don't think I ever will.

After breakfast, Abuelita and I discussed how challenging visiting my mom had been for me and how long of a journey it would be for Ma and I to get to a space where it wasn't push and pull. I know it was hard for Abuelita because her only daughter was in jail for what we believed to be the rest of our lives and then to make matters worse, she had to deal with my bullshit, too. All in all, Abuelita was proud of me for going to see my mother and was even grateful to Dré for encouraging me to do so.

We talked about Dré, too. Abuelita expressed her concerns, of course, but she also expressed that she was grateful for all he had done for us. It's crazy because the entire time, I figured she had no idea. Which makes the fact that she kept telling me that he reminded her of Daddy even more crazy. Like I said before, she wasn't too fond of Daddy. Of course Ma never told Abuelita that Daddy would put his hands on her, but Abuelita wasn't stupid. So between that, the fact that Daddy was outside selling drugs and the fact that Ma was doing time for his bullshit, Abuelita didn't really fuck with Daddy like that. She respected his role in my life, but compared to who she would tell me my grandfather was, Daddy was less than a man. The truth is, I felt like Dré and Daddy were alike but still very different.

Yes, they were both street niggas. But that wasn't some sort of unicorn lifestyle for a nigga like Dré from the D or a nigga like my daddy from New York. Regardless, Abuelita was happy that I found joy with Dré and she was super hype that because of him, I'd be able to start my own business. Her biggest concern was just making sure that the business was mine and not something I borrowed from Dré.

Overall, telling Abuelita about Dré was somewhat of a load off of my plate, but visiting Ma added double to that load.

Dré and I had been texting that entire morning, but I knew it was time for me to head back to the penthouse so that I could update him completely, so shortly after breakfast, Blanco and I went back home.

five
deandré.

THE FORTY-EIGHT HOURS that it took for me to visit
and process visiting my incarcerated mother and dead
father was an exhausting forty-eight hours to say the least.
It put me in a very weird space. You see, when everything
had happened, I became emotionally disconnected from
everything and everyone. Well, except Abuelita. But as far
as anyone or anything else went, it was all disposable to me.
In general, I was already a fairly private person because my
father had taught me to be that way, but I never really had
any issues expressing my true emotions to the people that
really knew me or whatever nigga I was dealing with at the
time. I mean, yeah, I was a kid and before I lost my parents,
there wasn't really much emotion to express. But even then,
Daddy had always taught me that when I started "having
little boyfriends or whatever", as he would put it, it was
important not to give them all of me. Oddly enough, he
would instill that in Ma's head, too. The way he saw it was
that if you give a man all of you, if he decides to leave one
day, he takes all of you with him. Daddy said that you give
a man enough to know that you are loyal to him and no one

else but you don't give him so much that he believes you aren't loyal to yourself.

"Loyalty is important to a man, but respect is crucial for a woman." Daddy would always say.

I'm still not too sure how I feel about that statement, but I guess it doesn't matter much now. Anyway, from the moment we laid my father to rest, my heart turned black. I was different. I felt like I didn't really exist. There was even a small period of time where I attempted therapy but it was pointless because I wasn't willing to share anything except my name with the therapist. No one could get through to me because I didn't allow them to. I wanted everybody to leave me the fuck alone because they all knew exactly what made me that way so why did they feel the need to constantly talk about it?

That all changed when I met Dré. Almost instantly. And it was probably because he was so much like Daddy. They were leaders. Protectors. Providers. Alpha men. Dré had a short, but powerful list of rules and regulations that he stood on; *Dré's Doctrine*, is what I used to call them, much like Daddy had a list of "codes". Dré instilled the doctrine into the whole crew on a regular basis the same way Daddy instilled the code into Ma and me, regularly.

Dré opened me up over the course of our relationship and made it easier for me to build walls around only the parts of my heart that felt pain, but it seemed as though visiting my mom and dad completely shattered every emotional wall I had built.

～

While Blanco drove us from Abuelita's house, back to the penthouse, I felt the urge to connect with him deeper than we'd ever connected before.

"Blanc, what's your family like? You've never said anything about them before." I asked curiously.

You could tell that Blanco was taken aback. "Shit, I don't really know, Lux. My pops dipped as soon as Moms told him she was pregnant and then she left me with my granny when I was about eight years old. I guess shit got too tricky for her. Granny had a heart attack when I was like ten or some shit like that and I just been making shit happen on my own since then. They put me in a group home but that shit was a dub 'cus the niggas in there were grimey. Dré was the first person to take me in and saw some shit in me I ain't see in myself. Him, you and the crew is all I know as family now." Blanco shrugged his shoulders when he was done speaking as if it wasn't a big deal.

"That's a lot, Blanc." My heart actually ached for him.

Blanco laughed a little, "Nah, ain't really shit to it. Don't none of that shit matter at the end of the day."

I didn't want to press the issue more than necessary, so I moved on to my next question. "What about your girl. You really fuck with her, or what?" None of the crew took his on again-off again white girl, girlfriend seriously, but I didn't want to give her too much, so I kept it cute.

Blanco's energy shifted from mildly defensive to a complete cotton ball.

"Ah, man." He looked over at me with a huge smile on his face. "She carrying my seed, Lux. She locked in for life now."

That was the last thing I was expecting to hear. "Ahh!" I screamed. "What is she having? Does the crew know? Why am I just now finding out?!"

"You know you're the first to know, Boss Lady. It's too soon to tell what she's having, but as soon as I know, that's when I'll tell the whole crew. Until then, we gone lock that one in the safe." Blanco said through laughter.

Hearing that Blanco was going to be a father lifted my spirits. Shockingly, there were no babies in the crew at that time, well, not any that we knew of. It was almost comical that the baby of the crew was going to be the first to have a baby, but I knew that Blanco would be a great father. He was the baby of our crew, but he held the capacity to run his own crew if he wanted to. I'm not sure if he knew that about himself, but I always saw it.

When we finally arrived back at the penthouse, Blanco yelled, "Ayo, D! The package is safe and sound!"

I playfully smacked the back of his neck and said, "Shut up, fool. Ain't no damn package!"

Dré met us in the living room and kissed me on the lips before dapping Blanco up.

"Blanc know what time it is, Baby! Always make sure the bag is secured!" He was obviously happy to see me.

"Oh, please! Y'all are so dramatic." I grabbed the back of Dré's neck and went in for another kiss. "Feed me." I kissed him. "I'm hungry."

Kissing me again, Dré said, "Nah, you greedy. Blanco told me Abuelita had breakfast boomin' this morning."

We all laughed and then Dré handed me his phone with the app to have food delivered, already pulled up. One thing about Dré, he always made sure there was food on the way as soon as I told him to feed me. For the most part, I was always fairly mild-mannered with him, but whenever we had to wait too long to eat, I turned into a monster. I have to admit, I was a spoiled brat because of Dré but I think the pain I carried around with me every single day kept me humble. Well, now that I say it out loud, it's giving spoiled and depressed, not really spoiled and humble. Whatever.

Our food had arrived about thirty minutes later and the three of us sat around the dining room table and ate while we joked with one another. The table was literally round, so we called it The Round Table. Real original, I know. We had sat around that table more times than I could count having meetings, eating dinner, playing board games, and some more shit, but for some reason, that day, sitting at that table had meant more to me than it ever had before. My heart was heavy but at the same time, I felt so much joy knowing that Blanco was going to be a father soon and so much gratitude knowing that I had Dré in my life. Sitting at The Round Table that day had me reflecting on everything Dré had done for me on a mental, spiritual and emotional level.

At first glance, you'd think Dré was a model or an athlete or some shit like that. I think D-Boy would have been the last thing anyone would have assumed he'd become because of his upbringing but it was for damn sure not anything you'd expect him to be if you met him. He had a different level of intellect. His mind was such a beautiful experience. One of my favorite experiences, actually. The way he processed things. The way he genuinely enjoyed learning new information. The way you could see him appreciate the intricate details of life as a whole, forced you to do the same. His heart wasn't as cold as you'd expect it to be, either. I learned that about him very early on because he was patient with me while I mourned the loss of my parents. His stillness was infectious. It demanded that I slow down. It demanded that I acknowledge the feelings I wanted so desperately to hide from. Then there was his leadership. His leadership is what created a sense of safety for me. He was always so confident in the decisions he made and the information he shared and with that, he expanded the minds of anyone willing to listen. Outside of Daddy, Dré was the first man to teach me something. I mean, I guess that isn't saying much considering how young I was when I first met him, but he taught me things that have stuck with me even today. I don't know that anyone else could have ever loved me the way Dré did. He loved me deep; down to the depths of my soul. He loved me raw; allowing me to strip down to the purest form of my being. He loved me free; allowing me to evolve into the highest form of myself. Dré's love gave me the power to heal and feel. It gave me the power to grow and glow. His love gave me the power to see and be seen. Because of Dré's love, I learned to listen but I also felt heard. Dré taught me the beauty in polarity, the power in stillness, and the strength in love.

My face must have had all of my reflective thoughts shown all over it because Dré said, "I don't know if you're looking like that because you love the food or because you love me, but I like it."

Blanco looked over at me and I shifted my eyes between the both of them before all three of us began to laugh hysterically.

As I finished my last bite of food, I said, "Man, I was just thinking about how much I love our little family." I rolled my eyes and smiled.

The boys were just about done with their meals too, so I began to clean the table off while they discussed business plans for the next day. There were a few dishes in the sink, so I started washing them while I thought about my mom and what she might have been doing in her cell at that moment. It was mid-afternoon so I imagined maybe she was in the yard or the rec area playing *Spades* with the other inmates. I wondered what she thought of me and how it felt for her to see me. To me, she looked the same, just sad and worn out. I wondered if that's how I looked to her, too, because I was definitely feeling that way.

Dré came and hugged me from behind, wrapping his arms around my body and nesting his head into the nape of my neck. "Come on. Do this later." He said as he reached to turn off the faucet.

I grabbed the hand towel that was to the right of the sink to dry my hands off. Leaning back into his embrace and turning my body so that we faced one another, I used my damp hands to grab his face for a kiss.

"You gotta tell me about the visit." He said with his lips on mine.

Truth be told, I thought that I was going to get away without having to mention any parts of the visit. I thought that if I displayed happiness and emotional stability to the best of my ability, Dré would allow me to skate by the conversation he knew I didn't want to have. I should've known better. Dré's ass don't ever, has never, and will never miss a fucking beat. Some part of me was annoyed because I just felt like I needed a break from all of that. The other part of me knew that I needed to face it while it was still pretty fresh in my mind and on my heart. Plus, I knew good and got damn well there wasn't a way to get around it.

Before I knew it, three hours had passed. For three full hours, Dré and I sat on the bedroom floor and talked through every single one of my feelings pertaining to visiting my mom and dad. Shockingly enough, I felt really free afterwards. It gave me a sense of emotional freedom that I didn't think was possible for me. It felt like I had hit a reset button and that's when I knew that Dré knew that talking through it was the best way for me to heal through it. It was another moment of appreciation for my man, only this time, I showed my appreciation by throwing that ass in a circle. We probably had the best sex we had ever had in our entire relationship, right there on the floor. I think we fell deeper in love that day. I think our bond strengthened that day. I think that was the day that I had realized that I never wanted to be without Deandré Lamont Givens.

six
lexington.

THREE MONTHS HAD GONE by before I physically saw my mother again. Over the course of that time, I answered all of her collect calls and replied to her letters but I was always very brief with her. I'm not sure why I couldn't just forgive her and give us a fighting chance to make up for old times while we built a new relationship under the new, far from ideal, circumstances. I knew that Ma had beaten herself up enough for the both of us each day that she sat in that jail cell, but for some reason, I couldn't find it in my heart, or maybe my mind, to forgive her. Honestly, I wanted to but I just couldn't. For the life of me, I couldn't figure out why I held on so tightly to the day that she decided not to take me to school because the reality of it is that everything that happened after that morning would have probably still happened exactly the way it did.

With that being said, it sounds insane to say that I would go sit at my daddy's grave for about an hour or so every single week and talk to him about how I couldn't forgive Ma. I could have just as easily had those conversations with Dré instead, but it felt like family business to me.

LOWKEE

There's some shit that just stays in the family. Some shit you don't share with anyone outside of the bloodline because of loyalty, because of respect, and because of solidarity. Granted, Dré was my family at that point and he knew everything about me but those conversations weren't meant to be had with anyone else besides my daddy. I can't think of one thing I hadn't shared with Dré about my life with my parents but I had become Lux Lex after everything happened. Lexington Rae Williams didn't exist anymore. I mean, how could she when the two people that created her, were either dead or as good as dead?

Each week, Dré or Blanco would take me to the flower shop for me to grab a new bouquet of blue roses for me to place on Daddy's stone. Blue had always been his favorite color and he always used to joke about how women should give men flowers too. He would always say that it wasn't about the flowers themselves, but the symbolism they carried. He felt like sometimes men should get flowers from the women in their lives just as a message that the woman acknowledged the man for who he was. I'll never get over not giving him those flowers while he could see them bloom. Daddy was a street nigga, but he had a big heart. Sometimes he was a monster, but behind those demons, he carried emotional intelligence and genuine empathy.

Even though he couldn't talk back, I felt like he was still instilling his emotional intelligence into my brain and embracing me with his empathy every time I sat with him. It didn't matter if I was talking to him about Ma, Abuelita, Sydney or whoever, each time I left him, I left feeling like I had all of the answers I needed.

It's hard to look back on this considering the fact that occasionally he would beat the shit out of Ma, but when Daddy was alive, he was always so patient and gentle with me. Whenever I made mistakes or needed guidance, he was right there to listen, correct and guide me. I think that's the reason sitting face to stone with him brought me so much comfort and insight. It's like it served as a space for me to give Lux Lex a break so that I could be Lexington without fear, shame or confusion. Daddy used to always tell me that a leader was to provide safety, stability and service and after he died, I would go off on him in my prayers at night because of that statement. Through a face full of tears and a heart full of anger I would tell him that he was a liar, not a leader. To me, there was no way in hell he could be a leader based on his definition because he died. For starters, he hadn't kept my mother safe. He certainly didn't keep himself safe. On top of that, whatever bullshit he had gotten us into got him killed, my mother locked up and put me into the deepest, darkest depression anyone could ever experience. Where was the stability and service in that?

It wasn't until I was sitting face to stone with him each week that I was able to release that anger and forgive him for falling short as a leader. Sitting with him each week helped me realize that leaders aren't perfect; they fall short of their duty sometimes. It took having one-sided conversations with my father's grave for me to realize that the man's duty to lead is less about perfection and more about impact. Daddy wasn't perfect by any definition of the term. In fact, he probably deserved a greater punishment than death for putting his hands on her and everything else he put my mom through. Death is easy for the dead. Death doesn't require accountability, responsibility or any other ability for that matter. Death just is. But leadership requires you to show up every single day, no matter what, and leave an impact. Leadership requires you to provide the service of stability through safety, no matter the circumstances. Daddy fell short of that while he was alive, but he made up for it from the grave.

It was unbeknownst to me at the time, but growing up, my father also taught me the ability to separate the person from the offense; being angry with him for hurting my mom, while still loving him for who he was to me. Impact, I guess. Maybe we can call it some form of duality, I don't know. To be honest, I'm not sure that I was fully aware that I needed to forgive Daddy, but when the forgiveness happened, I became fully aware. Daddy wasn't a perfect leader when he was alive, but when he died, his leadership was impactful enough for me to feel safe showing up as Lexington instead of the defensive Lux Lex I had become. Shit, I didn't even know that Lexington still existed. Daddy's leadership was impactful enough for me to realize that in order to forgive Ma, Lexington had to sit with her, too. Some parts of me were looking forward to forgiving my mother and other parts of me found sadness in it. Forgiving her meant releasing the anger and bitterness I carried toward her for being locked up in the first place and I knew that would lead to missing her; the old her.

Ma was always filled with so much joy and positive energy. Even when Daddy would beat her up, she'd wake up the next morning, patch herself up and then turn on some praise music while she waited for me to get ready for school. She'd bounce around my room praising the Lord while I chose my outfit for the day or had full blown church choir, kitchen concerts using a spoon as a microphone. Her smile was infectious – even on the days I knew she didn't feel like smiling. The embrace of her hug was so warm and nurturing it could tame the wildest of them all. Her patience with me and my daddy was unmatched and the grace that she embodied was present in every situation; good or bad. The truth is, when I was younger, my mother was who I aspired to be and seeing her rot away in a jail cell is far from who I ever imagined she would be.

~

I was leaving the cemetery one day and thought about how crazy it was that Daddy was teaching me so much about myself from his grave. God, I remember this day like it was yesterday. The air was crisp, yet fresh. It was cold outside and with every deep breath inward, the crisp air cleared all of my sinuses as it made its way down to my lungs. Dré had taken me that day and the energy was always very different when he took me to Daddy's grave than it was when Blanco took me.

Without ever saying a word, Blanco always made it a point to be extremely careful with me. Not physically, though. It was in the cadence of his voice when he would ask simple things like if I wanted to grab food. It was in how he made it a point to keep his eyes forward while he drove as if he was giving me some sort of privacy as I sat shotgun. Dré on the other hand wasn't going for any of that. He always wanted to know what I shared with Daddy, how I felt about things and what new self-revelation I felt like I uncovered. In theory, Dré was supportive, in reality, it was annoying as fuck. I don't mean to sound ungrateful or rude when I say that because if it weren't for Dré, I don't think I would have ever considered visiting my father and I for damn sure wouldn't have gone to see my mother, which means I would have kept a lot of pain and resentment buried deep inside of me. Be that as it may, the more I began to heal, the deeper I thought about putting forth a real effort to forgive my mother. Healing was hard work, though and it made me want to pack all of my pain away even more so that I could move on with my life. None of that mattered though. It didn't matter because regardless of my desire, I conformed to Dré's way of handling it. He wanted to talk about it, so we talked about it.

With that, on the way home from the cemetery, for the first time ever, I started to cry uncontrollably as Dré and I discussed my visit with my daddy. I was really losing my shit, too. It was so bad that Dré had to pull over so that he could calm me down. For the first time since I found out my daddy had died and the first time since my mommy had been taken to jail, I cried for myself and no one else. My heart ached for the little girl that was so pure that she held the capacity to love her father unconditionally, even though he consistently beat the shit out of her mother. My heart ached for the teenage girl that missed out on girl talk with her mother. My heart ached for Lexington; the piece of myself that felt alone, abandoned, and alienated because my entire life was ripped from underneath me – the piece of me that felt like I hadn't appreciated the good moments enough or grieved the bad moments at all.

"Why would they do this to me?!" I practically yelled. My mouth was full of warm saliva, my nostrils were slippery with a clear layer of snot and my eyes were so full of tears that I couldn't even see clearly.

Dré was sitting in the driver seat hugging me as tightly as he could as he leaned over the center console and cradled my body. I'm not sure if it was that he didn't know what to say or how to say it, or if I just didn't give him enough time to figure it out but he didn't say a word.

"They missed my graduation, Dré. They missed everything. Daddy said family is before everything and after nothing and they still left me here!" My body was shaking as I struggled to catch my breath through the tears.

As he squeezed my body tighter and began to rock back and forth, Dré replied, "I know, Baby. I know."

"I miss her so much. I miss her smile and her laugh. I miss hearing her sweet little voice and watching her get ready. I miss riding to school with her. Why couldn't she just take me to school one last time? Why did she have to change the plan?!" I cried as I started to create resistance between Dré and I.

With each attempt to pull my body away from his, he would just hold me tighter; almost restraining me.

Defeated, I released the tension of my hug and just allowed Dré to hug me. "We were supposed to open my salon together. They were supposed to be here." I was finally running out of tears.

Dré finally released the hug and used the sleeve of his hoodie to wipe my face – snot included. If that ain't love, I don't know what is. My head was pounding, my eyes were burning and my breathing was that of a child who had just thrown a tantrum. I couldn't even look Dré in the eyes. I don't know if I was embarrassed or if I just didn't have the energy but I couldn't do it. It was probably the most, the hardest and the worst I had ever cried since the day Abuelita and I received bad news after bad news. It was absolutely the most Dré had ever seen me cry. That was the day he met Lexington Rae Williams, the girl I had packed away and hid from the world, including myself, after Daddy died and they got Ma. Come to think of it, Dré built Lux Lex. Without even knowing, he created a persona for me to hide from myself.

"Lux, I got you, Baby. For life. You know that. We'll get through this shit. When you open the salon, we will make sure that your pops and moms are incorporated in every way possible. I know you feel alone. I know this shit is hard…" Dré was choosing his words carefully.

Before he could finish, I interrupted, "Lexington. Daddy named me Lexington because that's the street he grew up on. I don't know why, but he swore he'd never go back home again, he just needed a little piece of home with him wherever he went. That's what he always told me. Ma named me Rae because her daddy's name was Raymond. He died when she was young. I never told you that story before, but that's where my name comes from." My breathing was starting to become normal again. My heart rate was slowing down, too.

Before Dré could respond I said, "I want to go home now."

Just like that, without any objection, Dré drove us home. Even today, I have no clue what triggered me to have that emotional outburst. If I'm keeping it really, really real with you, it wasn't until that day that I fully understood what emotions I was harboring. It must have been some sort of trauma response for me to just completely block everything out. Ma used to always say, *you can't hide from your emotions Lexy, they always find you.* I guess she was right.

dré.

THE WEEK after my big Lexington reveal-emotional breakdown-cry like a fucking baby episode, Dré woke me up at the crack of dawn telling me to get dressed. I was confused because I was supposed to visit Daddy that day, but it was way earlier than I had ever or would ever go. I didn't ask questions though because Dré was in hustle mode. Anybody that knows Dré, always knew he was in hustle mode when his chain was tucked and his fitted was low. Now, typically when he was in that space, I was in the house and out the way. It had always been that way.

"Nah. I'm in the streets today, Lux. Stay tucked." He said to me the first time I had ever watched him tuck his chain into his hoodie.

But that morning was different. That morning, he tucked his chain and I damn near wanted to tuck mine too. But I didn't have one. Dré's energy was contagious like that, though. Whatever he was on, the whole crew was on and he never had to tell us a thing.

His fit was simple that day, too. Black fitted, black hoodie, black sweats, black *Yeezy's*. There wasn't anything in my mind that prompted me to ask him where the hell we were going so early, so I just matched his vibe. Black beanie, black hoodie, black leggings, black *Yeezy's* but I threw on a pair of hoop earrings and two rings just to set my shit off a little.

As I stood in the bathroom looking at myself in the mirror, he walked in and embraced me from behind. His embrace was warm. His long arms wrapped around my body as he leaned forward to cradle his face into the nape of my neck. The scent of *Ombré Leather* transferring from his hoodie to mine.

"I love you, Lux. You really my mothafuckin' best friend." Dré said as he kissed my neck between each word.

Confused, but fulfilled, I replied, "I love you more." I closed my eyes just to take in his scent and enjoy his embrace. "I couldn't do this life without you." I continued.

I was confused because hustle mode Dré hadn't ever really been boyfriend-best friend, Dré at the same time. Hustle mode Dré didn't attend to or engage in anything remotely distracting. Not to say that I was ever a distraction but when ya nigga is in his bag you just have to be his homie until it's time to lay down at night. Niggas don't have time to cater to emotions and shit like that when they're in their bag. But the real ones gone make sure you're very well taken care of once they secure the bag. That's how you balance a street nigga out; know when to be his friend, when to be his girlfriend and when the two can coincide. I say all that to say that for who I had known Dré to be when he was in hustle mode, the amount of attention and affection he was giving me that very early morning, was not on brand. Regardless, it was fulfilling. There was something special about the stillness of it all. The sun had barely risen and I knew Blanco certainly hadn't woken up yet because there was no music playing, he wasn't yelling at the video game and there were no sounds from the TV in the background. It was just me and Dré; standing in love and adoration.

We must have just stood there intertwined with one another in silence for a solid five minutes.

"You want to be me so bad, huh? You couldn't wait to black yo' shit out like me, huh? Don't even know where we goin', didn't ask no type of questions and it's early as fuck and you just want to be twins?" Dré broke the silence.

Laughter interrupted the stillness.

Still laughing, I said, "Yo! I don't know what you're on this morning! It's too early to be trying to put a fit together so I was on whatever you were on." I looked at him through the mirror. "Don't nobody want to be you, nigga. My shit looks better anyway." I said with a fake attitude.

Dré laughed and began to play fight with me. "Oh, ok, baby! Pop yo' shit!"

I began to play into my role even more. "You see me, shining? You mad 'cus you picked this outfit out for us and you don't look as fine as I do!" I stuck my tongue out and rushed out of the bathroom and into the closet to grab a purse.

When I came out of the closet, Dré was leaning up against the dresser, facing our bed with his arms folded, legs crossed and a smirk on his face. He looked happy; the kind of happy a parent becomes when you are about to open a gift they swore up and down they didn't get you.

For a moment, I looked at him with a smile on my face. "Bro, what's wrong with you today?" I laughed. "Why are we up so early? Why are you being such a creep?"

Even though he was being a creep, he was my creep. At that point in time, I had no idea why he was in such a great mood but I really enjoyed it. As I continued to laugh, I was hoping he would answer my questions as I walked closer to him. He didn't. I stood in front of him, grabbing his face with both of my hands and began to kiss him.

"You're my best friend, too." I said, in between kisses.

Dré unfolded his arms and gently grabbed my hands from his face and turned my body around, pulling me into him. "Look." He said.

Thinking he wanted me to look at him, I attempted to turn my body around to face him again. Instead, he used his hands to guide my head in the direction of the bed where a black box sat perfectly centered at the edge of the mattress.

Dré had only ever gone to one jeweler and all of the boxes that jeweler carried looked just like the one sitting on the edge of our bed.

My heart began to race and I could feel my cheeks getting warm as I became more excited. Dré's hands were still holding my head in place as if I needed any additional support, so I grabbed his hands and gripped them as tight as I could.

"You got me something?!" I said with excitement in my voice.

You'd think that man wasn't buying me new shit every week the way I got excited, but I always got that excited when he gifted me things. That's probably why he did it so often. If nothing else, Dré fucking loved seeing me happy.

He gripped my hips and moved me out of his way and then, he walked over to the bed to pick up the jewelry box.

Before he opened the box he said, "It was supposed to be one of your birthday gifts, but since you think your lil' fit is so fly, I figured I would buss you down a lil' bit. You know, add to ya flex." And then he opened the box.

My smile was probably shining as much as the fucking diamonds inside of that box. My body was stuck right where I stood. As happy as I was to see what was in that box, my eyes began to fill with tears and my bottom lip poked out like a little brat.

Tears began to fall. "Baby, you got that for me?" I was ugly crying with a smile on my face.

He took a step forward to hand me the box and wipe my tears dry. "You said Pops was going to get it for you, so I wanted to make sure that still happened. It's from me and Pops." He said.

With enough diamonds to light up an entire room, there sat a diamond encrusted chain that said *Lux Lex*. The same chain I spoke about when I was face to stone with Daddy. It looked exactly the way I imagined it would and it was bossy enough for Daddy's taste, too. It was perfect. Dré was perfect. No matter how many people he took care of, no matter how many different streams of income he had to focus on, whether they were legal or not, no matter what other types of issues he had to deal with, Dré never missed a fucking beat.

He kissed my forehead. "You like it?" He stupidly asked.

"Duh! I fucking love it! It's perfect! You're perfect! THIS! Is perfect!" I said with overwhelming joy.

Dré kissed my forehead and then began to undo the clasp on the chain so that he could place it around my neck.

He took a step back to admire his work. "I ain't gone lie, Babe. That shit shinin'!" He said with a smile of satisfaction on his face.

I screamed and then quickly covered my mouth so that I wouldn't wake Blanco in the next room.

I wanted to admire his work too, so I ran toward our closet so that I could look at myself in the full body mirror. While I was doing so, I heard our bedroom door open and then close again shortly after. The next thing I knew, Dré was standing in the opening of the closet door with a dozen blue roses in his hands.

Before I could even react he said, "I know it's still early, but let's go show Pops how we coming from now on. Plus, I got one more surprise for you after that, so we have to leave the house right now."

Looking in the mirror at my chain, and then at Dré and the flowers, I made a dramatic face as if I were crying, "This is the best birthday ever and it's not even officially my birthday yet!" I whined.

It only took me a few steps to hop into Dré's arms. He managed to catch me, lift me up and kiss me without ever putting the roses down.

"Thank you, Baby. This really means the world to me. I love you so much." I said as Dré walked both of us into the living room with my legs latched around his body as he held me in one arm and Daddy's roses in the other.

In the living room, I released my body from his, kissing him as my legs blindly searched for the living room floor.

"I wish Daddy could have met you. He really would've fucked with you." I said with a smirk on my face as I looked Dré directly in his eyes and grabbed the flowers from his hands simultaneously.

Dré smiled and then gently grabbed the back of my neck as he placed his lips onto my forehead for a kiss.

That morning had so many layers to it. It was a moment of extreme fulfillment and complete gratitude for Dré's thoughtful gift. It was bittersweet because I wanted even more for my daddy to be able to meet my man. I knew in my heart that Daddy and Dré would have had a great rela- tionship.

It was also the moment when I realized that unpacking my childhood and resurrecting Lexington Rae, didn't only open old wounds, it began to heal them. Beginning to heal the pain from my childhood created space for me to love Dré even deeper than I already did. It created a space for me to learn things about myself that I may not have learned any other way. Most importantly, it was beginning to lift a weight from my heart that I was so used to carrying that I forgot how it felt not to. And to my surprise, it created a deeper desire to heal my relationship with my mother.

My thoughts must have been written all over my face because suddenly, Dré gently lifted my chin and said, "Stop thinking so much. Come on. Let's go."

Before walking out of the house, he knocked on Blanco's bedroom door. "Yo! We out. Location's on. The spot at 2."

He didn't even wait for Blanco to acknowledge him. That's how things always went, though. Dré practically trusted Blanco with his life, my life and everything in between. After that, Dré double checked his pockets for his wallet, keys and both phones and then wrapped his arm around my neck and shoulders as we headed to the car.

In the car I held Daddy's flowers across my lap like they were worth a million dollars. Making sure he had fresh blues every week was always on the top of my list of priorities, which naturally put it on Dré and Blanco's lists too. Family business. The car ride over was free of tears. My poor Dré was probably on eggshells too, so I worked overtime to hold my shit together. I was still emotional though. Overwhelmingly, emotional.

"I want to take you to Abuelita's. I'm not going to have her forever and I need you to breathe the same as her at least one time before I lose her." I said out of nowhere.

You could tell that Dré was shocked by my statement

because he began to choose his words wisely. "Ok." He took a breath. "Ok. Bet."

I don't know what I expected him to say, but I didn't expect it to be such an easy conversation.

"You tell me when she has time and I'll be there. No matter what." He said as he placed his hand onto my inner thigh.

Interlocking my fingers with his I said, "Today. Let's go today. I know you and Blanc have shit to do in a few hours, so we'll make it quick, but we have to go today." I looked over at him and gave him an innocent smile because I knew that I was throwing a little curveball into the rest of his day.

By that time, we were pulling up to Daddy's gravesite.

"Don't worry about time, Lux. We got all the time you need. Pop yo' shit with Pops and then we'll pull up on Abuelita afterwards." Dré said as he put the car in park.

I opened my car door. "WE are going to pop our shit with Pops. Come on, let's go."

Besides the one time that I allowed him to sit with me at Daddy's stone, it had always been an unspoken rule that I visit Daddy 'alone'. Dré and Blanco would keep a close eye on me, but they never invaded my personal time with Daddy. This time was different though. This time, I wanted Dré to experience as much of Daddy as he could. I felt like he deserved that. Both of them did, actually.

Daddy's spirit was always so strong whenever I was at his stone and I had always felt like it meant that his spirit was grateful that I was finally making time to be with him. Yeah, I could feel his energy from time to time before I started sitting face to stone with him, but it was rare. For so long after he died, I just couldn't do it; any of it. If I would think about him I'd get mad and then sad so I would push the thoughts away. I was trying my best to forget that he had ever existed but I'd dream about him often and the dreams would feel so real that I wasn't sure if I was really experiencing them or not. It would happen the most when I would sleep at Abuelita's house, even if I had just closed my eyes for a second. It was like all of the time I spent fighting to forget Daddy, he spent fighting for me to remember him.

Anyway, as soon as Dré and I sat down with Daddy, the sun began to shine brighter. Dré noticed it too and was just as fulfilled as I was. It was like Daddy knew that both of us were there with him and he was happy that we were. For about an hour, we sat with Daddy and shared the story of how we met. We told him about my new chain and I made sure that Daddy knew that Dré had a plain Jane *Rolex*. Dré on the other hand, made sure that Daddy knew that we also had a couple of buss down's. Balance, I guess. Overall, it was beautiful sharing in that experience with Dré. I was grateful.

We cleaned Daddy's stone and left his fresh blues for him and then we made our way back to the car so that we could go visit Abuelita. I was nervous. My palms were sweating, my heart was racing and I could feel my breathing pattern being thrown off.

"Wait." I said as I completely stopped walking.

Dré looked back at Daddy's stone thinking that maybe I had forgotten something.

I took a deep breath. "When I told Abuelita about you, she told me that she already knew. But.." I took another breath. "The thing is that you're a lot like Daddy, Dré. Like … A LOT. And Daddy and Abuelita didn't really get along that well because she didn't love his lifestyle. Your life… OUR lifestyle." Tears began to fill my eyes.

Dré took a step closer to me. "Lux, we'll be fine. Abuelita loves you so much. I can tell. If things become uncomfortable for her, then I'll leave and let y'all have girl talk. But let's at least try. We won't know unless we try."

Dré was such an incredible man. Confident. Assertive. Fearless. He was a street nigga, but he took care of his family; he took care of me. He took care of me beyond material things. Of course that came with the lifestyle we were living, but it was nothing compared to the way he took care of my heart. Dré damn near knew from the moment we met that I had gone through hell and he did everything he could to make sure that I lived a comfortable life mentally and emotionally.

Anyway, he was right. At the very least, I had to attempt to introduce him and Abuelita. I didn't want to run the risk of losing that opportunity forever. Him meeting my daddy was never an option seeing as though I didn't meet Dré until well after daddy's death, but knowing they could never meet, made my heart heavy. I wasn't going to make that same mistake with Abuelita. If Dré never taught the crew anything, he for damn sure taught us not to make the same mistake twice. He preferred we didn't make them at all, but felt as though as long as we could right our wrongs, we would always stay ahead.

"Ok." I shook my head in agreement. "Let's go see Abuelita."

eight
abuelita.

ABUELITA WAS ALL I had left of my family. Yeah, Dré and the crew were my new family, but my roots were Ma, Daddy and Abuelita. My roots were the difference between Lux Lex and Lexington and I felt like Dré had just begun to meet Lexington on a deep level. Sharing pieces of my childhood with him over the years was really just a glimpse into who Lexington really was, so allowing him to sit face to stone with Daddy and then taking him to see Abuelita immediately after that, was mildly overwhelming. I'm saying mildly because I always tried my best not to display too many emotions surrounding my childhood, but the truth is that I was losing my fucking mind on the inside.

For one, there was no real way to tell how Abuelita would respond to me showing up to her house unannounced with a nigga that moved just like my daddy did. Not to mention I had just barely introduced the fact that Dré even existed. Granted, she was receptive to the idea of his existence, but seeing him inside of her house would make it real. Knowing some shit exists and seeing that it exists can cause completely different emotions to surface.

Secondly, Lux Lex didn't exist in Abuelita's house – ever. Whenever Blanco would pull up in front of Abuelita's, as soon as I opened that car door, I tapped into my roots. The purest form of myself; Lexington. Besides the fact that she and I shared a beautiful relationship prior to all the bad stuff that happened, we also shared that pain the same way. The way that she lost a piece of herself in losing my mother, was the same way that I lost a piece of myself in losing her. The only other person that shared the experience of receiving the news of my daddy dying, was Abuelita. For as long as I could remember and as far in the future as I could see, Abuelita had always been there for me. She's always been my safe haven. So yes, I showed up as Lexington when I was around Abuelita because that was the only place it felt safe and appropriate to do so. With that being said, I wasn't sure if I was prepared to show Dré that piece of me. The few weeks leading up to that day had already been a lot for both of us because of my emotions and what not, so knowing that I was getting ready to essentially be fully exposed created a new layer of emotions for me.

As Dré drove us to Abuelita's house, he didn't seem to have any reservations about meeting her, but in true Dré fashion, he could feel that I was losing my shit.

"Talk to me." He said as he reached over and caressed my chin. "Why are you so deep in your head right now?" He asked.

I wasn't going to lie to him. I never had a reason to lie to him about anything—feelings included.

"I'm different around Abuelita." I shifted my body in the passenger seat so that I was facing him. "Abuelita is all I have left." I quickly realized how insane that sounded when it came out of my mouth. "I don't mean it that way. I mean like.."

Dré interrupted me, "I know what you mean, babe.

Keep going." His smile was warm and reassuring.

"Sydney knows me as Lex, so she knows different parts of me, but Abuelita knows me as Lexington. Lexington Rae. She's the only person on Earth who.." I caught myself again. "Well her and my mom, but you know what I mean. I don't know, Dré. I'm not Lux Lex around Abuelita and I just.."

Dré let out a laugh. "Lux. Please. I'm not Dré to my mother when she texts you to check on me, am I? I'm *Deandré* every single time. Shit, I'm surprised she doesn't put *Deandré Lamont Givens* in those messages."

We both laughed.

Dré continued, "We aren't children anymore but that doesn't mean we've forgotten who or where we came from. We didn't completely change our names or identities and start living double lives, we just grew up. We are no longer products of our environments because we've decided to create the environments in which we want to be products of. That's it. To me, you're Lux Lex. Lux for short. To your mother, you're Lexington. Lexy for short. To your father, your abuelita and anyone else that knew you as a child, you're Lexington. Lex for short. All of those people make you exactly who you are right now."

My eyes began to water.

"I can't wait to meet Abuelita. Getting to meet another piece of you–the woman I want to spend the rest of my life with, my best fucking friend, my ride or motherfucking die, is lit as fuck. To be honest, I didn't think you'd ever let me meet her. I'm fucking honored, babe. This shit is lit to me. Sitting there with Pops this morning, watching you interact the way that you did– that shit was fire. It was a part of you I had never seen before today and I fell deeper in love with you for it." He continued.

The tears began to flow down my warm cheeks. I was

blushing. A chill ran up my spine.

He looked over at me and then back at the road and lifted his hand to gently wipe a tear off of my cheek with his thumb. "Of course you're not Lux Lex around Abuelita, man." He giggled." First of all, Lux Lex is mine. Second of all, Lux be running all types of plays and she nasty as fuck in the bedroom. Abuelita don't need to know her grandbaby be doing all that."

He caught me off guard with the bedroom statement. I began to laugh and playfully punched him in the arm. "Stop telling my business!" I said as I wiped the rest of my tears from my face.

Dré switched from laughter to a more serious tone. "We're good, baby. Everything is going to be just fine. I told you that if Abuelita doesn't fuck with me I'll sit in the car and give y'all time to chat it up." He gripped my thigh.

Taking a deep breath in my nose and out of my mouth I said, "Ok, well if this goes well, Lexington and Deandré have to make more dinner plans with your mother. I can't be the only one exposing myself." A big smile formed across my face because I knew Dré wasn't going to love what I had just said.

Dré began to shake his head back and forth in amusement and disbelief. "Wow. That's what we're doing? That's crazy. You ain't shit. But ok, deal."

I placed my hand out so that we could shake on it. Dré hated having to shake on things with me.

He had always been a man of his word but whenever I required him to shake hands with me, he knew that it meant he wasn't hearing the last of whatever he shook on.

By that time we arrived at Abuelita's house and I was surprised to realize that I hadn't had any thoughts of doubt or worry, thanks to Dré. Whenever I think back to this day, I always wonder if Dré's pep talk was his way of comforting both of us. Like, did he have any secret feelings of worry or doubt that he didn't share with me? I guess I'll never know.

As we approached the front door, I toggled with the idea of ringing the doorbell over using my key but ultimately decided to just use my key. I didn't want to induce any unnecessary concern for Abuelita because it was rare for her to have visitors that actually rang her doorbell.

Dré stood behind me as I slowly opened the door, which in and of itself was weird because he always held doors open for me. I'm not sure I had ever touched a door knob from the moment we started dating.

"Mami, where are you?" I called out before closing the door behind me.

Dré quietly took a step to the side of me.

Abuelita called out, "Hi, mijá! One second."

I looked over at Dré and smiled. I think that was the moment where I started to become excited about them meeting.

Abuelita finally made her way toward the living room. "Ah!" She squealed. "Mijá! Porque no me lo dijiste?!" She ran to her room as quickly as she could.

I was relieved. "Mami, you look fine! Come back!" I laughed.

Dré looked down at me. He was visibly concerned and confused while he motioned his hands in a way that questioned whether or not he should leave. It was sort of cute to see him in a space of uncertainty. He had always walked into every room like he owned the place and paid everyone inside to be there, so it was almost refreshing to see him in a space where he didn't hold all of the power.

With a smile on my face I said, "No. You're fine. She asked why I didn't tell her. She feels like she needs to be fully dressed when there's company."

Dré's eyebrows twisted. "Since when do you speak

Spanish?" He whispered.

I scrunched my nose up. "Ah. Yeah. Lexington." I bit my bottom lip. "For the most part I understand it, but I don't really know how to speak it." I almost started to laugh.

Dré had the biggest smile on his face. He was completely shocked.

Things were already going so much better than I had expected them to. "Come on, fool. Let's sit in the kitchen." I shook my head, laughed and grabbed his arm, pulling him toward the kitchen.

Abuelita walked into the kitchen at the same time as Dré and I. She looked up at him and grabbed her face in excitement.

"Oh, mijo. Hi! Come. Sit. Sit." She rushed to pull out a chair at the table.

My heart completely melted at how excited she was to see Dré. At that moment, I realized that Dré had encountered a new layer of Lexington by sitting face to stone with Daddy and meeting Abuelita, but I was also encountering a new layer of Deandré because baby was a whole teddy bear when he saw Abuelita.

It felt unnecessary but I said, "Mami, this is my boyfriend, Deandré. Dré, this is my heart and soul. Abuelita." I stood there with a smile on my face as I watched the two of them interact. Almost in shock.

Before sitting down, Dré touched Abuelita's hands as she attempted to allow him to sit down. Instead, he gestured for her to take a seat instead. Abuelita obliged, with pure gratitude.

"It's so nice to finally meet you, Abuelita. Lex speaks so highly of you and tells me how good of a cook you are all the time." Dré smiled as he placed his hand onto Abuelita's shoulder.

Abuelita pointed at the pantry. "Mija, grab my nice glasses and a bottle of wine." She instructed me.

I dramatically grabbed my necklace as if they were pearls and looked at Abuelita and then at Dré. "Oh, you got her pulling out the good stuff? She never pulls the good stuff out for me!"

Waving her hand back and forth as if to encourage me to move faster, Abuelita said, "Mija, detente!"

Poor Dré was as confused as I had ever seen him.

As I placed the glasses onto the table I said, "I'm joking, Mami. I'm joking." I grabbed the bottle of wine next.

Abuelita began to pour wine for each of us. "I'm so happy you're here, Lexington. I wish you would have told me sooner, I would have cooked lunch or dinner."

Finally taking a seat at the table I said, "I know. I'm sorry. It was sort of last minute. We took Daddy some flowers this morning and I just felt like today was the day that you and Dré should finally meet."

Abuelita passed Dré a glass first. "Thank you." He said.

I continued, "We don't really have much time today anyway, Mami. Dré has an appointment at two o'clock, but we'll come back tomorrow if you want to make us dinner. Is that ok?"

Before Abuelita could answer, Dré interrupted. "Actually, Abuelita, if you're not busy, you're welcome to come with us today. My two o'clock appointment is actually a birthday surprise for Lex." He didn't even bother looking over at me.

"Huh?!" I almost choked on my wine.

Abuelita cut in, "Oh, yes! Déjame vestirme!" She began to stand up.

I shook my head. "English, Mami." I said before taking a sip of my wine.

Dré looked over at me and then at Abuelita. You could

tell that he was thoroughly entertained by everything that was happening; my confusion about the appointment, Abuelita's excitement and just being present for all of it.

Abuelita smiled, "Sorry, mijo. I said let me get dressed. Of course, I'm going! Lexington never takes me anywhere."

"Oh, Abuelita! Please!" I laughed in disbelief. I was tickled that she was pretending to turn on me in order to appease Dré. I enjoyed it.

Abuelita moved faster than I had ever seen her little self move before. While she was in her room getting dressed, I rinsed the wine glasses out, placed them into the dishwasher and then put a wine stopper into the wine bottle. When I was done, I walked over to Dré and placed my arms over his shoulders as he sat in the chair.

"Another birthday surprise?! What is it?" I said into his ear.

He laughed, "Get real. It wouldn't be a surprise if I told you. Watch out." He gently lifted his shoulder in an attempt to shoo me away.

Abuelita came out of her room in one of her best dresses and it was honestly the cutest thing I had ever seen. Truth be told, she was right, I didn't ever take her out of the house but I hadn't really realized that until she mentioned it. A part of me felt some guilt for it but I was happy that Dré had invited her to whatever it was that we were getting ready to do.

"You look beautiful, Abuelita." Dré said.

She started to blush. "Gracias, mijo." She smiled.

I was amused by their interaction and how smitten Abuelita was. "English, Mami. And yes. You look absolutely beautiful." I laughed and kissed her forehead.

"Ladies first." Dré gestured toward the front door.

Abuelita wasted no time heading out of the kitchen and toward the front door and Dré was right behind her. He made sure she got into the car safely while I locked up the house. My heart was so full. My man sat face to stone with my daddy and had my abuelita all googly-eyed within the same twenty-four hours. None of that was planned, but it really created memories I would never forget, right before my twenty first birthday. The buss down necklace and whatever else Dré had planned for me was all great, too, but watching him interact with two of the people that meant the most to me, was more than I could have ever asked for. The way that he had fallen deeper in love with me after watching me interact with Daddy was the same way I had fallen deeper in love with him after watching him interact with Abuelita.

As I finished locking the front door, I turned around to head to the car. The windows were very tinted, but I had no problem seeing that Abuelita was sitting in the front seat and she was seemingly telling Dré a very important story. I couldn't even imagine what they were talking about, I mean, they had literally just met. It made my heart smile, though. Abuelita was on cloud nine and I knew she was probably telling him about a random DIY project she had planned for herself. By the time I was near the car, Dré had gotten out of the driver's seat so that he could open the back door for me. Man, my heart was so full. I smiled, gave him a quick kiss on the lips and gladly hopped into the back seat.

On the ride over to the mystery destination, I sort of zoned out in the backseat. I couldn't help but to think of Ma and how she would have loved seeing Abuelita interact with Dré. I wondered how she herself would have interacted with him, too. My relationship with Dré reminded me a lot of Ma's relationship with Daddy, minus the fact that Dré wouldn't dare put his hands on me. The way that they were best friends, the way that Daddy always taught Ma new things, the way that, with the exception of beating her up, Daddy treated Ma like a queen. That's how Dré and I were, too. The way that Ma was always down to ride for Daddy was the same way that I was always down to ride for Dré.

The difference was that I never would have taken a charge for Dré and he never in a million years would have allowed me to. My thoughts were beginning to weigh me down. Some part of me wished that Ma could experience those moments with Abuelita, Dré and I and some part of me felt resentment toward her for not being able to.

Luckily, just as my thoughts started to become intrusive, Dré began to park the car in front of a building. Abuelita was just as confused as I was because I had never seen the place before and it didn't look like any place Dré would ever take me on a date. Especially not in the middle of the day and especially not as a first date with Abuelita. I didn't bother asking any questions because I knew he wasn't going to answer any of them, plus Abuelita was telling him something about the church she and my late grandfather used to attend. I had to have been pretty zoned out during the car ride because I don't even know what led her to share that story with him.

"Abuelita, excuse me for one second. I'm going to step out to make a phone call. Don't forget where you left off." Dré said as he opened the driver's door.

As soon as Dré made his way out of the car and closed the door behind him, Abuelita turned around like a child excited to talk about her first day at summer camp. "Oh, mija! He's perfect for you. What a gentleman." She said with a smile on her face.

At twenty years old, after experiencing all of the tragedy I had experienced, I guess it didn't really matter one way or another if Abuelita liked Dré or not, but it meant a lot to me. With that being said, seeing the excitement in her face, hearing the joy in her voice, and feeling the way her spirit genuinely welcomed Dré's presence damn near brought me to tears.

My smile could have lit up a dark night. "That makes me so happy. I'm so happy you feel that way. He's so good to me, Mami. He really is. He's a good man.I'm so grateful that you got to spend time with us today. We have to do this more often. And get you out of the house more often." I moved closer to her.

Just as I moved closer to her, Dré opened both of our car doors at the same time.

"Ladies." He said.

You would have thought the surprise was for Abuelita because she was practically more excited than I was. Don't get me wrong, I was excited, but my mind was focused on trying to figure out what the surprise could have been, which I'm sure was the reason Dré didn't tell me there was another surprise in the first place. Lucky for him, Abuelita was there as a buffer so I couldn't be as annoying as I wanted to be.

Dré closed the car doors and then allowed Abuelita to hook her arm into the bend of his elbow. Literally the cutest thing I had ever seen him do. We were parked right in front of the location we were supposed to be entering, so Dré walked right up to the door and allowed me to enter first as he and Abuelita followed right behind me.

Right as I stepped into the building, all of the lights came on, music started playing through what sounded like surround sound speakers and the whole crew was standing inside with their phones out. My heart sank and my knees weakened, so much so that I had to shake my legs in order to regain my balance. I literally couldn't believe my eyes. The room was filled with white roses and there were blue and silver balloons tied to every single chair. Of course the water works began once again, but that time, it was out of pure joy and happiness. Dré had gotten me a hair salon with four booths, two washing stations, a front desk, a back room and a selfie station.

After about thirty seconds of standing in the middle of the salon while I processed what was happening, I turned around to see Dré and Abuelita hugging. My heart sank deeper into my chest. Abuelita had a face full of tears and a smile that I felt like I hadn't seen in years. I turned back around to look at the crew and I screamed and began to jump up and down. My up and down jumping quickly became a circle of jumps and when I made it around to Dré, he was finally done hugging Abuelita so I ran and jumped into his arms.

With my face nestled into his neck and my legs wrapped around his body, I kept saying, "Thank you, baby. Thank you! Thank you! I can't believe you did this!"

Dré hugged my body tight as he rubbed my back with both of his hands. "You're welcome, baby. You deserve the world." He said.

I lifted my face up from his neck so that I could kiss him on the lips.

He kissed me twice and then said, "It's all yours, babe. Everything is in your name. It's all trademarked, LLC'd and DBA'd. The first year is paid up, all you have to do is design it how you want to and get people in here. You deserve this."

The only thing I could do was scream, smile and cry. Dré had gifted me a hair salon, we were able to bring my Abuelita along for the surprise and the whole crew was there to capture the moment.

I had finally untangled my body from Dré's and gave Abuelita a hug as well. Dré gave all of us a salon tour and I fell in love even more; with him and the salon. Everything he had done was so intentional. He made sure that all of the intricate details we had discussed over time were included. The booth chairs were upholstered with a silver leather like material and diamond like embroidery. The capes were all navy blue with a silver *Luxurious Cabello* logo centered in the front. He included blue led lights to represent my daddy and had two empty picture frames at the booth that would belong to me so that I could put photos of Ma and Daddy inside of them. In the front desk area, there was a floor vase that carried two dozen roses that were a mixture of blue and white. It fit the name perfectly: Luxurious.

After the tour, Blanco had a few bottles of champagne chilled and prepared for a celebratory toast. I'm not sure when he had time to do this, but Dré also made sure that there was a bottle of the same red wine Abuelita had been drinking at the house before we left. By that point, she was completely enamored. You couldn't tell her that Dré didn't plan this day specifically for her, too because he had her feeling so special. I told you, the man never missed a beat. Some of that credit belonged to Blanco because he's the one that always made sure shit got done whenever Dré called a play, no matter how last minute it was.

Getting the keys to my salon was one of the best days I had had in a very long time. From beginning to end, it was a day full of pure bliss. Dré had really outdone himself for my birthday and it was still about a week away. Watching Dré and the crew interact with Abuelita in my new salon was such a surreal moment. It felt so good to be exactly who I was at that moment. I was still Lux but I was also Lexington. My two worlds had finally become one and I loved every second of it. We all stayed in the salon for at least three hours while we danced, drank and enjoyed each other's company.

nine
ma.

AFTER LEAVING THE SALON, Dré and I took Abuelita to dinner so that she and Dré could spend more time with one another. Per her request, of course. Although it was as if I wasn't there, I really enjoyed spending time with Abuelita outside of the house. Even more so, I enjoyed how much she enjoyed Dré's company; I was worried for no reason at all. Dré allowed my abuelita to talk his ear off without ever appearing to be uninterested or irritated. Come to think of it, he never even looked at any of his phones either. The whole way home she ranted and raved about how nice the restaurant and how the staff was top tier. I loved that for her. I still wish I would have facilitated their introduction to one another sooner so that Abuelita could have experienced more of the lifestyle I was living.

When we finally arrived back at her house, Dré and I walked Abuelita inside. Truth be told, I could have walked her in on my own, but Dré wasn't having it. He had been helping take care of Abuelita financially for years because she's someone that I love but he never had an emotional connection with her prior to that day. You couldn't tell either of them that they hadn't been family since birth after that day though and because of that, Dré naturally became her protector the way he was mine. After making sure she was settled, Dré waited for me in the car while Abuelita and I had a quick girl talk about everything that had transpired that day.

"Oh, Mija. Dré's a great guy. I can't wait to tell tú madre about this." She said with joy on her face and in her spirit.

I gave her a hug and said, "I'm glad you enjoyed him, Mami. He means a lot to me. You mean a lot to him, too."

Abuelita began to speak in Spanish but she was speaking too quickly for me to understand. The only thing I knew was that it had something to do with my mom.

"Mami. English." My face displayed confusion because I genuinely didn't understand why she was speaking so quickly.

Her eyes began to swell with tears. "Visit your mother, mija. She misses you so much. She loves you and needs you. Visit her, sweetheart. Please."

The events from the day must have overwhelmed Abuelita with emotions because I felt as though the tears and the urgency for me to visit Ma were extremely misplaced after the day we had just had together.

Wiping the tears that fell down her cheeks, I said, "Mami, what just happened? Why are you so sad?" I embraced her body once again, hugging her tighter that time.

Abuelita wrapped her arms around my body in return. "I'm just so happy for you, mi amor. I know your mother would be just as happy. All we've ever wanted was for you to be happy and to feel loved unconditionally. Your mother did her best, Mija. I know she did. She became the best woman she could ever be so that you could have the best version of her. She is not perfect, Mija. But she loves you. Please visit your mother again."

To say the least, that wasn't how I expected our day to end, but Abuelita was my angel and not only did I respect her opinions, I respected her feelings as well.

"Mami. Mami" I said, as I gently grabbed her face between both of my hands. "Stop crying. You don't need this stress. I will visit her again. I promise. I'll go as soon as I can. Just stop crying. Please."

Abuelita wrapped her hands around both of my wrists. "Oh thank you, Lexington. Thank you." She began to smile.

"Abuelita." I sighed. "You haven't cried in years. Are you going to be fine staying here alone tonight? Should I tell Dré that I'm staying with you?" I asked as I wiped the last of her tears away.

"Oh por favor. Estoy bien." Abuelita said.

With a smile on my face, I shook my head in disbelief. "Oh Abuelita. What am I going to do with you, Mami? Ok. Well my phone is always with me and here.." I grabbed a pen and paper off of the small table near the front door. "This is Dré's number. You can call him any time. But if you need me tonight, then call right away. Don't try to be Superwoman and get through it on your own. Ok?" I handed her the paper with Dré's number written on it.

"Thank you." She was calm.

I think that the only reason I felt comfortable leaving Abuelita alone that night was because she had stopped crying and she seemed to have felt some relief once I told her that I would go visit my mother again. I mean, I knew that eventually I'd have to go see Ma again because I really wanted our hearts and my mind to be on the same page. I wanted us to heal. I just didn't necessarily want to go through all of those emotions days before my birthday and being that I told Abuelita I would make it happen as soon as I could, I knew that it would absolutely have to happen before my birthday.

One thing Dré always taught me through his actions was that if you say you are going to do something, whether it be good or bad, you do it. If what you said you'd do was something good, then you've built trust and authority within that relationship. If what you said you'd do was something bad, you still follow through because you're still building trust and authority within the relationship. There's definitely a different type of trust and authority being built if you have to stand on something negative you said, but it teaches people not to play in your face and establishes the authority that you are not to be underestimated by any definition of the word.

Dré would always say, "If I say I'll do something, niggas know it's going to get done. I don't care if it's good or bad, I stand on everything I say."

Based on the stories he's shared with me during our many three a.m. couch conversations and car rides, I knew that he had done things he didn't want to do, simply because he said that he would. I always believed that those stories were where his growth, maturity and careful consideration came from; dark memories, heavy mistakes and lost souls.

Anyway, after making sure that Abuelita locked the door behind me, I noticed that Dré was leaning against his car while he waited for me the same way he always did when he waited for me at Daddy's grave. It was very different from how Blanco would wait. Like I told you before, Blanco would sit in the car with the burner on his lap, ready for whatever. Dré was trained and ready to go, too, but he was like a frontline soldier while Blanco was more like a sniper. In general, our crew was very low profile, yet still well known and well respected in the spaces we needed to be. However, Dré believed that regardless of the fact that the streets and community respected us, you could never be too sure that someone wouldn't switch up. *Complacency creates chaos*, he always told us.

As I walked from Abuelita's front door toward Dré, we made eye contact but didn't say a word to one another. We had both fallen deeper in love that day and the passion in our gaze was the first moment we really had alone to truly acknowledge those feelings. When I finally approached him, I threw my arms around his neck, grabbing the back of his head with my right hand and pulling his head closer to mine so that we could kiss. His hands gripped my ass and then transitioned up my back as he caressed my body underneath my hoodie. The touch of his skin against mine paired with the taste of his tongue, sent chills up my spine.

I stopped kissing him, "Thank you for everything." I said.

"You don't have to thank me, baby." Dré said as he continued to caress my back.

"I do. Thank you for everything that you are to me. That you do for me. For how you made Abuelita feel today. All of it. I love you." I shifted my hand from behind his neck, to cup his cheek and ear instead.

He smiled, "Gracias, baby." He was certain he was using the correct word.

We both laughed.

"English, papi. You just said 'thank you', fool." I rolled my eyes as we headed to the passenger side of the car.

"Man, I can't believe you never told me you speak Spanish. I guess I should have known but damn. Dré said playfully as he opened my car door.

The entire car ride home, Dré and I held hands. Every so often he would lift my hand to his lips and kiss it without saying a word.

Blanco was already home by the time Dré and I had arrived. It appeared that he had showered and changed his clothes. "What's good, bro?" He said as he and Dré slapped hands.

Dré greeted Blanc with his right hand because he was holding my hand with his left.

Blanc continued, "Y'all good tonight? I'm 'bout to step out for the night but I can shoot back this way if need be."

"Nah, bro. You good. Handle ya business. We're inside tonight." Dré said as we continued toward our bedroom.

"Alright, bet. We locked in with TMoney tomorrow, so I'll be back before then." Blanco said as he headed out the door.

TMoney was the newest, youngest member of our crew. He was essentially taking over the role that Blanco occupied when I first met Dré and Blanc; the runner. TMoney was going to be the little homie that handled all of the small details that were necessary but tedious. As far as I knew, there was no initiation process other than just pulling your weight and proving yourself to be loyal, reliable and trustworthy. Anyone who was a part of the crew came with a heavy recommendation from someone closely connected and they always had some sort of fucked up upbringing that ultimately they needed healing from. I guess we were all a bunch of fucking misfits with good hearts and hustle mentatlities and money was our therapy. Go figure.

For the rest of the night, the only sounds that filled the penthouse were that of music blaring from the speakers and the sound of me moaning with every stroke. We fucked in the shower, the bathroom counter, the closet floor and in the kitchen, too. Damn near everywhere except the bed.

When we were finally done, we sat on the floor, naked, Dré's dick still inside of me as the walls of my vagina gripped him and just expressed our love for one another. He told me how much I meant to him and how I had helped him grow into the man that he was in that moment. He told me that we would only be doing our trap shit for another year or two and then we would be completely out of the game and be able to start our family. He also told me how proud of me he was for accomplishing all that I had accomplished despite all of the turmoil I had experienced in my life and promised me that none of it would be in vain. Eventually, he carried me to the bed and we slept peacefully as our naked bodies wrapped around each other like vines on a fence. From start to finish, it was probably the most beautiful day I had ever had.

The next morning, Dré was already showered and on his way out of the door with Blanco by the time I had woken up. They had the meeting with TMoney as well as a couple of other plays to run and Dré liked to touch bases at as many of the stash houses as he could from time to time, so I assumed he'd be gone for a majority of the day. I didn't mind though, it gave me time to write out all of my ideas for the salon and call Sydney and share all of the great news with her.

"Bitch! Guess the fuck what!" I said as soon as Sydney answered the phone.

She sounded unamused. "Girl. Don't stress me out today. Tell me." Sydney said dryly.

Ignoring the dryness of her tone, I said, "Dré got me a salon!! We are about to have a full blown business! Doing hair! Selling hair! All of it!" I was excited all over again.

There was a brief, confusing silence on the other end of the phone and then, "So basically, Dré got himself another spot to launder money through." She took a deep sigh. "Lex, I thought you were going to wait until you could afford this place on your own." Sydney said.

"Actually, everything is in my name and he doesn't need 'another' business to launder money through. Trust me. We're good. I thought I was calling my best friend to share good news, but I guess not. I was going to see if you wanted to ride with me to visit Mom, but it sounds like you need a nap or something, so I'll link with you another time." I made sure not to give Syd even a second to slip a word in.

Sydney's tone changed slightly. "Lex, don't start. You know I'm your.."

I quickly interrupted her, "Nah, it's all good. I'm not even tripping. I'm going to hit you later though 'cus I need to get ready to pull up on my mom."

Without waiting for Sydney to respond, I disconnected the call. My feelings were hurt. As far as childhood friends went, Sydney was the last of the bunch for me. That wasn't the first time she had said some low key hater shit to me but it was the first time I had even scratched the surface of addressing it. Remember, Dré stopped liking her when she said some slick shit to me in the car on the way to see my mom the first time because he felt as though she was jealous of me. She was my best friend though and I refused to believe that someone that came from where I came from, been through what I've been through and watched me experience the things I've experienced would ever hold the capacity or see reason to be jealous of me. It just never made sense. Unfortunately, her dry tone and underwhelming excitement for me in a moment of what felt like an achievement for me, was something I couldn't ignore. It was actually the moment that I decided I would never speak to her again; cold turkey. It doesn't matter who a person is to you, if they can't celebrate your wins like a win of their own, they shouldn't be around at all.

Whether or not Sydney was taking me to see my mother, my mind was made up that I would be seeing her. Dré and Blanco had taken the *Benz,* so I sent Dré a quick text that said: *You were right. Syd is a hater. She's cancelled. Taking the Rover to go see Ma for a bit. Locations on.*

I knew Dré was in the field handling business, so I didn't really expect him to do anything more than read my text and take a mental note. Instead, he replied, *Fuck her. Proud of you. Tap in when you touch down.*

After that, I was on my way to visit my mother again but on my own, which had never happened before. I felt like it was a milestone of sorts. It took me about an hour to arrive at the penitentiary but it was an hour full of brainstorming for *Luxurious Cabello,* thinking about all of the hater shit Syd had ever said and done and thinking about how grateful I was for Dré. When I was finally parked, I placed all of my belongings out of sight even though the windows to the *Range Rover* were super dark. My nerves began to kick in. I was nervous because the last time I had visited my mother, it wasn't exactly a great visit and this time, I'd be sharing more with her because I knew that Abuelita had already started priming her. Regardless of my nerves or how much I dreaded the idea of sharing my life with my mother, there was no turning back.

The walk from my car to the metal detectors felt like a marathon. My heart was racing, my palms were sweaty and my mouth was dry but I had to be a woman of my word. Being a woman of my word wasn't the only reason I was following through with the visit. In my heart of hearts, I really did miss my mom. I missed the old days. I missed having her next to me all of the time. I guess some part of me was fearful that things wouldn't go as smoothly with her as they did with Daddy but the other part of me knew that wasn't even close to realistic. It wasn't like Daddy could argue with me about anything or refuse to take account- ability for his actions. My heart just forgave him and I needed to do the same thing with Ma.

Waiting for her to be escorted to the visitation area by the guard felt like hours. Apparently jails create some false sense of time for me. Anyway, when she finally sat down, I could tell that she was doing her best not to cry. I could tell because I was doing the exact same thing. Before Ma got locked up, we were damn near the same person; Daddy always called us twins. I could feel her energy the same way she could feel mine and before either of us could get a word out, tears began to stream down her face.

"Hi, baby." She stopped talking to clear her throat. "I'm so happy you came." She said.

I channeled my inner Dré and did my best to choose my words wisely. "Hi, Ma. How you holding up in here?" Truthfully, I didn't know what else to say.

She wiped the tear that rested at the tip of her nose. "Ah, you know. Day by day. No other choice, really." She looked down at her hands and smiled.

I looked down at my hands, too.

Ma continued, "It's almost your twenty first. Can you believe it?! I know you have big plans."

For some reason, that triggered me. Lux Lex is where I feel safest but I wanted to show up as Lexington for my mom that day. But hearing her say that and knowing that she had already spoken to Abuelita made me feel like she was being fake. I didn't want fake love or fake interest in or about my life from her. I just wanted her to show up authentically.

I just stared at her for a moment without saying a word.

I tried to choose my words as carefully as possible but I'm not sure I did a great job at that.

"My boyfriend planned everything." My tone was as dry as Sydney's tone.

"I heard. I hear he's a pretty stand up guy. Congrats on your salon, by the way." Ma was finally showing up authentically.

"Thank you. I'm super excited about it." I was trying my best to refrain from any harsh tones.

Ma was doing her best to ignore my dry tone. "I'm happy for you. I really am. I wish I could have been there to experience it with you."

We just sat there in silence again while the sound of laughter and joy bounced off of the walls from the other families spending time with their mother, sister, girlfriend or whomever.

"Lexy, baby. He sounds charming. He really does. I'm grateful that he's taken care of you and Mami for all these years. It sounds like he's a lot like your father was when I first met him." Her tone was that of the start of a lecture.

"Ma. Please. Don't." I took a deep breath so that I wouldn't get myself worked up. "Don't do that. Just let me be happy, Ma. Ask me about my plans for the salon. Ask me about my plans for the future. Ask me about anything. But please, please don't even entertain the thought of telling me what my boyfriend, who you've never had the opportunity of meeting, and probably never will, is like. You knew exactly who Daddy was and you still ended up here. You knew exactly who Daddy was and you still abandoned me for him." My voice was low and stern and my eyes were beginning to fill up with tears.

The little color Ma had left to her complexion began to flush. "I'm sorry, baby. I'm sorry that I abandoned you. I'm sorry that I've missed so much of your life. I'm sorry that I can't be there for you the way that I'm supposed to. If I could go back to that day, I would. I swear to you I would. I would go back and take you to school instead of doing the bullshit that Daddy and I had planned." Ma's eyes didn't even have time to fill up with tears because they were flowing freely.

I was silently crying, too. My heart was so heavy yet free. 'I'm sorry' followed by every reason she mentioned, was exactly what I needed to hear from my mother. Before I could get a word in, she continued on.

"Baby, whether I had taken you to school that day or not, Daddy and I would have followed through with our plans. There's no way for me to know whether or not the outcome would have been different had I taken you to school that morning, but this is where things are now. This is the outcome we got. Daddy and I were involved in things and with people that we shouldn't have been. That day was supposed to be the day that ended all of that for us. We were supposed to run one last play and then turn our lives around but neither of us expected for it to end the way it did." Ma's tone was the same sweet tone I remembered hearing right before she would tell me to close the bedroom door.

Hearing her tone took me back to a place and time that I hadn't visited even in my dreams in quite some time. It took me back to our old apartment where life was mostly easy and free of pain. But her words confused me. Her words were full of implications and left room for way too many assumptions.

"What did you do? Where were you? What happened?" I asked through a face full of tears.

Ma shook her head in disappointment. "It doesn't matter, Lexy. None of it does. All that matters to me now is doing what I can to make up for lost time."

"You can't make up for lost time, Mommy." You could hear the defeat in my voice. "The time is gone. We don't get it back. Daddy is gone. We don't get him back. I don't know how to move forward from here." I began to wipe the tears from my face.

Ma was stepping out of emotion and into logic. "We move forward with love and forgiveness, Lexington. The only thing that gets me through each day in this hell hole, is thinking about how much I love you. Forgiving myself for ending up here is the only way that I've been able to love myself again. But.."

"But what, Ma?" I realized I was louder than I intended to be. Lowering my voice I said, "I don't know how to forgive you. I miss my mommy. I miss my twin. I feel like once Abuelita goes, every piece of my childhood is gone. Everything that I have to hold onto the foundation of who I am will just disappear when Abuelita goes because I don't have Daddy anymore and it feels like I don't have you either." I was almost whispering.

Ma pleaded with me, "As long as I have breath in my body, you have me. I don't know how to help you forgive me, but I'm willing to try. I'm willing to put in the work. I just need you to open the door to me, Lexy. Tell me it's ok for me to be a part of your life again."

My heart, mind and spirit were exhausted. I had had enough emotions for one day but I didn't want to end things on a bad note. "I don't know, Ma. I'm not sure. This is just too much for me. I just need time, ok? I'll come back after my birthday, I promise. I just .. I just need time."

I took a breath. "Thank you for apologizing. It really means a lot to me." I said as I stared directly into her eyes.

"I love you, Lexington." Ma said.

Before standing up I said, "I love you too, Ma. I'll come back soon, ok?"

Before I could stand up completely, the guard was already at our table placing handcuffs back onto my mother's wrists. The sound of the metal clicking into itself as it locked around her wrists sent chills through my body and forced me to move even faster so that I didn't have to see her that way; in captivity. My mother lived freely for as long as I could remember. Even the mornings after she had gotten the shit beat out of her, she did her best to keep her spirits high and her energy free. Hell, before she took that charge for my father, I had never seen her being shackled to anything or anyone that even threatened her mental, emotional or spiritual freedom.

By the time I made it back to my car, I realized that I had forgotten to let Dré know that I had made it safely. My phone had ten missed calls and five text notifications so I didn't even bother reading any of the texts, I just called Dré back immediately.

He answered on the first ring. "Yo. What the fuck!" He was whispering, but his frustration was loud.

"Babe, I'm so sorry. I got here and started to get nervous and completely forgot to text you." I said anxiously.

Still whispering, he said, "Damn, Lux. I been watching your phone sit in this one spot for all this time, nervous as shit. You can't forget the rules, babe. I made them for a reason."

I felt awful. "I know, baby. I'm sorry. I'm safe. I'm fine. I made it here. I saw Ma and I'm getting ready to go home now."

Dré was still whispering. "Alright, hit me when you get there. We'll talk tonight."

"Why are you whispering?" I asked.

It was definitely not the time for me to pull a jealous girlfriend card, but Dré ain't ever whispered on the phone with me before. We've never even had any incidents of him cheating or even flirting for that matter, but as he always said, complacency creates chaos, so sometimes you just have to make sure.

"'Cus I'm in a meeting and you're stressing me out. Go home. I'll be there soon. I love you." He whispered but his demands were stern.

"I love you, too." I replied with a smile on my face. Something inside of me enjoyed the sternness in his whisper.

Dré was my perfect balance. Every problem I caused or encountered, he had a solution. Any time I was nervous or disheveled, he provided peace and order and whenever I got on his last damn nerve, he still made sure I knew that he loved me. Without even knowing how my visit with my mom went, Dré was able to help me pull myself together while still respectfully expressing his own concerns and that's one of the things that no matter what, I will always be grateful for.

I spent my drive home thinking of ways to facilitate peace between my mother and I the way Dré helped me facilitate peace between my heart and my mind. As I played our visit back in my mind, I realized that Ma represented freedom to me for my whole life and then suddenly, she was any and everything but that. She literally had her freedom revoked, she was snatched away from her only child, she lost her man and best friend and she could only hear her mother's voice through a telephone. It was the drive home from visiting her that helped me realize that in order to forgive my mother, I was going to have to unlearn the free woman I knew her to be so that I could accept the woman that she had to be.

Ma was far from free physically and seeing her the way I did during that visit had shown me that she was far from free mentally, spiritually and emotionally, too. The same way I was held captive to my emotions and the loss I had endured was the same way Ma was held captive to all of those same things. The difference was that I was able to compartmentalize my captivity so that I could go on with my life. Ma didn't even have that option. It was heartbreaking to see and too much to process right before my twenty-first birthday so I decided that I would push it to the back of my mind until it was time to face it again. Another Lux Lex luxury – one that my mother would never be afforded.

deandré lamont givens.

LATER THAT DAY when Dré and Blanco arrived home, I was sitting at the round table with my laptop having a glass of the red wine that Abueita enjoyed, while I listened to *My Little Love by Adele*. Somehow, I had decided that if my mom could express herself in a song, it would probably be that one.

Blanco called out, "Sup, Lux!" As he headed directly to his bedroom from the front door.

Only lifting my eyes from my laptop, I hollered back, "Big Blanc!"

Dré walked into our bedroom to place all of his belongings down like he always did. That wasn't normal for him. Usually, he'd kiss me before he did anything else but I knew that he was bothered that I forgot to text him.

As I sat there and researched decor ideas for my new shop, memories from my childhood played on a loop in the back of my mind. I'm pretty sure Dré could tell that I was deep in my thoughts because instead of pressing me like I thought he would when he came out of the bedroom, he made his way over to me and softly kissed my cheek. After that, without saying a word, he grabbed a wine glass from the kitchen, poured himself a glass of wine, pulled a chair close to me and sat down with his legs facing my body. The smell of his cologne lingered in the empty space between us and created a sense of security within my mind.

We didn't say a word to one another, but I looked away from my laptop, slightly leaned into him and gently kissed his lips. I allowed my lips to rest on his for a moment before I turned away. As I began scrolling through websites again, he nestled his head into my shoulder as he watched the screen.

"I'm sorry." I said without missing a scroll.

Dré didn't say anything in reply.

I stopped scrolling and took a sip of wine and a deep breath. "I didn't mean to scare you. I know the rules, so I don't really have an excuse."

Dré lifted his head from my shoulder. "We gotta talk." He said before downing his entire glass of wine.

My heart began to race because I knew that I had stressed him out by not letting him know that I had made it safely, but I didn't think it warranted much of a talk beyond me taking accountability and apologizing for my mishap.

Slowly closing my laptop I said, "Babe, please. I don't have the energy. I just want to hang out with you and not think about anything other than my new shop and celebrating my birthday."

Dré was visibly agitated. His demeanor was different than I had ever seen. It was like he was uncomfortable in his skin and it very quickly began to rub off on me.

"Wait. Talk about what? What's going on?" I asked with concern and confusion.

Dré grabbed my hand as he stood up from the chair. "Come on."

A million bad thoughts raced through my mind as I

followed Dré from the dining room into our bedroom. Outside of forgetting to send a fucking text message, I couldn't think of any reason he would have been acting the way he was. Not only that, bad news was the last thing I needed.

As we entered our bedroom, he slowly closed the door behind us. "Sit down. He said as he pointed to the bed.

"No." I said.

I folded my arms and looked directly into his eyes. "Dré, what the fuck?!"

He took a deep breath into his nose and out of his mouth and then interlocked his fingers behind his neck. My heart began to race even faster and my stomach grew a pit. At that point, I had no choice but to sit down at the edge of the bed because my legs felt like they were going to give out. My thoughts were racing but I couldn't formulate any words.

Dré was looking at me but his mind was somewhere else. It was like he was looking through me. His heart must have been racing as quickly as mine was because I could see his chest rising with each breath that he took.

Finally, "I know that I said we were out of the game in a year – two max." He began.

By that point, I was super confused.

He continued, "I don't want you to worry, but I can't keep this from you. You are literally my right hand." He stopped talking.

"Dré." I said sternly.

He anxiously licked his lips and blurted out, "Lux. Fuck." He took a breath. "One of the stash houses got raided."

It was like the wind was knocked out of me. I exhaled and placed my hands on my knees and looked down at the floor.

"Jay was there with TMoney, so they both got hemmed up. None of it connects back to us right now but it for sure means that shit is hot right now." Dré continued.

It was somewhat of a relief to hear that the house didn't connect back to Dré and I but I knew that wasn't the last of what he had to tell me, so I didn't even bother asking any questions.

"That means we got about six more months of this shit. Really, less. You need to stay at Abuelita's for a minute. You can facilitate but not participate – me and Blanc will handle everything." He sounded defeated.

"Dré, no! I'm not just going to.." I interrupted.

He cut me off. "Lux, LISTEN!"

I'm not sure Dré had ever raised his voice at me before that moment, but I knew that it meant that things were a lot worse than he was telling me.

"Look, if shit goes bad, you're the only person that knows how to do everything." Dré dropped down into a squatting position and placed his head in the fold of his arms. "Lux, if shit goes bad, you're the only one I trust to keep shit afloat." He looked up at me.

I could feel a lump forming in the back of my throat because seeing Dré that stressed out and not being able to console him in a real way, hurt my heart. It wasn't the time or place to start crying though. Dré needed his best friend, Lux, not the girlfriend.

We sat in silence for a moment.

"For now, you're at Abuelita's. We all have new phones and we're only using video chat, no regular phone calls, locations off, check in every hour. This is our last night at the penthouse, so take no more than two duffles of whatever you want to take with you. There's cash in the whip and your account is good, too. Me and Blanc will be at the spot downtown. You take the Rover because it's in your name and not connected to any of this shit but you need to stay low, Lux. Complacency creates chaos and that's the last thing we need right now." Dré shifted his position from a squat to sitting on the floor.

The only thing I could do was listen. Essentially, Dré was preparing me for my worst nightmare; losing him.

He continued, "Get the salon together. It ain't no pressure, but over the next six months or less, me and Blanco will run it up while you focus on the salon and the trucks. Whatever the salon and trucks bring in will be what you keep for yourself over the next few months. The bag in the whip should hold you and Abuelita over though. Between stocks, crypto and our other investments, we'll be fine but I need this six months to just flip and stack to make sure of that."

I took a deep breath. "Why are you sitting me out? We've been doing this shit as a unit for how many years now? Why are you switching it up?"

Dré shook his head in disappointment. "I already gave you that answer, Lux. If they get us how they got Jay and TMoney, you're the only person that can feed the whole crew. You're the only person that knows where every spot is, how to contact every plug and run every play. If both of us are out, then the whole crew is out. We are playing chess, baby. We *play chess, or* we *get check'd*. Gotta protect the queen at all costs. It's that simple." He looked up at me.

"Ok. So then it's three months. Not six. You and Blanco have three months to do whatever the fuck you need to do and then we're out. The whole crew. We're done. We move out of this city. We throw all of these phones away and we start legit. Three months, Dré. That's it." I fought back tears as I laid out my demands.

To my surprise, Dré was receptive. "Ok. Three months. But you gotta hold shit down on your side, Lux. We can't fuck this up. We can't get lazy but we can't get greedy either."

Offended, I said, "When the fuck have I ever been lazy or greedy? When have I not held shit down on my side?"

He exhaled through his mouth and clicked his lips. "I'm not saying that you haven't held shit down or that you're lazy. Fuck. I'm saying that WE can't fuck this off. You can't participate how you been doing. You can't be outside with me like that right now. We can't be on no type of simp shit and trying to lay up together or none of that. The next six … three, the next three months are strictly business. I have three months to make sure me, you and Abuelita are good for life and that means three months to make sure the whole crew is in a position to be good for life, too. So that fucking attitude that you just tried to throw my way is out. We don't have time for that shit."

"What about Jay and TMoney? What are we doing about them?" I asked, ignoring his last two sentences.

Dré took another deep breath, "They'll be out by Monday. That's already in motion. TMoney is damn near a baby in this shit, so that's easy. When he's out, there's a bag waiting for him and he can move however he wants to move. There's a spot and a bag waiting for Jay in Miami. The nigga not new to this but he hasn't put in as much time as the rest of the crew, so that was the easiest way to close that shit out." he said.

My thoughts were beginning to race again. "Ok." I said in agreement.

Dré had lifted himself up from the floor and stood on his knees in front of me as I sat on the edge of the bed. He placed his arms around my body and his head into my lap, finally switching from being my OG to being my boyfriend. It was his way of letting me know that it was safe for me to transition from best friend to girlfriend and that was exactly what I did. Embracing his body like he did mine, I placed my hand into the top of his shirt and began to rub his back as he cradled into my body. Tears began to flow from my eyes onto the back of his shirt, leaving little damp spots each time they landed.

"I can't lose you, Dré. I can't watch you be in handcuffs. I can't watch the crew be dismantled. I don't want to be without you. I can't go through that again." I cried out.

Dré quickly shifted himself from his knees to his feet and picked my body up. My legs wrapped around his body as he turned and sat on the bed, with me on top of him.

Wiping the tears from my face, he said, "You won't, baby. Three months. We just need to stack and stay low for three months. We're going to be fine. You can start looking for places in whatever city you want. We can open a new salon and let somebody else run this one once shit gets poppin'. Abuelita can come live with us and take care of our babies while you're at the salon and I'm in my home office investing in stocks and real estate. Everything that was supposed to happen in one or two years is going to happen in three months instead. You won't lose me, babe. We just gotta play chess right now. Thug this shit out so we can come out on top. That's it." He began to kiss all over my face.

Normally, Dré was able to calm my nerves when he reassured me the way he had just done, but there were so many reasons why it didn't work that time.

"So for the next three months, I'm only going to see you every hour for a quick video call and that's it?" I asked as more tears began to stream like a river down my cheeks.

He knew how fucking wild that sounded. "Don't think of it that way. Think of it like this, for the next three months, you'll be learning how to own and operate *Luxurious Cabello* and run a trucking business with three trucks, three drivers and dispatchers. For the next three months, you'll be on your boss shit more than ever before. After those three months, I'll make sure that you never have to work another day in your life if you don't want to. That's on me."

My heart was heavy but ultimately, I knew that everything that was being presented to me came with the territory of the life I had signed up for. I knew that everything that Dré had taught me over the years was in preparation for the very moment we were experiencing. The same way that I felt as though every member of our crew was capable of taking what Dré had taught them and using it to run their own shit, was the exact same way I was going to have to take all of his teachings with me if shit hit the fan. After all of the work I had done to pull Lexington out of the dark, Lux Lex was the piece of me that Dré needed the most. It was the piece of me that I needed in order to survive.

Dré and I had all types of stash spots that couldn't be traced back to either of us. He had always made it a point to place duffle bags full of cash in different locations so that we were never without, no matter the circumstances. He had always taught me exactly how to run every single money play he had, whether it was illegal or not, so that if he ever ended up in a grave or a cell behind our lifestyle, I could manage without him. I guess we never considered how I would handle my emotions without him. I guess that's the same way I imagine Daddy probably never considered mine and Ma's capacity to manage our emotions without him.

After Dré told me that I'd never have to work again if I didn't want to, I wrapped my arms around him, squeezing his body as if it would be the last time I was ever able to hug him.

In an attempt to lighten the mood, I said, "You don't

buy me a whole hair salon and then tell me I never have to work again if I don't want to. It doesn't work that way."

He laughed, "Nah, you don't even have to work there if you don't want to. You can train some bitches to do what you do and let them run shit up for you. You can kick your feet up and relax when we're out of this shit, baby. I promise you that."

The rest of our day was mostly spent in bed, with only the sounds of our voices filling the room. We just wanted to enjoy each other's company before we spent the next three months apart. That time was just as much for me as it was for Dré because although his family was alive, free and fully capable of holding space for him, he felt as though outside of the crew, I was all he had. The same way that even though I had Abuelita and sort of had Ma, too, I felt as though he was all I had. We needed each other to survive. We needed each other to be free. We needed each other to feel safe.

By the end of the day, Dré had ordered take out for us, Blanco included, and we enjoyed one last round table dinner with the three of us. Apparently, Dré and Blanco had already decided that no one else in the crew would know what the plan was because it left less room for fear or fuck ups. I know that Dré really felt the pressure of pulling everybody out of the game on top of adding more onto my plate. I would imagine Blanco felt pressure of his own knowing that things were about to change so drastically with the crew on top of him walking into fatherhood. Money had never been an issue for any member of our crew. Dré made sure of that, but it was about time for each of them to spread their wings and fly on their own; whether they knew it or not and whether they were ready or not.

Dinner was different from our normal take out nights,

for obvious reasons, and we couldn't ignore the awkward-ness or fake the funk. Well, I wasn't willing to, anyway.

"Blanc, three months. Not six. We handle all of this shit in three months and we start fresh, ok?" I said as we all ate our food.

Blanco placed his fork down, looked up at me and then over at Dré.

Dré shook his head as if to let Blanco know that he was in agreement with me.

"Alright, Lux. Three months." Blanco replied.

He started to pick his fork up to continue eating and then he paused. "D." He looked over at Dré. "I got a little boy on the way." He smiled and stared through Dré off into space. "Three months, OG. Three months." He continued to pick up his fork.

Part of me was hoping that Blanco had kept his great news to himself because I knew that in a time like that, it only added to the pressure that Dré was already feeling.

Shocked, Dré replied, "Nigga! That's great news!" He held his hand out to dap Blanco up.

Blanco smiled and shook Dré's hand and then smiled at me, too.

"Three months, bro. Three months." Dré reassured Blanco.

That was it. The three of us finished our dinner together and then we began to transition into the three month play. Blanco loaded his and Dré's bags into a rental car and headed downtown to the spot they would be staying at, while Dré loaded my *Range Rover* with the items I was taking with me to Abuelita's. He and I drove separately so that he could head downtown immediately after seeing that I was safe. Truth be told, he could have just gone down-town without making the stop at Abuelita's, but I think he wanted to spend a little more time with me and say hello to

Abuelita. Plus, if you haven't noticed by now, Dré's protective nature hardly allowed him to let me do things on my own on a normal day, so there was no way in hell he was about to send me off on my own for three whole months. Especially because shit was hot and he had just felt the stress of not knowing where I was when I forgot to text him.

We made it to Abuelita's house fairly quickly and Dré carried three of my four bags while I carried the fourth bag. I didn't take many clothes, shoes or purses with me because Dré said that we would just buy all new shit when everything was over. He didn't want the penthouse to look like we were literally on the run if for some reason things went bad. When we were packing our bags he said, "This shit is material, we'll get it all back. Take the jewelry, some clothes, shoes, panties and bras and shit. It's just three months."

And I didn't argue with him.

Of course, Abuelita was fucking elated to see us. Well, to see Dré, really. So much so that she almost missed the fact that we were carrying duffle bags with us.

She finally noticed my bags. "Mija, what's going on?" She asked after greeting Dré.

That was the moment that it all began to sink in for me. I was doing my best to keep my composure but Dré must have seen my heart drop and my face must have shown all of my emotions because he very quickly answered Abuelita's question.

"Abuelita, Lexington is going to stay here for a few months." He smiled as he looked at me. "We are going to buy a house soon and it just makes more sense for me to save a few months worth of rent while we make that happen. Is that okay with you?" He asked as he placed his hand on her shoulder.

Abuelita clapped her hands in excitement. "Oh, sí! Of course! This is her home, mijo." She waved her hand at me, suggesting I put my bag down.

Dré quickly grabbed my bag off of my shoulder. "Thank you, Abuelita. You know, if you're up to it, when we move, we'd like for you to come live with us." He said as he placed all four of my bags in front of what he assumed to be my bedroom.

Before Abuelita could respond, I interjected. "Hey, hey, hey!" I put on a fake smile. "We don't even have the house yet, don't scare her off just yet!" I said.

The truth is that I wasn't concerned about scaring Abuelita off. I was actually worried about how heartbroken she would be if she thought she was moving in with us in a few months and it never happened. It was one thing for Dré and I to harbor unannounced feelings of fear and anxiety but I didn't want to add any additional pressure to myself by listening to Abuelita talk about future plans when she had no idea what it was going to take to achieve them. Not to mention the slightly high probability that they may never be achieved.

Dré laughed as he gracefully made his way back over to Abuelita, but I could tell that he didn't appreciate the underlying tone of uncertainty in my statement.

"Ok, ladies. I'll leave the two of you to enjoy the rest of your evening. I've got some work to do so that I can make sure we get this house." Dré said as he kissed Abuelita on the forehead and hugged her, but never taking his eyes off of me.

"Ok, mijo. Be safe. Please." Abuelita said as she leaned into the hug.

With a smile on his face, Dré said, "Always, Abuelita. Siempre."

Shocked, I burst out in laughter. I'm not sure when he had found time to add a Spanish word to his vocabulary, but it was clear that he was incredibly proud of himself for doing so.

"Who are you?!" I said through laughter.

He quickly replied, "Me and Abuelita 'bout to have whole conversations in Spanish at the house, watch."

We all shared a laugh and Abuelita began to hug Dré tighter.

"Ok, mami. I'm going to walk him to his car. Want to have a glass of wine with me after?" I asked.

"Si, mija." Abuelita said as she headed toward the kitchen.

Dré and I made our way toward the front door.

As we stood in the doorway, my emotions began to rise. My heart felt like it was pounding through my chest. Dré could sense all of it. He cupped my face into the palms of his hands, rubbing my cheeks with his thumbs.

"I can't believe we're doing this right before my birthday." I could barely look at him.

He lifted my face so that I had no choice but to look into his eyes. "Just three months, baby. Only three. I'll make it up to you. I promise."

My eyes began to swell with tears. "I'm sorry." I shook my head. "It feels like I'm being ungrateful after everything you just did for me. I'm not. I promise. I just.." A tear fell down my cheek landing at Dré's thumb.

"I just don't want to lose you too, Dré. I can't." My voice cracked as I attempted to fight back more tears.

Dré gently kissed my forehead and then titled my head back so that he could kiss my lips. "I know, Lux. I know."

Although my head was tilted back, I closed my eyes so that I didn't have to look at him.

"Look at me." He said.

I opened my eyes and tears began to fall.

"Three months. Hold your head for three months. Nothing is changing between us but everything is changing for us. It's not how we planned, but this is why I've always expressed the importance of knowing how to pivot the play. It's a quick pivot but when we're out we can look back and laugh at how we *finessed* this shit." Dré's voice was low and his tone was reassuring.

There was nothing for me to say.

Dré leaned forward and whispered into my ear, "Nothing and nobody is more important to me than you. You're my best fucking friend. You're going to be my wife. You're going to raise my children. I love the fuck out of you, Lux. Hold me down for three months. Just three."

Chills rushed my body as his lips gently touched my skin while the bass of his voice rang through my ears. I grabbed his wrists and squeezed them as tight as I could and then threw my arms around his neck and hugged him even tighter.

"Three months. Three fucking months, Dré. That's it. I don't care if the crew wants to stay in this shit when it's over. I don't care if Blanc wants to keep going. I don't care about anybody else. YOU are done in three months." I cried.

Dré pulled me closer into him. "I got you. I promise." He said.

For a few moments, we just hugged one another without saying a word. I could feel his heart pounding as hard as mine was. We were both nervous but he wasn't willing to allow me to see or feel the pressure that he felt, but I could feel it with every beat of his heart. Finally, we released one another and Dré walked out of the front door without another word.

There was no way in hell Abuelita could see me as worked up as I was. Before joining her in the kitchen, I had to pull myself together as best I could, so I stood in the doorway for a few moments until my heart rate decreased and all of my tears dried up. Thankfully, it worked.

Abuelita and I enjoyed each other's company for the rest of the evening as we drank wine and baked cookies. It was actually a refreshing moment for me. It was a moment where I was able to just ease my mind for about an hour or two before I was forced to sit with my thoughts before bed and the wine helped me fall asleep much faster than I would have.

The next morning was rough. My body felt heavy and mentally, I was exhausted. I wanted to just stay in bed the entire day but I knew that Abuelita would have too many questions that would very easily turn into concerns and I just didn't have the energy for that. I made the best of the day, helped Abuelita with little chores around the house and then we crashed on the couch and watched movies all day. For Abuelita, it was heaven. We hadn't spent a day like that together in so long that she just enjoyed my company. Truth be told, I enjoyed her company too. I was fighting one hell of a battle on the inside; missing Dré already and worrying about him, too.

Six days later, on my twenty-first birthday, Abuelita woke

me up with a beautiful display of one dozen, long stem red roses that were practically the same size as her. My mind was in so many other places that I had actually forgotten that it was my birthday. Go figure, right? I guess knowing that Dré wouldn't be there made it so that I wasn't really concerned about it anymore. Each birthday that I had spent with him prior to twenty-one was always so special. I had always woken up to a grandiose birthday gesture of some sort. One year it was the Range Rover, another year it was my Roley, and another year it was one hundred thousand dollars in cash.

In all honesty, year twenty-one was no different because I mean, he gifted me a salon. Oftentimes I wonder if his reasoning for presenting it to me before my actual birthday was because he knew that shit was hot or if it was pure coincidence. If I were to ask him, he'd say, *nothing is coincidence, Lux. Shit happens exactly how God planned for it to.* So, who knows.

"Abuelita, these are beautiful! You didn't have to do this, Mami. I love them!" I said with a raspy voice, barely moving in bed.

She laughed. "No lo hice, mija. Get up! Come see!"

Abuelita telling me that she didn't get me the flowers was a little surprising to me but she didn't even give me time to enjoy the roses she carried because she was already on her way to the kitchen by the time I could even get myself out of bed.

As I crossed the threshold of the kitchen entrance, Abuelita was placing the roses she carried onto the kitchen table with another dozen of beautiful white roses. They were absolutely beautiful. There was a small card pierced by a plastic rod, hedged in between the roses.

The card read, *Feliz Cumpleaños. 3 MONTHS. I love you. -Dré.*

My heart smiled. "Read this." I said to Abuelita through laughter.

I'm not sure why I was even remotely surprised that Dré found time to have two dozen roses delivered to my abuelita's house on my birthday. The most shocking part was that the message on the card was written in his handwriting. Not because I assumed he didn't physically go to the flower shop himself but because Dré writing in Spanish was by far the funniest thing he had ever done. I knew that he was intrigued by the fact that I understood Spanish, but between his moment with Abuelita before he left for three months and the card, it was obvious that he was completely captivated.

"What's three months, mija?" Abuelita's voice interrupted my thoughts.

Just as I searched my mental rolodex for a believable answer, I could hear my phone ringing in my bedroom.

Grateful that I was being saved by the phone and excited because I knew it had to be Dré, I screamed "Ah!" as I ran to my bedroom.

Quickly rubbing my unbrushed teeth with the sleeve of my shirt and aggressively pulling the hair tie out of my hair, I answered Dré's video call.

"Hey, birthday girl." He said with a smile on his face.

Smiling back, I said, "They're beautiful, baby. I love them."

"I'm glad. Did they put the card in there?" He asked.

"They did!" I laughed. "You swear you speak Spanish." My smile was from ear to ear.

It had only been a few days apart, but it felt like it had been years since I had seen him. I was trying my best not to cry and I succeeded, but it was hard. I just wanted him there with me. It didn't matter where we were, I just wanted to be together—breathing the same air.

Dré giggled. "I do. Shit, I probably speak more than you already."

"Oh, you're spicy today, I see." I said sarcastically.

"You right. My bad. It's your birthday, let me chill." He shot back.

He just stared at me for a moment as his smile faded away.

"I love you, baby. I miss you. I'm sorry I'm not there today." He placed the phone upward so that it was facing the ceiling away from his face. He sighed deeply.

He brought the camera back to himself. "There's a card on file at our spot. Take Abuelita there tonight for dinner. Enjoy it. Take lots of pictures so that we can print 'em and post 'em up at our new spot."

I appreciated his efforts, but my heart was broken. "Ok. I will. I love you." I took a deep breath. "I miss you so much already." I said.

"I know. Me too. Don't focus on that today, though. I just want you to have a good day. I'll check in with you in an hour. After tonight, you have to get up and start handling business, babe. Three months, remember?" His words were slow and well thought out.

"Three months." I rolled my eyes.

"Thank you" He said with a smile.

The call ended.

I placed my phone face down onto my pillow and then closed my bedroom door so that I could cry. Dré wanted me to have a good day and made every effort to make sure that I did, yet somehow, I was still devastated. All of the things he had done to make sure I was happy, were all great things. However, none of them were his presence. Only a few days had passed and I already missed him like crazy. I needed his hug to hold me together. I needed his kisses to keep me going. I needed his mind, to ease mine.

I stayed in my room for about ten minutes just so that I could cry, pull myself together and make dinner reservations for Abuelita and I. When I finally came out, Abuelita was damn near done making breakfast tacos; one of my favorite dishes of hers. The rest of our day, including dinner, was fine. It was a simple day. One that was full of both love and grief for me, but I got through it.

For the next month, I worked my ass off to get *Luxurious Cabello* up and running. I was never really much of a fan of social media and Dré felt as though it was sloppy to give people the amount of access social media provided given our lifestyle. So, we just never had any social media. But, with a new business and all the free marketing I could do on social media, I had to set up an account. For the most part, the salon was ready to go, I just needed to fill it with staff and clients. Dré's trucking company was an easy task. It had already been up and running for about a year and I was typically the one handling the day to day tasks during that time. Dré and I would split the tasks when his schedule allowed him to but it was mostly overseeing the company as a whole and making sure all of the drivers and dispatchers were paid out each week.

Between getting the salon ready for business, checking in with Dré every hour, handling the trucks on my own and keeping Abuelita entertained enough for her not to ask questions about Dré, I was pretty busy. I hadn't even had time to sit with Daddy or visit Ma. Luckily she and Abuelita got their phone calls in on a regular basis, so Ma knew that I was staying at Abuelita's house. Dré and I would mostly talk about business when we spoke.. There was no time for emotions, really. I'd update him on each of our business endeavors and he'd add his input and that was pretty much it. Well, he would always let me know that he was proud of me before we got off the phone and we never hung up without telling each other that we loved each other, but that's as far as anything emotional ever got. It was probably better that way for both of us because I know that the distance was as hard on Dré as it was on me.

The most challenging part of all of it was probably the fact that Dré's mom had been texting me more than usual. See, when Dré got all of us new phones, he didn't share his new number with his mom. I shared mine, of course but it just wasn't enough for her. Even though Dré was always really cut and dry with his mother in text messages and refused to get on an actual call with her, I think that she still felt connected to him when she texted his phone directly. I'd imagine she was beginning to feel a way that she wasn't able to text him because she didn't have his number and to make it worse, I was suddenly becoming cut and dry with her too. To be honest, I considered telling her that we had broken up so that she would just give me space until Dré and I had things figured out. Ultimately, I decided against that because my heart wouldn't allow it. I may never know the truth behind the friction that Dré had with his family but for some reason, I always wanted him to be open to a relationship with his mother as if my relationship with my own mother was something worth admiring.

One morning, Dré skipped our call and it threw my entire day off. Some part of me was angry because checking in every hour for about five minutes each day was already not enough and skipping one of those calls made it worse. The other part of me was concerned because it didn't make sense that he would skip a check in. He's too thorough. He had always been big on *sticking to the plan, staying the course, only pivot if it's necessary, but never miss a step.* Skipping a check-in call went against that but I tried not to let it get to me because there were so many other things that I had to focus on. Three months, remember? To be honest, that first month went much quicker than I expected it to because of how busy I was and I was grateful for that.

Anyway, he ended up skipping calls that entire day. I was worried. I was frustrated. I was even a little bitter so I told myself that I would make time to visit Daddy's grave so that I could just find some sort of balance in the midst of everything that was going on around and within me. I won't lie, I cried myself to sleep that night. It was the first time in a month that I had done that but not speaking to Dré when I was supposed to, really hurt my heart.

The next morning, I was woken out of my sleep to the sound of my phone ringing from across the room. I damn near fell out of my bed trying to get up so that I wouldn't miss his call. I knew it was Dré because he was the only person that I had been talking to besides business associates and they would always text first. When I finally picked up my cell phone, it wasn't Dré's photo on my screen. Instead, the screen read *No Caller ID.* I didn't put too much thought into it and there wasn't really much time to do so anyway because the phone had already been ringing for a while.

Assuming it was Dré on the other end of the line I said, "Hi, baby!" Cheerfully.

"You have a collect call from: Complacency Creates Chaos. To accept, press one." An automated message said.

My heart sank. The rest of the automated message became inaudible to me. It was Dré. He didn't sound like himself because he was clearly defeated and upset, but I knew it was him because of what was said. So, let's back-track for a second.

The night that we decided that we'd be out of the game in three months, Dré told me that if he ever called me and the first thing he said was complacency creates chaos, it meant that shit had gone bad. He said that it didn't matter how calm he sounded, what number he called from or what else he said afterwards, I was to get rid of the phone and wait for him to contact me. I can hear his voice as if he's standing right next to me whenever I think of that day. "Lux, I'm dead ass. If I say it, kill the phone and just lay low. Don't come looking for me. Don't go to any of the spots. Just stay low. Handle business as usual, but don't make any other moves until you hear from me. I'll contact you. You do not, under any circumstance, try to contact me. That's what he told me when we prepared for shit to possibly hit the fan."

The phone fell out of my hand, bounced off of my lap and tumbled across the room. Tears filled my eyes and my heart sank to the pit of my stomach. The sound of Dré's voice played over and over again in my mind while I was frozen in time. My world literally came crashing down inside of me; my heart might as well have exploded out of my chest and my stomach might as well have fallen through my ass. My head was pounding and my vision was obstructed by the pool of tears that sat in my eyes. The sound of beeps that indicated the call had ended snapped me out of my misery causing me to fall to my knees and gasp for air. My sobs were quiet but I could hardly catch my breath. It was my worst nightmare, all over again. They got Dré.

eleven
lux lex.

ABOUT TWENTY MINUTES had passed after receiving the collect call that told me everything, well almost everything, that I needed to know. It didn't really matter how it happened or what happened because the end result was the same; Dré was in jail. Twenty minutes was really all the time I had to fall apart and pull myself back together because I couldn't break Abuelita's heart again but also because I had very specific tasks to complete. The first one being to get rid of my phone.

It took me about ten minutes to brush my teeth, throw on some sweats and a fitted cap and start the day I hoped I'd never have to start. I can't count how many times Dré had gone over the just-in-case plan he had put together for me under the assumption that he would be the only one taken away. My heart was in shambles and my mind was racing millions of miles per second, but I had to stay strong. Before leaving the house, I kissed Abuelita on the cheek as she sat in the living room enjoying her morning tea while watching the news.

"Love you, Mami. I'm running late." I said without

giving her a chance to look at me, ask me any questions or engage at all for that matter.

As I opened the front door, my thoughts became intrusive.

What if the police are surrounding the house, waiting for me to come out? What if my car is gone? Did they get Blanco? Maybe he's posted out front waiting to tell me everything I need to know.

It certainly wasn't the time to be afraid or to play mind games with myself. I knew that I had to be on my shit like never before.

"Come on, Lux." I said aloud to myself.

Taking a deep breath into my nose and out of my mouth, I forced myself to shake any feelings of fear, doubt or apprehension and slowly stepped across the threshold. I felt like I was transitioning from a place of safety inside of Abuelita's house into the wilderness beyond her front door. As the front door latched shut behind me, I lowered my head, only lifting my eyes to scan the block below the brim of my hat. Nothing appeared to be unusual and there were no cars on the block that I hadn't ever seen before so it appeared to me that everything was fine.

Dré had always taught the crew to scan the block. That meant, whatever block you live on, whatever blocks you frequent and whatever block you're ever active on, you scan it and become familiar with the vehicles that are either always present or present when you arrive. To take it a step further, he encouraged us to try our best to memorize at least the first two alphanumeric characters on as many plates as we could. I'm not going to lie, that shit had always seemed ridiculous in the past but as I stood there not knowing what our futures held, I scanned the fucking block. That was the thing about Dré – even if we didn't agree with some of his teachings or we felt like they were just impossible scenarios, he continued to press the issue and for the first time ever, it finally made sense why.

After I scanned the block, I swiftly walked to my car. As soon as I sat in the driver's seat, I started the engine and locked the doors.

"Niggas can catch you off guard, but you're never unprepared. Remember that, Lux." I said out loud to myself as I envisioned the day Dré said that to me.

"What the fuck, Dré!!" I said loudly. It wasn't a question. It was just an emotional outburst. I slammed my balled fists onto my thighs.

After a moment, I was able to gather myself and I began to pull out of Abuelita's driveway. Surprisingly, I didn't listen to any music as I drove to the river. There was a pier not too far from Abuelita's house that had a boardwalk over top of the water and I was to go there, pretend I was taking photos of the scenery, factory reset my phone and then allow it to fall into the water. That had always been the plan if we ever had to lay low and as much as I hated it, I stuck to the plan. My entire body trembled as I watched my cell phone slip through my fingers and splash into the water. I had only had that phone for about a month because Dré had gotten rid of all of our phones when the stash house got raided.

Symbolically speaking, releasing the phone into the ocean on my own, both carried and released so much weight. It meant that I was tapping completely into Lux Lex in order to protect myself, fend for my family and make sure that I didn't let Dré down the way that he had never let me down. I wanted to jump into that fucking water with my phone. I wanted the river to whisk me away and wash away all of my pain. Instead, I watched as it sank deeper into the water until I could no longer see its shadow and then I walked over to a set of lockers the pier housed.

Locker *555* had a combination lock attached to it. Before reaching for the lock, I made it a point to discreetly check my surroundings to make sure that I hadn't been followed or wasn't being watched and then I fidgeted with the lock, entering code *0209*. My heart began to race before pulling down on the lock to confirm that I had entered the correct code. I took a long, silent, deep breath and pulled down as I exhaled. I did it. Inside of the locker was a key and an envelope, just like Dré said there would be. I didn't take any time to open the envelope because he was firm in just grabbing it and leaving, if things had ever come to that point, so that's what I did. I placed the envelope and the key into the front pocket of my hoodie, replaced the lock, spun the dial, ensured that it was secure and headed right back to my car. By that time, all of my emotions had escaped me. Dré had spent so much time in the past preparing me for that day and because of that, I felt confident in everything I had done. It was time to boss up and hold my nigga down the way he had held me down for so long.

From the river, I drove about an hour away to a condo that was fully furnished and untouched. It was something that Dré had tucked away for situations exactly like the one we were in. Truth be told, I don't know whose name was on the paperwork or how he ensured that the payments were sent on time each month. I wasn't involved in the purchasing process in any way. For all I know, it could have actually been paid for in cash. Hell, now that I think of it, I don't even know if it was purchased prior to me meeting Dré or at some point after. Not that it mattered then and it certainly doesn't now. I had only been there once before and the purpose of me being there that one time was just so that I wasn't completely unfamiliar with the location if we ever needed to use it.

Maybe this goes without saying at this point, but Dré was involved in a lot more than just selling drugs and I was never involved in whatever the 'a lot more' included, I just knew that it existed. He never wanted me to feel as though I was out of the loop in any of his endeavors, whether legal or not, but he also felt as though there were some things I just didn't need to know. According to him it was safer that way and I had no reason or desire to question that. Anyway, with the exception of excessive dust, the place looked exactly as I had remembered it. Being sure to lock the door behind me, I stood in the landing and just took everything in.

The condo was much smaller than the penthouse but it still carried Dré's energy and it made me feel safe. When Dré and I first started dating I would always tell him that if I couldn't feel his energy when he wasn't physically present, he wasn't really my man. When I was a child, my daddy had always taught me that you could feel a leader's presence even when he wasn't present and it was something I had taken with me into adulthood.

Standing in the condo was the first moment since receiving the phone call that I had actually felt safe and it was the first moment that I had taken a moment to process my current situation in its entirety. Dré wasn't present, but his energy was and that was going to have to be enough to help me navigate through the foreseeable future. There I was, standing alone in a condo filled with nothing but furniture. It only took a moment for all of the emotions that had escaped me earlier in the day to come crashing down. Reality began to set in. I knew that Dré would make sure he got in contact with me, but I also knew that it could take days or even weeks before that happened.

As I stood there, alone, my stomach began to ache and my heart became heavy. With my arms straight down to my sides, I kept my head up as I looked around the compact condo while tears rolled down my cheeks. I was weak. Physically. My body involuntarily leaned forward and I was forced to place my hands onto my almost hyperextended knees as my elbows locked into place. My sorrow was loud. Each gasp for air and painful cry echoed between the walls of the condo Dré had secured in case of an emergency. I was standing in the middle of the emergency without a phone to call for help; literally. I allowed myself another minute to drown in my sorrow and then I took my hat off, tied my hair up, rummaged through my purse and removed the envelope that I pulled from the locker. I sat down where I stood and began to count the money inside.

Twenty thousand dollars. That was what Dré had put aside as an initial payment for a lawyer and bail but I wasn't supposed to make any move until I heard from him. No lawyer. No contact with the crew. No bailing him out. No phone calls and no visits. Nothing. I hid the envelope on top of a package of frozen meat and then wrapped foil around them both before placing it back into the freezer. I had driven an hour away from home to hide twenty thousand dollars in a freezer.

Part of me wanted to stay there for as long as I could. I wanted to sleep there for a few nights because I thought it would be the only place where I would feel Dré's energy. I thought it was the only place that I would actually feel safe. He had given me his word so many years before that, that no matter what happened to him, he would always make sure I was good. And for a moment, being in that condo seeing it look exactly as it had looked when I was there with him, and counting the money that he swore would be in the locker, made me feel good because even without physically being present, he still stood on his word. Based on what Daddy considered a leader, Dré was a damn good one.

Obviously, I didn't stay. I couldn't. For one, I had to go get a new phone. But two, Dré specifically told me that I wasn't to stay there because it was only a hideaway house. *Our* hideaway house, yes. Meaning, not one person in our crew knew that it existed but I wasn't to stay there for longer than necessary. *Stash and shake,* he would always joke. Before leaving, I made sure that I had all of my belongings, including my hat, took a moment to bask in the small spark of Dré's energy that I could feel and then locked everything up. It was almost a saddening feeling to leave but I had to shake that shit off and keep it pushin'.

When I finally made it back to my side of town, I had to stop by the phone store for a new phone and decided that I wouldn't give Dré's mom the new number because I didn't have the heart to tell her that her son was in jail. After I got the phone, I made a pit stop to pick up some food, flowers and wine for Abuelita before heading back to her house. As much as I despised doing this, I was going to tell her that the flowers and wine were from Dré. It sounds like a ridiculous lie but I wanted so badly to maintain some sense of what I thought would be normalcy. Had I not introduced them to one another, I wouldn't have had to worry about it but, the timing of it all caused me to finesse things that probably didn't even need to be *finessed.* Ironically, in grabbing the flowers for Abuelita, it reminded me that I was supposed to visit Daddy and I made a mental note to put it on my list of things to do the following day. Crazy how that works, right? I went from seeing Daddy face to stone with fresh roses every week like clockwork to having to put it on my to-do list because my mind was consumed with whether or not Dré would ever come home and how I would explain it to Abuelita if he didn't.

Abuelita was so fucking happy to see me when I arrived back home, in part because I showed up bearing gifts *from Dré* but also because I had run off so quickly that morning that she hadn't really gotten time to enjoy my company. Even then, unfortunately, I didn't really have time to sit and chat with her because I needed to make sure I reached out to each of my trucking business associates to give them my new contact information and ensure all of the day-to-day tasks were running smoothly. It was a tedious task that felt unnecessary but seeing as though I had gone through two phones over the course of one month, I didn't have any other choice. Business must go on. Luckily, as far as the salon went, I only had to worry about deliveries being made and those were already prescheduled. There was no real need to contact anyone with updated contact information so my only concern was to make sure that I was at the salon on time the following day when everything would be delivered.

When things were normal, running the trucking company and handling a few other day to day tasks was a breeze for me but those same tasks partnered with every-thing else going on felt a little overwhelming. At the time though, I was grateful that I had so many things occupying my mind because I knew that it would only take a second of mental freedom or one wrong question from Abuelita to cause my mind to spiral out of control. I needed to keep my momentum going for my sanity and for Dré.

At the end of what was easily the hardest day I had encountered since the news of my father dying, I finally had time to watch a movie with Abuelita. But the first thing I did was shower. I needed to shift my energy from Lux Lex to Lexington so that Abuelita wouldn't sense that I was struggling. I tried my best not to cry while I showered but I shed a few tears. For a moment, I got lost in my thoughts because I was worried about Dré of course, but I was also worried about Blanco. There was no way for me to know whether or not 12 had picked him up too, if he was on the run, or worse. When my thoughts became that dark, I knew it was time to get out of the shower in an effort to stay out of my head.

It only took me a second to throw on some sweats and once I was dressed, I popped some popcorn for Abuelita and I to share and poured both of us a glass of wine. I'd say I got through a solid ten minutes of the movie and listened to about five minutes of how Abuelita's day went before I fell asleep. She must have known how exhausted I was because she didn't bother waking me so that I could climb in my bed. Instead, she threw a blanket over me and gently kissed my forehead. I'm not sure if she knew how chaotic my life had become that day, but she knew that I needed my angel because she didn't leave my side. She cuddled up on the reclining chair right next to me and we slept in the living room together.

The next morning, the smell of bacon traveled through the house, waking me out of my sleep. My mind was awake, hell, I'm not even sure it ever went to sleep, but my body was heavy. The pressure of a ton of bricks was stacked on top of my chest making it hard for me to breathe. There was so much pressure that my heart was pounding in my stomach as if there wasn't enough room in my chest. My vision became blurry as my eyes filled with tears. I was afraid. I couldn't breathe. I was awake but I couldn't move. As I gasped for air, I grabbed my throat with both hands while tears rolled from my eyes landing inside of my ears. There was so much weight on my chest that I literally thought I was going to die. There was a disconnect between what I was commanding my body to do and what was actually happening.

I took another gasp for air and yelled, "Get up!" out loud.

I could hear myself gasping for air and see my body struggling to move but I had no control over what was happening. My mind was racing and I kept telling myself not to die on Abuelita's couch.

"Please!" I yelled and then gasped for air.

"Mija?" I could hear Abuelita from the kitchen.

I released my hands from my throat and covered my mouth instead. One hand on top of the other. For some reason, I didn't want Abuelita to hear me struggling to breathe. It felt like I was literally fighting for my life and as badly as I didn't want to die on Abuelita's couch, I didn't want her to walk in on me dying even more. Covering my mouth only made it harder to breathe and each gasp for air became louder than the last.

"Lexington!" My abuelita screamed.

The sound of glass shattering forced my hands away from my mouth. My body was still heavy, paralyzed even, but the sound of glass shattering meant that Abuelita could see me dying or was dying herself. Either way, I couldn't see her but I wanted to save her.

With my arms down to my sides and tears still running down my face I yelled, "Get up!" once again.

My sobs were louder each time.

"Please!" I yelled.

"Mija!" Abuelita screamed as her soft hands grabbed hold of both of my wrists.

Her touch instantly brought calm over my body and I began to cry hysterically. The pressure of the bricks had been lifted but I still laid there as I cried out loud. Abuelita released her grip on my wrists and began wiping my tears as she shushed me like you would a baby.

"I'm here, sweetheart. Shh. I'm here." She said as she caressed my hair.

My heart finally traveled back into my chest, my breathing finally went back to normal and my tears had finally begun to dry up.

I placed my hand over Abuelita's hand as she continued to rub my hair. "Mami, I'm sorry."

"Shh." She replied.

"No, really. I'm sorry, Mami. I was so scared. I had a dream about Daddy. I'm good. I swear." I lied.

Three lies in less than twenty-four hours and two of them were back to back. I didn't have a dream about Daddy and I for damn sure wasn't doing good by any definition of the term. Lying in general was something that I hadn't ever really made a habit of but lying to Abuelita was something that I definitely didn't do at all other than when it came to Dré. For as long as I could remember, she was the one person I could tell anything, no matter what. But I had to lie to her. I had to lie to her because I didn't need anything else to worry about. I had to lie to her because I didn't want to scare or stress her. And I had to lie to her because I didn't really have any real answers to the questions I knew she'd have. I had to lie to her to protect everybody.

I tried to get up to prove that I was as good as I swore I was but my body couldn't catch up with how quickly my brain was moving. As I attempted to stand up, blood rushed to or from my brain so quickly that I became lightheaded and it forced me to lean into Abuelita's body, knowing that she didn't have the strength to hold me up.

"Lexington! Enough!" She said sternly.

She placed her hand on my thigh, applying as much

pressure as her frail body would allow her to and said, "Siéntate!"

She told me to sit down and she meant it. I knew she did. There was no way for me to deflect from what had just happened and Abuelita wasn't going to pretend she didn't know that something was wrong.

At that point, I had already started lying to her, so I knew that whatever question she had, my answer was going to be a lie. That's the reason I don't like lying. One lie has to turn into a hundred more lies. The truth is much easier to keep up with but I waited patiently for her to press me.

"What the hell is going on?" She asked.

I was shocked. Abuelita hardly ever cursed. I mean, *hell* hardly qualifies as cursing but it was definitely more razzle dazzle than I was used to hearing out of Abuelita's mouth.

Without hesitation I answered, "I dreamt of Daddy. He was lying in the middle of the street after his accident and I was trying to save him but I couldn't. I didn't have the strength he needed. I didn't have strength at all. It was like my body was paralyzed – like I had a ton of bricks on my chest and I couldn't get up to save Daddy. I just kept yelling for him to get up. Pleading with him. But I couldn't. We were both dying but there was no reason for me to be dying."

Well, my lie was only partially a lie. The truth was that I really did have that dream, but I had it years before that. In fact, I had bad dreams about my parents pretty often but none of them woke me out of my sleep the way the pressure of my real life had woken me up that day. Somehow, I decided that it was less of a lie since all I had done was change the timeline.

"Oh, Mija. It must be because you're sleeping on the couch. Your body remembers that day. Your body remembers that trauma. You need proper rest, Mija. Please. Eat breakfast and then rest in your bed." Abuelita grabbed my hand and squeezed it as she attempted to encourage me to rest.

"I have to get to the salon, Mami. I have deliveries coming today. I'll rest later, I promise." I kissed the side of her forehead as I slowly stood up from the couch.

She sucked her tongue at me and let out a deep sigh.

"Abuelita, don't worry! I'm fine. I'm taking breakfast to go, but I'll be home to have dinner with you. I promise." I forced a smile.

Without giving Abuelita an opportunity to reply, I quickly walked to the bathroom so that I could wash up and throw clothes on for the day. I kept it simple; black hoodie, black sweats and black boots–hustle mode. I grabbed a black bag big enough to fit my laptop, notebook and planner so that I could attempt to get as much work done as possible while I waited for all of my deliveries to arrive at the salon.

On my way out of the house, I met Abuelita in the kitchen and kissed her forehead as she handed me a to-go container with pancakes, turkey bacon, scrambled eggs and breakfast potatoes. I knew that she wasn't happy that I was leaving but she knew that she couldn't stop me.

As I walked toward the front door, I noticed a pile of glass shards swept aside. It stopped me in my tracks because I had realized that the fear Abuelita felt when she saw me on that couch, forced her to drop the glass she held in her hand. My heart ached; for both myself and my grandmother.

I turned around and said, "I love you, Mami. I'll see you for dinner." I looked her in the eye.

"Be safe, Mija. Please." Her voice was stern yet shaky.

As I sit here and remember that day, I realize now that more than likely, Abuelita knew way more than I thought she knew, but she was respecting my space and privacy. God, I love that woman.

There was nothing healthy about the way I handled that situation. There wasn't really anything healthy about the way that I had handled any of the traumatic experiences in my life. They were all swept under the rug the same way that fucking rollercoaster ride had been swept under the rug. There was no time or space for healthy healing mechanisms. I had to cope and move the fuck on. The way my life was set up was far from simple, but let's not forget: you *play chess or get check'd* and Dré taught me how important it was to protect the Queen at all costs – getting check'd could cost me my life.

twelve
blanco.

LEAVING Abuelita's house that morning was bittersweet. On one hand, it was the alone time that I desperately needed because my mind was in complete chaos but on the other hand, I needed the calming energy that she embodied. It was a contagious energy that only she could spread. An energy that was powerful enough to move a ton of bricks from my chest so that I could breathe again and electric enough to keep the lights on in all of my darkest hours.

As I drove to my salon, I had to step out of myself as Lexington, the girl who had just had a mental breakdown on her grandmother's couch and into myself as Lux Lex, the woman who ran businesses, kept her composure, and held shit down until her man came home. It was a sick transition to navigate, but it was the only way shit was going to get done.

The drive from Abuelita's house to the salon was only about fifteen minutes but of course, it felt like it had taken me hours to get there. When I finally pulled up, I sat in my car for a moment and just reflected on how happy I was to be starting my journey as a professional braider and salon owner. It was something that I had dreamt of, prayed for and worked toward for years and Dré made it happen. Ma and Daddy knew that it was something I wanted and had promised for so long that they would help me achieve that goal but life snatched them away from me before they could even attempt to help me. I mean, shit, if I'm honest, I didn't really think it was a feasible goal until I met Dré. Not that my parents weren't capable because I know that they were absolutely capable. But because I was still young when Daddy was alive and Ma was free. Braiding hair at Abuelita's house or having Syd taxi me around the city to braid the hair of girls from our school was as far as my knowledge in the world of entrepreneurship went.

My moment of reflection quickly shifted into thoughts of how when I met Dré and he brought me into his world, it expanded my mind in ways I never knew possible. He was much more than just a drug dealer – he was a businessman and for every lesson he taught me about the streets, he taught me about being an entrepreneur. That was the thought that fueled me that morning. It gave me the confidence I needed to trust that with everything Dré had instilled in me, I had everything it took for me to own and successfully operate *Luxurious Cabello*. At first, the fuel that fired me up had me ready to hop out of my car and handle as much business as I could while I was at the salon.

The flame quickly died out right before I hopped out of my car to head into the salon as I realized that I was checking my rearview mirrors in an effort to see where Blanco had parked his car. In the past, if I fought Dré or Blanco for my right to go out into the world on my own, Blanco would still follow behind me like a fucking chaperone. Dré didn't think it was safe for me to move around alone. For a moment, I had forgotten that things were the way that they were. For a moment, it completely slipped my mind that Blanco wasn't parked a few cars away keeping an eye on me. For a moment, my thoughts about Dré allowed his energy to be so present within me, that I forgot that he wasn't actually there. For a moment, I felt free. It was a fleeing moment as the sound of a car honking its horn brought me back to reality. It was a reality that reminded me that I was in fact free in a physical sense but held captive to my thoughts and fears of a life without Dré. Not only that, but it also brought me to a reality where I had started to worry about Blanco, too.

Blanco had grown so tall and handsome over the years. He had grown his hair out and started those annoying little sponge curls. His smile was infectious but you could tell that he held painful secrets if you looked deep enough into his eyes. He developed his own sense of style but he navigated through life very similar to Dré; with confidence and grace. Blanco had lived with Dré for as long as I could remember; dating all the way back to when they came into my shoe store that day. Usually, when Dré took a new member of the crew in, he'd have them live elsewhere but report to him on a daily basis. It was different with Blanco though. Something about their relationship was different than any other relationship Dré carried. The love and respect ran deeper on both sides. Blanco was young, but wise. He was loyal. He was teachable. He was Dré's protégé. I'm not sure how they met or how long they had known each other before they came into my life, but whatever Dré saw in Blanco was enough to keep him closer than anyone else. Hence, why Blanc lived with us. Dré never said it out loud, but he almost protected Blanco the same way he expected Blanco to protect me. There was always a line that Blanco didn't cross and a space that Dré didn't give him access to, but it was always clear that if or when

Dré chose to walk away from the streets, Blanco would own them if he wanted to.

For me, Blanco was like a little-big brother. I say little-big because he was so much taller than he was when we first met but he was younger than me. At Dré's command, he protected me with his life. At first, he was all business. I'm assuming it was out of fear of and respect for Dré but he wouldn't look me in the eye when he spoke to me and he would only speak when spoken to. I hated that. It took some time for me to get him to understand that I was as much his family as Dré was before he began to trust me. Eventually, he was able to find the medium between brother and business. Yeah, if we had to put a title on it, I was technically Blanco's boss because Dré was, so there was a line there but we still shared a different bond. The same way he shared with me that he had a baby on the way before he shared it with anyone else is the same way he shared lots of personal things with me before he shared them with anyone else. We spent a lot of time together on our own though, so it always made complete sense. Plus, Lux Lex or Lexington, sister or boss, I'm still a woman and men share different parts of themselves with women.

Anyway, like I was saying, I knew that Blanco wouldn't be parked anywhere near the salon and it started to make me feel alone. In the span of about two minutes, I went from feeling empowered and capable to scared and under qualified. I knew that the same way I had a strict plan of action to follow in the event that Dré got locked up, was the same way that Blanco had a strict plan of action to take if he was still on the outside. Granted, the chances of Dré getting hemmed up without Blanco were slim and I didn't know anything about what Blanco's plan of action included. What I did know was that neither of our plans included interacting with one another until we heard from Dré. See,

Chess, remember? We protect the queen; me. If Dré was locked up and Blanco wasn't, we always knew that there was only a matter of time before that changed and that meant that Blanco and I didn't need to be in the same place at the same time.

I reached over to grab my bag and scanned my rearview mirrors one last time before I opened the car door. I wasn't scanning for Blanco, I was scanning the block the way Dré had taught us to do. My heart sank to my stomach as I attempted to take a mental note of every license plate, make and model of every vehicle that I could see. With my bag on my lap, I placed my hands on the steering wheel, locked my elbows so that my arms were completely straight and placed my head in the space between my arms where the straps of my bag poked through. I felt like I was losing my mind. Truthfully, with the amount of trauma I had experienced in my life as a whole, I probably was. But on that day in particular, I was trying to stomach the fact that Dré was in jail somewhere, chances were that Blanco was too. The rest of the crew probably had no clue and Abuelita was at home worried sick about me. I took a deep breath in my nose and out of my mouth, lifted my head from my arms and rummaged through my glove department for a pair of sunglasses.

Daddy's rule of never allowing a nigga to see that he had you pressured up was at the forefront of my mind as I walked toward the door of my salon. It was a short walk from my car, but there was no real way for me to know whether or not I was being watched so I made sure that as soon as I opened that car door and stepped foot on the pavement I did so as the queen that I was. If they, whoever they were, were watching me, they weren't going to be able to see my red, puffy eyes because my sunglasses shielded them. They weren't going to be able to gauge my fear because it was packed away. As far as anybody who was somebody knew, Lux Lex was still that bitch and nothing was going to change that.

The wind touching my face as I opened my car door was refreshing. I threw the straps of my bag over my shoulder, and then quickly glanced around again before closing the door and activating the car alarm. Nothing seemed out of place and I was relieved by that. The fear I had packed away almost began to show itself as I attempted to place my salon key into the keyhole. My hand was shaky and unsteady but there wasn't any time for me to be acting like a little bitch so I muscled through and finally unlocked the door. The automatic lights activated as soon as I began to walk toward my work station and I immediately felt as though I was in my element.

Being that I was lowkey paranoid and I wasn't technically open for business yet, I considered locking the door but opted against it because I didn't want to have to deal with unlocking it each time a delivery man arrived. There were industrial sized boxes of shampoo and conditioner scheduled to be delivered first and I was most excited about that. One thing I always hated when I was growing up was that I couldn't wash or blow dry anyone's hair. In my opinion, it was and still is very tacky for braiders to require clients to come washed and blow dried already. Like, girl, give them a whole experience or don't do it at all. The other shipments contained blow dryers, hot tools, braiding hair racks and customized *Luxurious Cabello* aprons for the stylists and capes for the clients. The plan was to provide everything a stylist would need to work in my salon, whether they were fresh out of school or a seasoned vet.

It felt good to be in the salon. My mind was in a million places but I was able to find solace there. I pulled my laptop from my bag and placed it on the counter top so that I could begin researching Cosmetology schools. It sounds crazy but, I wasn't a licensed cosmetologist when Dré gifted the salon to me. He felt as though I could get the salon up and running, hire employees, rent out the booths and sell my braiding hair while I went to school. Everything I knew about hair and hair maintenance was self taught so school was just a formality and I didn't need a license to run a salon. On the other hand, there were still a number of other licenses that I needed to obtain in order to run the salon and sell my products and the plan for the day was to get all of that research done while I waited for my deliveries to arrive.

While I was writing down the pros and cons of the different schools I was interested in, Blanco crossed my mind again. I knew that he and I weren't supposed to communicate with one another until we heard from Dré but not knowing whether he was in or out of jail made me uneasy. As my thoughts of Blano's well being became louder, I realized how quiet the salon was and walked toward the front so that I could turn on the bluetooth speakers. I threw a playlist on shuffle and the first song that came on was *Run It Up by DB Bantino*. It was perfect for the headspace I was in prior to thinking about Blanco.

Dré always used to tell me that whenever I felt over-whelmed or under prepared for a situation I got myself into, I needed to take a second to breathe deep and ask myself what he would do in that situation. *Use me as your playbook*, he would always say. When I think about it, Dré had prac-tically trained me to handle just about anything. With that in mind, I stood in the middle of the salon, took three deep breaths and forced my thoughts to slow down.

"What Would Dré Do?" I said out loud.

Immediately I rushed to my laptop and began to type *inmate search* into the search engine. It was at that moment that I realized that I didn't even know Blanco's real name. After all the years, time and secrets I shared with him, I never once asked his real name and he never shared it. My heart sank. For half a second, I couldn't catch my breath. As I sat down in the chair that would soon be where my clients sat, with my laptop on my lap, tears began to fill my eyes. I couldn't believe that there was something so simple that I didn't know about someone that meant so much to me; a name. A name holds so much history. A name holds so much lineage. A name holds so much power and I didn't know Blanco's real name. I knew why we called him Blanco but that only carried the history, lineage and power of one space of his life; the streets.

There wasn't much else for me to do seeing as though I didn't know Blanco's real name. I couldn't search for him in any capacity because as far as I had known, he had never gone to jail before and if he had there was no real way for me to know. I sat there for a moment and reflected on how Blanco must have felt knowing that I didn't know his name and assuming that I never cared due to the fact that I never asked. Lucky for me, I didn't have much time to reflect because my first delivery arrived, scaring me out of my thoughts.

"Ma'am?" A pubescent voice said from behind me.

Realizing I had my back to the door, something that Dré always frowned upon, I used my foot to turn the chair around so that I could put a face to the voice I heard. A white boy, who must have been all of eighteen years old, stood at the front of my salon with a clipboard in his hands.

"Uh, yeah. You need something?" I said, attempting not to sound as startled as I was.

My tone must have startled him because he fumbled over his words. "Uh. Yeah. Yeah. Yea– I.." He almost dropped his clipboard.

"I'm looking for Miss Lexington Williams." He finally said.

I stood up quickly. "What for?" I asked defensively.

The boy lowered his eyes to his clipboard. "I've got a few boxes to deliver to this address, ma'am and Miss Williams has to sign for them. They're – they're – they're heavy boxes, so if I could get a signature first, I can load them up on the dolly and place them wherever she'd like." He said nervously.

My heart sank as a rush of adrenaline left my body. In my right mind, I knew good and got damn well that 12 or the Feds would never calmly walk in a spot the way that boy had done but for some reason, everything inside of me was telling me that it was my last day on the outside. Paranoia was very clearly getting the best of me.

Through nervous laughter I said, "Oh. Boy. Why didn't you just say that?" I began to walk over to him.

"Sorry, Miss. I've been standing here for about two minutes with no response from you so I wasn't sure I was in the right place." He was visibly confused.

Two minutes? I thought to myself. *He was standing there for two minutes?* Realizing there wasn't much time to toggle between thoughts or account for one hundred twenty seconds, I grabbed the pen and clipboard from his hand, scanned over the document and signed on the highlighted line.

"My bad. It's been a long morning. Here you go." I said nonchalantly as I handed the items back to him.

"Thanks, Miss." He smiled. "I'm going to load the dolly up and then you can let me know where you'd like for me to place the boxes."

Without saying a word, I shook my head in agreement.

While the young boy was outside, I scanned around the salon to decide where he would be placing the boxes. I just wanted him to drop whatever it was and get the fuck out. Hearing him say that he had been standing in my salon for two minutes without me responding made me realize that I was being careless. I was so used to Dré and Blanco protecting me that I didn't really pay attention to the details the same way they did and I didn't like that. It was scary in general but the fact that Dré was locked up and I had no clue whether or not anyone else from the crew was or not, it was an eye opener that I needed to be on my shit more.

Just as I decided that the boxes could be placed in a small storage room to the back of the salon, the young boy returned with four large boxes stacked on top of each other on his dolly.

"Oh, you can bring them back here." I called out.

I knew better than to enter the room with him, so I just pointed him in the direction he needed to go. That white boy caught me slipping once but I wasn't going to give him a chance to let it happen twice. Dré used to always tell us that a nigga only had to catch you slipping one time for him to end everything you've risked your life for and thanks to the little white boy delivering my industrial sized shampoo and conditioner for the salon, I knew exactly how true that statement was. I mean, I was obviously overreacting because he was just a delivery boy but I promised myself that I wouldn't take that chance moving forward. There was too much at stake and too much I wasn't yet aware of.

For the next few hours, I filled out an online application for the cosmetology school I had decided on while the rest of my deliveries had come. Toward the end of my day, as I was packing up my laptop and preparing to close the salon down, a white girl with blonde hair and ocean blue eyes walked through the doors. She looked familiar but I couldn't remember where I had known her from. She was wearing an oversized T-shirt with sweatpants and a pair of

Yeezy's. The same pair that Dré had purchased for Blanco when I met them for the first time. As the front door slowly closed behind her, she just stood there, looking at me with her piercing blue eyes.

I knew that she wasn't a delivery girl because all of my deliveries had already arrived, she wasn't dressed like one and even though I couldn't remember where I knew her from, I knew her from somewhere. There was nothing in that salon that could protect me, but I wasn't going to allow her to believe that I was alone and unprotected so I reached into my bag as if I was reaching for a gun.

"Is there a problem?" I said. Looking her right in the eyes.

She looked back at me and tears began to flood her eyes. I didn't understand her tears. I didn't know her well enough for her to come into my salon crying about shit that probably didn't make a difference to me and no one besides the crew knew where the salon was at that point. To say I was confused is an understatement.

"Where's Blanco?" Tears rushed down her face.

Maintaining my eye contact with her, I said, "Who's Blanco?" With a straight face.

It only takes a nigga one time to catch you slipping for him to end everything you risked your life for and I wasn't going to give her that chance. I acted brand mothafuckin' new and I didn't feel bad about it.

"Lux. Please. It's been too long. This isn't like him. He's always with you." She begged.

When she called me Lux, everything immediately made sense, well, almost everything. The baggy t-shirt and the tears made sense but not her presence as a whole. The girl standing in my salon was Blanco's on again, off again, but currently pregnant girlfriend. The thing that had me confused was how she knew where to find me. Dré and the crew had come to the salon but we hadn't made any announcements or had a grand opening or anything of the sort at that point and I knew that Blanco wouldn't have just randomly told her about the salon. That wasn't something Blanco would do. It wouldn't have even made sense for him to tell her because it didn't really have any relevance to her – well, not that I knew of. Remember, I didn't even know Blanc's real name or anything about his family, so that should tell you how serious he was about keeping certain things private – even if I didn't understand why they had to be that way. I had seen his girlfriend around a few times, enough to know that I had seen her somewhere before, but he didn't bring her to the house often, if ever, and he hardly brought her to any of the family nights we would have with the crew, which was why I barely recognized her.

On top of that, the few times I did see her, she had been wearing crop tops or form fitting clothing, not a baggy t-shirt and sweats. It was obvious that she had come to my salon in fear and likely as a last resort. I can only assume that her hormones had taken over and she was losing her mind.

Before speaking, I took my hand out of my bag. For one, there wasn't actually a gun in there and I could only pretend for so long but two, I wanted to make sure that the girl felt safe.

"What's your name?" I asked.

"Stacey." Her voice shook.

I was praying that's what she said. I wouldn't have remembered her name if she hadn't said it, but I knew that I would remember it if she did.

I wasn't sure what she knew about Blanco's life, who she thought he was, how she thought he made his money or anything else for that matter, but it wasn't my place to share any information with her.

I answered her question with a stale voice. "I don't know where Blanco is, Stacey. I'm sure he'll come home when he's ready."

"Don't fucking lie to me!" She yelled.

Miss Stacey had lost her shit for a moment and that was one thing I wouldn't tolerate from anyone.

"Look, bitch. I told you I don't know where the fuck he is. I don't know you and I don't owe you shit. I'm not here to keep tabs on your man. You want to know where he is? You figure that shit out on your own." There was no more sympathy in my voice.

As I walked towards her, I continued, "And if you ever come to my fucking salon again, Blanco will be looking for you instead. Get the fuck out!" I stood right in front of her.

Stacey looked at me through the pool of tears in her eyes and shook her head at me in disgust as she turned and walked out of my salon.

Truthfully, it wasn't necessary for me to be that rude to her. I didn't even want or need to be that rude to her because I actually felt her pain. I actually understood her tears, her fear, her confusion, all of it. I understood completely. The issue was rooted in what I didn't understand; how she found me. The fact that she pulled up to my salon, after, as far as I know, never having been there before, really added another level of fear to my heart. It was uncomfortable knowing that someone who I knew close to nothing about, knew exactly where to find me.

When she walked out of the salon, I locked the door behind her, being sure to keep an eye on her so that I could see what vehicle she got into. Unfortunately, for as far as I could see, she didn't get into a vehicle and I'm not sure if that's because she didn't have one or if Blano taught her not to park in front. Whatever the case, it placed enough fear in my heart for me to finish closing the salon up, hop into my car and get to the hideaway house as quickly as I could.

When I arrived at the hideaway spot, I didn't waste any time. I went there for one specific thing. I flipped all of the couch pillows, searched through all of the frozen containers, opened every drawer and rummaged through every cabinet until I reached the closet. In there, inside of a shoebox, I found exactly what I had driven there for – a gun. Dré had never mentioned it being there, but I knew my man and I knew that it had to be in that condo somewhere. Hell, there was probably plenty more hidden in places I didn't consider looking but all I needed was one. Dré was never big on me having one of my own, but he was huge on making sure I knew how to fully handle one; everything from cleaning it to shooting it and he made sure I never missed.

He always used to say, "If you pull the burner out, you gotta buss. Ain't no threats. You TTG."

TTG means trained to go and between the delivery boy telling me that he was behind me for two whole minutes before I acknowledged him and Blanco's pregnant girlfriend walking into my salon like we had been friends forever, I wasn't feeling very TTG.

Once I found the gun, I just sat with it for a moment. I remember thinking that it didn't feel right for me to have a gun because Dré and Blanco were usually the ones that carried. My thoughts traveled on to how Blanco used to sit his gun right on his lap when he would sleep outside of Abuelita's house and wait for me overnight. And then it dawned on me. I ran to the living room and searched my bag for my phone so that I could check the time.

"Fuck!" I said out loud.

I realized that I had been late for dinner with Abuelita.

"Fuck. Fuck. Fuck!" I said to myself.

I was frustrated. It wasn't like me to prioritize anything over Abuelita and I had done it twice in the same day. It felt like my life was completely falling apart and I had no idea how to fix it. I needed to hear from Dré because I was feeling lost without him. I snapped out of my frustration for a brief moment as I rushed around the condo slamming every pantry door and drawer that I had opened. Just out of an abundance of caution, I also opened the freezer to make sure that my frozen meat money was still there. At that point in my life, I didn't trust anything to stay the same and there was no real way for me to know whether or not anyone else had run through my safe space.

When I was finally done putting everything back into place, I grabbed the gun, put it in the bottom of my bag, underneath my wallet and laptop, and briskly walked back to my car. I was in a tricky space where I wanted to smash down the freeway so that I could get back to Abuelita's as soon as possible and knowing that I needed to abide by all of the traffic laws because I was basically riding dirty. None of that shit ever mattered when Dré was home and it was pissing me off. I was starting to become upset with him for leaving me out to dry. I couldn't understand why the fuck it was taking him so long to tell me what to do next. And again, I didn't know where the fuck Blanco was. If his girl didn't even know where he was, then I figured he had to have been on the run. There was no other explanation and there was no way for him to contact me because I had a new phone.

Before I knew it, I was back home. I was so deep in thought on the way there that I'm not even sure if I stopped at red lights or not. When I pulled into the driveway, I noticed that the house was dark. I mean, Abuelita's curtains were always closed, but you could always tell whether or not the lights were on. My heart sank as I turned the engine off. My mouth became dry and my lips felt chapped as I began to breathe through my mouth. I waited for all of the lights on my car to power off and then I slowly lifted my bag from the passenger seat onto my lap and reached for my gun. I scanned the block as much as I could from where I sat in the driver's seat and then I slowly opened the car door and gently closed it behind me. In an effort to remain as quiet as I could, I didn't even bother activating the alarm. My palms were sweaty, but I held the gun in my hand, positioned down right in front of my stomach. My bag was positioned on my shoulder as secure as it could be.

As I got closer to Abuelita's front door, my heart began to race. I was worried someone was either inside or worse, someone had taken her. I'm not sure where those thoughts had come from because although Dré was pretty heavy in the drug game, he never had any real enemies. Not any that would kidnap my grandmother anyway. Before unlocking the front door, I took a deep breath. I was still trying my best not to make too much noise so that I didn't announce my presence before I had a chance to figure out what was going on inside. As I opened the door, I could smell the remnants of the dinner Abuelita had cooked for us and instantly felt sad. I couldn't believe I missed dinner.

The house was quiet and dark. From what I could see, it didn't appear that any of the furniture or anything else was out of place so I pulled my phone from my bag and used the flashlight to quickly glance around the room. Everything looked completely normal but when I turned the lights on, my grandmother was nowhere to be found. Usually, if she made dinner and was expecting my company, she'd leave a plate on top of the stove underneath the stove light so that I'd see it. There was no plate and no light.

"Mami?" I called out.

Nothing.

The only place I hadn't checked was her bedroom and I didn't want to walk into her bedroom with a gun drawn but I didn't want to be unprepared either. I placed my bag down on the couch and then stuffed my gun into the front pocket of my hoodie and held it there.

"Mami!" I called out once more.

Before opening her bedroom door, I took a deep breath and slowly turned the door knob handle. As I peeked through the crack in the door the light from the living room allowed me to see Abuelita lying in bed, sound asleep. Though I was relieved to see that she was safe, I knew that I had fucked up.

I gently touched her shoulder. "Abuelita. I'm late. I'm so sorry, Mami. Things got.."

"Mija." She threw her hand up as if she didn't want to hear what I had to say. "Get some rest." She said.

"Ok, Mami. Lo siento." I leaned in close to her and kissed her cheek.

I knew that I had fucked up. I knew that Abuelita was hurt that I didn't honor our dinner date. I knew that she was worried about me and I knew that my life was spiraling out of control. At that point, there wasn't anything else I could do except promise myself that I wouldn't put my grandmother on the back burner again. Of all the pain and turmoil I had experienced in life, Abuelita was the one place or person that allowed me to feel free of that. She was the one person that had never abandoned me. She was the one person that had never let me down. And what did I do in return? I let her down.

I felt like the biggest asshole on the planet but even in

the midst of being bothered by my actions, or lack thereof, Abuelita was right. I needed to rest. Leaving her room, I quietly closed the door behind me and grabbed my bag on the way to my room. I didn't usually lock my bedroom door, but that night, I did so that I could figure out where I would hide my gun. I sat on the edge of my bed, holding it in both hands as if it was some sort of platter and just stared at it. To be honest, I don't think I had any thoughts. For the first time that day, I didn't feel or think about anything. I lifted my childhood full size mattress and placed my gun between the box spring and mattress, unlocked my door and slept in my clothes. I didn't even bother pulling my blankets back. I needed to rest my mind, my body and my spirit and that's exactly what I did.

The next morning, I woke up extremely early so that I could grab Abuelita some flowers and her favorite red wine. Part of me was hoping that she wouldn't be awake so that I could surprise her, but the other part of me was hoping that she was so that I could hug her.

When I was done getting dressed, I considered whether or not I should pack my gun with me and decided that it wasn't necessary since I was just running a quick errand. I stood still so that I could check to see if I could hear Abuelita moving around the kitchen; I didn't. I felt like a child sneaking out of the house when I tip-toed across the living room and snuck out of the front door but it was important to me that I made it up to her. I had never missed dinner when I said I would be there and I had never experienced the Abuelita that was disappointed in me. It was obvious that I was going to have to learn a very clear line between who I had to be for Dré and who I really was for Abuelita.

It took me about thirty minutes to grab flowers and wine and get back to the house and I knew that Abuelita would likely be awake by the time I returned but I still tried my best to sneak back inside just in case she was still sleeping.

"Good morning, Mami." I said as I closed the door behind me.

She was sitting on the couch flipping through the channels and barely looked over at me.

She was dry in her response. "Good morning, Mija."

"I got these for you." I handed her the flowers and placed the bottle of wine on the floor next to her. "I'm sorry for missing dinner, Abuelita. It won't happen again. The day got away from me but I will make it a point to pay attention to the time." I said as I sat down next to her.

"You should have gotten me two bottles of wine if you're going to stress me out this way." She didn't even crack a smile.

Her sarcasm lightened the mood and was just what we both needed.

"I'll be sure to bring you another bottle AND not stress you out. How's that?" I smiled.

She placed her flowers up to her nose and took a deep breath in. "That's a good deal. I'll take it."

I nudged her shoulder with mine. "Oh, good. I didn't have anything else up my sleeve besides making you breakfast."

She burst out in laughter. "Oh, dios mío! That would be more stressful than you standing me up for dinner. Two bottles of wine will be enough, thank you."

I laughed and politely took the flowers so that I could

place them in a vase for her and grabbed the bottle of wine so that I could place it in her wine holder.

Luckily, it didn't take much more than just being present and taking accountability for my fuck up for me to get back on Abuelita's good side but I wasn't willing to risk that again. She was literally all I had left.

THE NEXT TWO weeks of my life consisted of going to the salon every day to handle all of my business. When things were normal, I didn't have an office. I ran all of our businesses right from our living room but with things being the way they were, I decided that the most productive thing for me to do was use the salon as my office. That way, I was able to make all of my phone calls, check on all of my truck drivers, and be present in the salon so that I could begin the hiring process for my stylists. Not to mention, one day I had to fill in for one of the truck dispatchers and besides it being something that I didn't want Abuelita to know about, it was also a job that I had never even imagined I'd have to take care of. Dré always said that if I was going to run the trucking company instead of allowing him to outsource, then I needed to be prepared for all of the bullshit that came with it and he was fucking right. Mind you, it was just a four hour shift that needed to be covered but it was probably the longest and most unproductive four hours I had spent in the salon since I stepped foot in there. Even though it was starting to become stressful because of the circumstances, I was grateful for the trucking company because it was probably the only sense of normalcy my life had at the time. And, if nothing else, it was going to keep a steady stream of income until everything was sorted out with Dré.

Anyway, there was a lot to figure out in regards to how I wanted to run the salon, what vibe I wanted to set and what type of stylists I wanted to hire. There were so many different options for me to consider and it was low key overwhelming but the good kind of overwhelming. The kind where every road leads to a bag, you just have to decide which road is the smoothest and stretches the furthest. There was also a back room inside of the salon that was cute, secluded and big enough for me to rent out to a lash, brow, wax or nail girl. I've always been about my money, so the truth of the matter was that I wanted to figure out a way to rent it out to all four girls. Since I still hadn't heard from Dré and I knew that when I finally did it probably wouldn't have been the time to ask him which type of girl I should rent the space to, I had to have another *what would Dré do* moment with myself. I fucking hated having to do that. To me, it was stupid since he could have just fucking called me to let me know that he was doing fine or tell me what to do next or just let me hear his voice.

Instead, he left me out to dry. He left me just like my mother and father had done and I was starting to hate him for it. But for the record, I decided that I was going to rent it out to all but the nail girl. The other three girls would all be able to use the same table for their clients to lay on while they received their services and I figured I could allow each of them to rent the space out for a few days out of the week. If Dré was around, he would have told me that it would ensure that the rent for the space was being paid on time because it would be easier for the girls to have consistent clientele on a day-to-day basis rather than a monthly basis.

My assumption was that if they were renting space from me, it was more likely that they were just beginning their solo journey rather than them being a full blown entrepreneur with the ability, finances or clientele to open up their own spot. I mean it was that or they didn't have a sponsor. Most bad bitches with salons have a Dré type nigga in the cut somewhere sponsoring all of their dreams.

Another two weeks flew by and by that time, it had been well over a month since I had heard from Dré and it was starting to weigh heavy on me. The first couple of days it didn't bother me because I was so busy. Hell, I hadn't even really had any real time to go visit Daddy. Well, if I'm honest, I didn't make any time to go visit him. Somehow, Dré being away made it hard for me to visit Daddy and eliminated my desire to visit Ma all together. I'm not really sure how they tied into one another but it was what it was.

It wasn't long before I began to feel depressed. Like, extremely depressed. Barely making it through the day type depressed. One morning, I slept way longer than I usually would because I was in a dream. I was at Daddy's grave, but I couldn't find his stone. I felt like I was in a maze and every single time I hit a corner that I thought would bring me out, I was trapped deeper in the maze. I kept screaming but I knew that no one could hear me because I couldn't even hear myself. Tears were streaming down my cheeks as I continued to search for my father's stone but it was nowhere to be found. And then out of nowhere, I realized that I was holding a bouquet of blue roses in my right hand. I was dragging them and the petals were falling from the stems with every step that I took.

"Lexington!" I heard Daddy's voice say.

I kept trying to follow his voice but every turn that I made, I ended up nowhere. It was just me and myself standing in the middle of a cemetery trying to find my father as if I hadn't sat face to stone with him dozens of times before that.

"Lexington!" I heard again.

My body jolted.

"Lexington Rae!" Daddy's voice said again as he grabbed my shoulder and jolted my body.

That was the moment that I realized that it wasn't Daddy's voice that I was hearing, it was Abuelita's. She was trying to wake me up but I must have been so lost in my dream that I didn't hear her voice, I heard Daddy's instead. Once I realized what was happening, I placed my hand on top of her hand as it rested on my shoulder.

"Good morning, Mami." I said through a yawn.

"Mija! It's two o'clock in the afternoon! What are you doing here?" She sat down at my back.

I smiled, "You told me to get some rest."

"Ay. Mija. Please. I also said don't stress me out!" She stood up from the bed.

"Lo siento, Mami." I said as I blew kisses at her.

She began to walk out of my room and then stopped at the door.

"I don't even know. Do I make you breakfast or lunch?" She said sarcastically before walking away.

"Brunch!" I yelled out.

I was making light of the situation, but I knew that I was in a bad space. It wasn't uncommon for me to not have access to him in a dream but I hadn't dreamt of Daddy in a long time and it weighed heavy on my heart just like missing Dré had started to do. My heart was breaking all over again for new reasons and the same reasons.

With everything I had left inside of me, I tried my best to get out of bed so that I could meet Abuelita in the kitchen. My body wouldn't let me. As soon as I tried to stand up, my knees became weak and the next thing I knew, I was on my knees using my elbows on the edge of my bed to keep my balance. I couldn't tell you whether or not I was crying loudly but I was certainly crying hard. So hard that I didn't hear Abuelita come back into my room.

She kneeled down next to me, "Mija. Qué pasó. Por favor. Tell me." She begged.

I removed the weight of my body from my elbows and wrapped my arms around Abuelita's body.

"We're done, Mami." I cried. "Dré and I are done."

"Oh, baby." She hugged me tight.

"It's over, Abuelita. He left. It's over for good." I continued to cry.

And for about thirty minutes, my sweet grandmother sat on my bedroom floor and consoled me as I cried over a breakup that never actually happened. That's right, I told her yet another lie. We already know that one lie will always turn into more lies and since I was in an ongoing situation, I knew that an entire portion of my life was going to have to be a lie from that moment forward. I hated that for me. I hated doing that to Abuelita.

"Te quiero, Mami. Thank you for always being my rock." I said when I finally stopped crying.

Look, I'll keep it real with you, I'm not really sure if my dream was the reason I was crying or if missing Dré was the reason.

"This is our family, Mija. You don't say thank you. We are all we have left with your mother being away. It's just us out here. We have to stick together. Please don't keep things like this from me, Mija. I cannot help you heal if I don't know that you're broken." She said as she wiped the remaining tears from my cheeks.

Which, of course, sent my heart through the wringer again but I held it together. We sat there in silence for a bit longer until Abuelita stood up.

"Let's go. I'm sure you've worked up an appetite. Your *brunch* is ready." She held her hand out as if she had enough strength to pull me up from the floor.

Hearing her place an emphasis on brunch made me laugh and reminded me yet again why I loved that woman so much. Even in the worst moments of my life, she was able to find a way to shine a light that helped me find my way out of my darkness and I couldn't be more grateful for that. Both then and now.

After brunch, I helped Abuelita with a few chores around the house and then spent the rest of the day in my room. I was down, but work still needed to be done. Once I accomplished all of my regular tasks that were bringing in a consistent cash flow, I sat down on the floor next to my bed, with my back leaned against the side of it. As badly as I wanted to attend cosmetology school so that I could make everything official with *Luxurious Cabello,* I wasn't really sure where the money for tuition was going to come from. If things were normal, five to ten thousand dollars on schooling wouldn't have meant shit to Dré's pockets but without him, without knowing how long I'd be without him and not knowing how long I'd have to make the money from the trucking company stretch, it was starting to look like I wouldn't be working in my own salon.

My thoughts began to race because I wanted so badly to find an alternative. I wanted so badly to be able to prove to myself that I had what it took to live out my dream with or without Dré or anyone else for that matter. Before I did anything else, I connected my phone to my small bluetooth speaker, my headphones were somewhere buried in my bag and I had no desire to stand up to rummage through my bag, that was across the room, to find them. Typically I'd prefer to listen to music as loud as the speaker will allow, but you know Abuelita doesn't tolerate that shit in her house, so I was going to have to settle for lower volume on a cheap bluetooth speaker. Hardly the same as the surround sound Dré and I had in the penthouse but life was changing for me and I needed to embrace what it was.

The first song that began to play on shuffle was "4 Walls" by *VEDO* and *Natasha Mosley*. It wasn't exactly the right song for the mood I was in but I just needed sound to fill the room so that the sound of my thoughts would drown out a bit. My notebook and *Sharpie* pens were within reach so I grabbed them and began to write out all of the Cosmetology school alternatives I could think of. The list was short: apprenticeship and junior college. Both of which were no option at all for me. They would both take entirely too long for the timeline I had in my head and my heart. Listen, Dré spoiled the fuck out of me. If there was a timeline in my head or in my heart, he made sure that every deadline was met; no questions asked.

In an effort to reset and release some of the anxiety that I felt, I straightened my legs out, placed my notebook and pen on my lap and stretched my neck from left to right and then in a full circle. All of the stress I was carrying sat in my neck and shoulders and the weekly massages I was getting when Dré was home were obviously canceled due to unforeseen circumstances.

Just then, Abuelita lightly knocked on my bedroom door. "Mija, you ok?" She asked as she peeked her head inside of my room.

With a half of a fake smile I replied, "I'm good, Mami. Just getting some work done for the salon. I'm going to need your help when we finally open up."

"Oh, how exciting! I can't wait!" She was so excited.

"I love you, Mami." I said as she gently closed the door after pulling her head out of the doorway.

Abuelita loved being a part of anything that allowed her

to feel useful and besides saving money by having her in the salon, I wanted someone that I could trust working the front desk. My only concern was her safety. I hadn't forgotten that Stacey walked into my salon with ease and more freedom than I was comfortable with and the idea of anyone else being able to do that made me nervous. Again, my thoughts shifted to the fact that if Dré and Blanco were around, it wouldn't even be a thought I'd entertain but I had to keep reminding myself that my life was very, very different and may very well have been the new normal forever.

Funny enough, it wasn't even on my list of things to-do at the moment to figure out who would be working the front desk but as usual, Abuelita's presence solved problems; even a problem that hadn't presented itself yet. Even though I was sitting in one spot in the middle of my bedroom floor, my entire life was all over the fucking place. All at once, my brain was overloaded with thoughts of fear, confusion, and ideas on how I was going to succeed. I didn't have any more brain power for the day. I didn't have the capacity to think anymore thoughts or feel anymore feelings, so I powered my little speaker off, placed my phone on the charger and climbed in my bed. It didn't feel like I'd get any sleep but the idea of just laying in bed doing nothing, including thinking, was more appealing than anything else at that moment.

Have you ever fallen asleep without realizing you were asleep until you woke up? That's obviously what happened to me. The sound of my phone ringing is what woke me out of my sleep, because I thought it was my alarm and I knew that I hadn't set an alarm. It wasn't an alarm though, my phone was ringing.

"Hello?" I said before even placing the phone to my ear.

I was genuinely confused.

"Baby." Dré said from the other side of the phone.

My heart sank. I sat up in my bed and fixed my hair as if he could physically see my appearance.

My voice shook. "Dré." I was almost in tears. "Oh my gosh. Where are you? I'm coming to see you right now! Where are you?"

By that point, I was aimlessly walking around my room, moving items around trying to figure out what I was going to wear to go see him.

"Lux. Slow down, Mama. Slow down." Dré was calm and careful with his words like always.

Usually, the calmness of his voice and the way he selected his words would ease my spirit and bring me from a ten to a one in no time, but that morning, it triggered me. It sent me to a place I had never been with him before.

"Where the fuck are you?! Why did it take you so long? What am I supposed to be doing out here? What the fuck, Dré?" The questions came out just as quickly as the thoughts happened.

There was silence on the other end of the phone. I realized that I needed to check my tone and instantly regretted the energy I had just given him. His silence had me thinking he disconnected the call.

"Dré." I said.

With more calmness than he had ever had before, Dré said, "Lux. Two deep breaths."

Naturally, I complied and began to cry.

"I know, baby. I know. We'll get through this. We've gotten through everything. EVERYTHING." Dré said.

"I miss you so much. I'm so lost without you. I'm so scared. Stacey came to the salon looking for Blanco and I didn't even know that bitch knew where the salon was, Dré. Who's going to protect me if you're not here?" I spewed.

Dré cleared his throat. That was a rare occurrence, but it was something that he did when he was experiencing more rage than he would like to admit. I could hear him taking those two deep breaths he told me to take.

"Ok. Ok. I'll deal with that. Blanco is here too. She's probably just as lost as you feel right now. But the difference is that you're not lost, Lux. I'm your map, baby. I'm going to tell you exactly what to do and how to do it." He finally said.

I took two deep breaths in my nose and out of my mouth. "When can I see you? I need to see you. I need to look at you and touch your skin. I need to see with my own eyes that you're doing fine in there. Please." I tried to sound as calm as I could.

"Write this number down." He completely disregarded everything I had just said to him.

Frustrated, I picked up my notebook and pen from the night before, ripped the cap off of the pen with my teeth and wrote down the number Dré gave me.

"Now what?" I said with an attitude.

"Now write this address down." He replied with no regard for my attitude.

I wrote down the address and intentionally sighed loud and hard into the phone.

"Relax, Lux. I need you on top of your game right now." He said.

Shaking my head in disbelief, I said, "It's really hard when you're not here, Dré."

"I know, baby. Give me time. That address is where I'm at. Come see me next week between noon and four o'clock. No jewelry. Take an *Uber.* Just keep doing what you're doing until you see me."

"Ok. I love you." I felt better.

"I love you, too. You TTG. Stop stressing." He said in an attempt to reassure me.

We disconnected the call. My heart was filled with so much joy just from hearing his voice. Some part of me felt relieved knowing that Blanco was inside too. I mean, the alternative was that he was on the run and that's really no way to live. Besides, if he was on the run, I don't think Dré would have been able to help him, so as crazy as it sounds, jail was the best option for Blanco at the time.

fourteen
lux lexington.

HEARING from Dré and knowing that I was going to be able to go visit him was all that I needed to bring me out of the slump that I was in. After I spoke to him, I spent the next few days pampering myself so that I would look as fine as I did before things got weird. I mean, he was in there surrounded by a bunch of grown ass men so it probably didn't matter how I looked, but I wanted to make sure I gave him something to look at and dream about.

On the day that I was going to visit him, I woke up at about six forty-five in the morning feeling anxious. Not the good anxiety that you feel when you're excited to see someone, it was the bad anxiety. For some reason, I felt like things weren't going to go the way they were supposed to and whatever that meant, meant that I wouldn't be able to see Dré. There was no real reason for those thoughts to invade my mind other than all of the unfortunate events leading up to that day but they were completely taking over. Of course there was nothing I could tell Abuelita because I had already told her the lie about Dré and I breaking up. I knew that she was the only person on Earth that could have

181

brought me out of that space of anxiety that I was in but what was I supposed to say? *Oh, hey, Abuelita. I know I told you that Dré and I broke up, but I'm actually going to visit him in jail today where he was taken after he was arrested for what I assume to be drug charges and I'd really appreciate it if you could help me calm my nerves.* Not a fucking chance.

Anyway, when we had spoken on the phone, Dré told me that I could visit between the hours of noon and four o'clock as if he didn't know that I would be at the front doors by eleven fifty-nine. I was up and in my thoughts way too early and I knew that I wasn't going to be able to go back to sleep so I was greatly considering popping Abuelita's bottle of wine open and drinking the entire bottle just so that I could find some fucking chill, but I didn't want to get so drunk that I missed my chance to see Dré. Instead, I decided that it was time to go see my daddy. I hadn't seen him in a while and I missed being in his presence. I missed sitting face to stone with him and receiving answers to questions that I didn't think I'd ever have the answers to.

It was too early for me to stop at the flower shop to pick up fresh roses and I was sort of bummed about that, but I was in a time crunch and I figured Daddy would just be grateful I finally showed up again. Since I didn't have time, I rummaged through the duffle bag at the bottom of my closet that I never took the time to unpack when I first moved back to Abuelita's house. It's funny because I knew that Dré never would have tolerated no shit like that. He was a neat freak and a germaphobe and there was no way in hell he was going to let me slide for allowing a bag of clothes to sit on the closet floor for a day, yet alone more than a month. As I started to pick through the clothes I was looking for, I laughed to myself thinking about what Dré would have said. He always used my looks as a valid reason as to why I shouldn't have done whatever stupid thing I did.

He would have said something like, "You too damn fine to be leaving clothes in a bag for a month. And you fa sho too fine to have that shit on the floor. Get 'cha fuckin' life."

Hearing his voice in my head saying, getcha fuckin' life, brought me to tears. But like always, there was no time for that so I fanned my hands back and forth in front of my eyes until the tears dried up. I wanted to go see Daddy because I knew it would give me some sense of normalcy and balance before seeing Dré. It would also kill time while I waited for the clock so that I could go see my man. It's crazy how time moves like a fucking sloth when you're in a rush but on days like the one when I forgot about dinner with Abuelita, it just fucking flies by.

I knew there was a blue hoodie with matching sweatpants in that bag somewhere and I had finally found it. I felt like it was the perfect substitute for the blue roses I'd typically take with me when I saw Daddy, so I wanted to wear it. When I was done putting it on, I threw my hair up in a bun and watched my reflection in the mirror that hung against the back of my bedroom door. As I twisted my bun around in an effort to center it more, I started to think about Daddy. I wondered if his spirit was really somewhere in the sky missing me or if I had been sitting face to stone imagining that I felt my Daddy's energy like I was in some sort of fairytale world. I shook my head at myself because literally nothing in my life was making sense and none of it felt real. It's like I was the main character in my own nightmare and I didn't know how to change the channel.

It was a short drive to the cemetery and I almost considered not even putting my seatbelt on until I remembered that Daddy probably wasn't wearing his when he died and I was afraid that the beeping sound the car made when it reminds you that you haven't put your seatbelt on, would trigger me. See, Daddy never had his seatbelt on when he was alive and Ma would always be on his head about it because she didn't like hearing that beeping noise. I'm not sure if I was afraid it'd trigger me into a rollercoaster of emotions from thinking of Daddy's death or if it'd trigger me into missing my mother but I wasn't willing to find out.

It felt like it had been so long since I'd been to Daddy's grave that it almost felt weird being there. Not to mention, no one from my fake security team was nearby to survey the land of the dead while I sat there and had heart to spirit conversations with my father. Regardless, it felt good to be there. Can you imagine how shitty my life had to be for me to say that it felt good to be at a cemetery and really mean that with all of my heart? Anyway, as I walked over to Daddy's gravestone, I checked the time from my phone and then took two really deep breaths in my nose and out of my mouth so that I could calm myself down the way Dré had taught me. After my breathing exercise I felt eager to sit face to stone with Daddy so that I could tell him about the circus that was my life.

"Hi, Daddy." I said as I sat down in front of his gravestone.

I took in the smell of the crisp, morning air and used my pointer finger to draw a heart in the morning dew that was all over his stone. My words and thoughts had escaped me but I felt at peace. It was like there were so many things I wanted to tell him but it almost didn't even feel necessary once I was finally face to stone.

About five minutes had passed before I finally said anything.

"Well, Dré's in jail." I said softly. "I miss him a lot." My voice cracked and my head lowered in shame.

I took a deep breath and looked up at the stone as if it could talk back to me.

"I'm going to see him today." I continued.

"And of course, I'm nervous." I chuckled with my mouth closed and a gust of air escaped my nostrils.

I looked up to the sky and took another deep breath. "And, to make it all worse, I lied to Abuelita. So life is – life is really fucking shitty right now, Daddy. I don't know what to do. I'm sad. I'm angry. I'm confused. I'm scared. It's too much. All of it." I looked at Daddy's stone again and threw my hands up in the air.

"So here I am. I'm a mess, but I'm here. I'm sorry it took me so long. I didn't forget about you." I felt ashamed. "I could never forget about you. Life has just been really hard lately and I'm struggling to get through each day."

For the next two hours, I just sat face to stone without saying another word. That was part of the peace in visiting Daddy; stillness and silence.

Finally, it was time for me to head back to Abuelita's so that I could drop my car off, change clothes and wait for an *Uber* to pick me up. While I was driving, I thought about what I wanted to wear. See, Dré was a face guy. Of course he wanted me to be fitted, but less was always more to him. He didn't mind a full set of lashes or tinted eyebrows, but he preferred minimum makeup and didn't like pounds of hair. Which, considering the circumstances, was a good thing because paying for lashes and brows had already felt like too much.

As I pulled into the driveway, I finalized my thoughts on my outfit and started to become anxious about seeing Dré;

the good kind, though. So anxious that as soon as I opened the front door, I realized that I hadn't paid attention to any of my surroundings before I had gotten out of the car. It didn't make a difference but it was another reminder that I needed to keep all of the things Dré had taught me in the front of my mind because the purpose of him teaching me the things he did was so that I could protect myself whether or not he was around. There wasn't anything I could do to change the fact that I hadn't scanned the block but I took a mental note, once again, to do better moving forward.

"Hola, Mami!" I said with excitement as I walked into the living room.

She was surprised to see me, but happy nonetheless. "Oh, hi, Mija! I thought you were still sleeping. Tienes hambre?" She asked.

"No, Mami." I said as I leaned in to kiss her forehead as she sat on the couch. "I'm in a hurry. I've got a meeting today!"

If it isn't obvious yet, whenever I didn't want Abuelita to question my statement, I'd hurry out of the room or change the topic as quickly as I could so that she didn't have the opportunity to do so. It was becoming a dirty habit those days but it felt necessary. Telling my grandmother that I had a meeting to attend was a little white lie. I mean, technically, I was going to a meeting, I just didn't disclose what type of meeting it was. Half a lie is better than a whole lie, but I know that no lie at all would be best. I wish that my life afforded me the luxury of not lying to my angel, myself, or anyone else for that matter, but that wasn't the reality of my life at the time.

Whatever the lie, I was truly excited to finally see my fucking man. My wardrobe options were slim, so I had decided on wearing a black long sleeve bodysuit, one of the few items I actually unpacked and properly placed on a clothing rack, a pair of ripped black jeans and some patent leather thigh high boots that were about four and a half inches high. Without hesitating, I grabbed the bodysuit from the hanger and put it on before I grabbed my jeans and unboxed my boots. I stood in the mirror and looked back at my reflection. Somehow, a different version of myself stood there that day. The woman that stared back at me was somewhere between Lux and Lexington. *Lux Lexington.* She was both empty and full of emotion.

At some point that morning, I had set an alarm on my phone for ten forty-five so that I could stay on task. Even though I was anxious to see Dré, I knew that my memory, my concept of time and my ability to properly manage it were a bit flawed. It didn't make sense to me at the time because I had always been on top of my shit, Dré's shit and Blanco's shit too. But, today, I understand that anxiety, depression and extreme trauma changes you in ways you never even considered. The amount of pressure I was under in the present time combined with the amount of trauma I had experienced over the course of my life caused me to be less mindful of things because I was subconsciously working so hard to just .. exist. Anyway, I liked who was looking back at me in the mirror that day. Somehow, I felt empowered. I felt powerful. I felt capable. Somehow, knowing that I was going to see Dré gave me unwavering confidence.

Before putting my pants on, I sat down on the edge of my bed, closed my eyes and took two deep breaths in my nose and out of my mouth. I began to envision a chess board. For some reason, the vision was crystal clear as if it was right there next to me. The board was glass and there were clear and frosted pieces that were glass as well. Funny thing is that I had never actually played chess a day in my life, but I could hear Dré saying: *Always think ahead of your opponent, Lux. You're the queen, don't move too soon. You know what it is. You play chess or get check'd.*

Just as I heard his voice say that, the frosted king on my imaginary chess board toppled over and brought me back to reality.

"No time for emotions, Lux." I said out loud.

I quickly jumped into my jeans and stuffed my legs into my boots. As I took one last look at myself in the mirror, I wished that I could put my chain and a pair of hoops on to set my outfit off, but I remembered that Dré specifically told me not to wear any jewelry. It was fine though, I felt good in my decision to wear all black and I felt good in my decision to wear that bodysuit.

Still looking in the mirror, I ran my hands across my torso and smiled at myself. Really, I was smiling at how much I knew Dré would like my outfit. It was simple and I was completely covered but he loved it when I wore bodysuits because he loved to bend me over the bathroom counter, pull the crotch of my bodysuit to the side and fuck me from behind. The memories sent chills up my spine so I knew that the visual would give him something to dream about.

Before I left my room, I sprayed myself with the only bottle of perfume I had taken from the penthouse. And just as I was about to walk out of my bedroom and love on Abuelita for a second, I realized that I didn't want to allow an Uber driver to pick me up from Abuelita's house. In my mind, it left her too vulnerable. Immediately, I decided that I would drive myself to my salon and get picked up from there. That way, if for whatever reason anyone had been looking for me, they'd assume that I was at the salon or in the general area, leaving Abuelita out of whatever chaos was intended for me.

"You look beautiful, Mija." Abuelita said as I approached her in the living room.

My heart melted. "Thank you, Abuelita. I'll be back in a few hours, ok?" I kissed her forehead again before leaving.

This time, as soon as I closed the front door, I scanned the block. My mind was clear and it allowed me to feel a sense of bravery. Nothing appeared to be out of the ordinary, so I hopped in my car and smashed all the way to my salon. When I made it there, I went inside and turned on the lights but I left the curtains closed while I waited inside for my *Uber* to arrive. At my workstation, I placed my small purse inside of the cabinet doors and then locked the doors. There was no need to take my purse with me, I just needed my ID and a little just in case cash.

Once my driver arrived, I considered shutting off the lights before heading out, but decided that it'd be better to keep them on so that it appeared as though someone was inside. I was probably doing too much but with the number of mistakes I had already made without consequence, I needed to start training myself to be overly cautious but not paranoid. Complacency creates chaos, right?

A black sedan pulled up in front of my salon as the driver waited for me to climb in the backseat so that we could begin our hour-long drive. By that time, it was already eleven thirty, which meant that I wouldn't arrive until about twelve thirty. I didn't love that but I had no one to blame but myself. The driver tried his best to have small talk with me but I wasn't the least bit interested in what he had to say. Unfortunately, it took him about ten minutes to realize that. Now that I think about it, it probably would have been in my best interest to chop it up with him because the way my nerves had my stomach doing cartwheels was out of this world. I wasn't having it though.

LOWKEE

There was nothing for me to discuss with a stranger and all I could think about was: *what if they don't let me see him?*

One very long hour later, I had finally made it to Dré's location. It was such a surreal moment to be there. It didn't feel right. Especially because images of my mother kept popping into my head. I knew that visiting Dré wouldn't be the same experience as visiting Ma, but if I'm honest, I was already tired of it before I even stepped foot inside the stupid place. I was already tired of going through metal detectors. I was tired of signing fake names on the sign in sheet. I was tired of seeing Dré in jail scrubs. All of it. I was already exhausted and we hadn't even done any real time yet.

After going through the entire sign-in process, I sat down in the visitors area while I waited for a guard to bring my man to me. Every time the door clicked, my heart would skip a beat and then it felt like it would beat double time when the prisoner that walked through the door wasn't Dré. Three prisoners walked out before they finally brought Dré out and when they did, my heart dropped as I stood up to greet him.

"You look good, Mama." He said as the guard adjusted his handcuffs so that he could sit at the table.

The only thing I could do was smile. My heart was so full.

We sat down at the same time. Neither of us saying a word.

"I miss you so much." I finally said.

Dré leaned forward, placing his forearms on the table and then discreetly looked around the room before he said,

"You look so fucking good. You know I love bodysuits." He licked his lips.

That was exactly the energy I was hoping for when I had gotten dressed that morning so if there was nothing else done right while Dré was away, I showed up and showed the fuck out that day.

"Thanks, Baby." I said with sex on my mind and in my eyes.

"When are you coming home?" I whined.

Dré took two deep breaths in his nose and out of his mouth and that's when I knew that whatever came out of his mouth next, wasn't going to be anything I wanted to hear.

He broke eye contact with me and looked down at his hands as he interlocked his fingers. "It'll be a while, Lux."

"What?!" I said louder than I should have.

"Not here." He demanded.

"What do you mean 'a while'? What's a while? Why a while? I did what you told me to do. The legal fees are on ice. Just tell me what to do and I'll do it. We don't have *a while*, Dré." My voice was shaky as I fought back tears.

I could see how quickly Dré's thoughts were moving as he leaned back in his chair and stretched his legs out underneath the table.

Choosing his words carefully he said, "I already spoke to my team. Don't worry about the fees. It's covered."

I looked down at my hands as a single teardrop escaped.

"Look at me." He whispered sternly.

I complied. Barely.

He continued, "You need to get your license, so use that bread to knock the tuition out. Get that salon going as soon as possible."

I was defeated. "And what if I can't, Dré? And why am

I using the bread for tuition when we obviously have other things to worry about?"

Every ounce of confidence and empowerment I had felt earlier that morning had completely dissolved.

"Do you trust me, Lexington?" Dré said as he leaned forward.

My eyebrows shifted and I rubbed my lips together with whatever lipgloss remained. I'm not sure Dré had ever called me Lexington and he for damn sure had never asked me if I trusted him.

I stared at him for a moment. "With my life, Dré." I finally replied.

"Ok." He shook his head in agreement as he took a deep breath. "We have to pivot, Lux. It's the only way we come out of this on top. Everything is a pawn now. I need you to play the game exactly as I tell you. You're the only way out of this." He said as he stared directly into my eyes.

I bit the insides of my cheeks out of nervousness but I didn't break eye contact with him.

"What about Blanc?" I asked.

Dré chose his words extremely carefully. "It's me and you, Lux. We have to focus on ourselves before we focus on anybody else."

I was confused. Dré had never been the type of person to leave someone behind. And Blanco meant the world to Dré, so I had to make sure that I didn't misunderstand what was being said.

Dré could obviously sense or visibly see my confusion. "I'm going to get him out of here, too, but I can only focus on one thing at a time. Don't stress yourself out. Please." He said calmly.

That made more sense and gave me some peace.

"Ok, so what's the play? How do we pivot?" I asked dryly.

It's as if he'd been waiting for me to ask that question the entire time. "Listen, let me tell you something.." He paused for a moment. "At some point, preferably between now and the time it takes you to get home, you need to realize that how fine you are, is one of your greatest assets. You've been able to walk into rooms and politic with people that I haven't been able to because you're fuckin beautiful. You're smart as hell. You're resourceful as fuck. And you get shit done, and all of that is important but that's not how these bitches are surviving right now. Niggas are not outside saving smart, resourceful bitches that get shit done. They're saving the ones that are pretty to look at and fun to play with."

By that point, I was completely lost. "What's your point, Dré?"

With a look in his eyes that I had never seen before, Dré said, "In order for us to win this game, you gotta start finessing these niggas."

"Meaning?" I replied with no thought.

Dré had the audacity to have an attitude. He shifted his body around in his chair and scrunched his nose at me as if I was some sort of imbecile.

"Meaning that there's no time for emotions, Lux. Meaning that you're going to have to spend some money on clothes and shoes and shit, go outside and get in these niggas pockets. You know how to penetrate a man's mind, so you do that enough to penetrate his heart and gain access to his wallet. When you get what you need, you move on. You don't become attached to these niggas, you just get what you can and you move the fuck on. Do you understand what I'm telling you?"

Offended, I said, "So you want me to be a prostitute. Got it." And then I rolled my eyes and shook my head in disgust.

"Don't fucking play with me." He said aggressively. He caught his tone and checked himself.

With a less aggressive tone he continued on to say, "Lux, you don't listen. I said penetrate his mind. That means that once your LOOKS have his attention, then you can use your wisdom and wit to get in his pockets. Not once did I say give my fuckin' pussy away." Dré's face was stern.

Tears began to fill my eyes.

"What's the point of this, Dré? How is this a pivot? How does this get you out of here?" I waved my finger in a circle to showcase that *here*, meant jail.

Dré took a deep breath. "Do you think I got us where we are without finessing niggas along the way? You know I didn't. You've run damn near every play with me, Lux. I've taught you everything you need to know. We still have plays to run but we have to move a lot differently now. When it's time, you'll tap in with a new plug but for now, we pivot."

His energy shifted and he was beginning to feel more like the Dré that I knew. "Men spend money on women. Men invest in women. Men help women. So we gone use that to our advantage. We gone get everything we can from whoever we can and stack until I'm out of here." He promised.

"The trucking company is doing well, Babe. And I'll do everything in my power to get the salon up and running so that it can start bringing in money ASAP. I promise." I pleaded with him.

"I believe you, Baby. I do. Remember we were supposed to run it up for three more months? It was going to take me three months to put us in a position to make sure the crew was good, buy us a house and set us up for the rest of our lives. Three months. That's it. Look at how quickly that changed. We have to pivot, Mama. We don't have a choice." Dré chose his words carefully.

I was speechless.

He took two breaths in and out of his nose again. "Lux, at minimum, I'm down for five years."

I let out a loud sigh and tears rushed down my cheeks.

"I need you, Lux. You have to run this shit up so that we can be solid when I come home. And when I get home, it's up. When I get home I'm going to make sure I make good on everything I said before I got here. But you gotta hold us down until then, Mama." Dré began to look around the room again as discreetly as he could.

I looked down at my legs so that I could hide the fact that I was crying from whomever Dré thought was watching us, which was probably every guard in the room.

It took me a moment to gather my thoughts and dry my tears but I finally said, "Ok." I shrugged my shoulders. "I'll figure it out." I looked up at him.

Dré let out a sigh of relief. "That's my girl. That's the fucking energy we need. Just hold this shit down until I'm home. You don't have to figure it out alone. I'm here. I'm calling you every chance I get. I want you to come see me every week so that you can give me the run down on these niggas and I can tell you how to finesse them. And I want you to send me letters and pictures and shit so that I can have a piece of you in here with me. We're going to get through this, Baby. I promise you that."

I stayed silent. I shook my head in agreement to ensure Dré that I was listening, but my thoughts were all over the place.

"And Lux, you know I don't fuck with Syd, but she's going to have to be a pawn in this game. You need her as a wingman right now. You know exactly who she is and you know that shit isn't going to change, so keep her at a distance but allow her to feel like she's close. Don't tell her shit. Just do what you need to do. When I say that there's no time for emotions, I mean that shit across the board. Everywhere except Abuelita." He said.

I didn't even bother acknowledging his statement at that point. My brain was exhausted and it was nearing time to wrap up our visit.

I took a deep breath and said, "Well, this isn't how I expected this visit to go. I mean, I'm glad I saw you. I'm glad I got to hear your voice. I don't know what I was expecting, but it wasn't this. I wish you could just come home." My eyes met his but I was in a daze.

"Five years, Lux. I just need you to hold shit down for five years." He said with confidence.

I giggled sarcastically. "Dré I barely survived two months without you. Do you understand that? I barely survived." My eyes became watery again but my voice was filled with anger.

"It's different now. You been TTG for years. Your hustle is different. Your mind is different. You've survived all the worst. Ain't nothin' to this shit, Lux. Not shit. You know what the fuck it is. When I'm out of here, we'll sit on a beach and laugh about the niggas you finessed and the plays you ran. We're a team, baby and I'm on the bench right now. Run the play." His words were sincere and somehow comforting.

And just like that, we were out of time. We had to tell each other we loved each other and end our visit. My mind was racing as I left the facility but my heart was at ease. I was so deep in my thoughts that I walked out of the visitation center and walked through the parking lot of the facility aimlessly scanning for my car. After about five minutes of searching, I started to panic until I realized that I hadn't driven myself there, I *Uber'd* like Dré told me to. It was a simple mistake but one that pulled me out of my head, like every mistake I had made up until that point had done. Go figure.

It only took me a second to request a car and while I sat there waiting, I just kept thinking about Dré telling me that there was no time for emotions. It was a challenging thought for me because I had finally gotten to a space where I thought I found a balance between Lux and Lexington and within that same eight hours, Dré had completely thrown me out of alignment. Not to mention the fact that ultimately, he was telling me to finesse men for money without fucking them and I had no fucking idea how I was going to make that work. But for years, Dré took care of me, provided for me, protected me and poured into me. Shit, I probably wouldn't even be here today if he didn't breathe life back into me when he did, so I felt like it was my duty to do the same for him. That's what partnership is, right? Balance. Reciprocity. Yin and Yang. In our case, *Bonnie & Clyde*.

There wasn't really much else to think about. Dré was my man. For as long as I had known him, he had never led me in the wrong direction and I had no reason to believe that just because his circumstances changed, that his ability to lead would differ in any capacity. A leader is a leader, regardless of the circumstances.

At the exact moment that my phone notified me that my driver had arrived, the black SUV pulled up in front of me. Before I stood up from the curb, I took two deep breaths in my nose and out of my mouth and I made the very conscious decision to hold shit down for the next five years.

Once I climbed in the car, I didn't even bother greeting my driver. I wasn't in the mood to have pointless conversation with a stranger. As a matter of fact, the only thing I could think about was how I was going to reunite with

Sydney. We hadn't spoken in months. There had been times in our childhood where our friendship had fallen off but it had never lasted more than a week or two. It was different though. We were adults. We lived completely different lifestyles. And it was very clear that she wasn't fucking with the lifestyle I had chosen for myself.

"Fuck it. No time for emotions. Run the play." I thought to myself.

I typed and erased at least four different messages before sending Sydney a text that said, *hey girl.*

To be honest, I didn't really know what I'd say once she replied and I wasn't really in the mood to go through all of the small talk that comes after months of not speaking to someone you consider a best friend. But what I did know was that the web of lies I had been telling Abuelita was about to be nothing compared to the web I was about to weave Syd. I didn't really know the play at that point in time, but the rules were simple: *play chess or get check'd.*

fifteen
romeo.

DURING THE REMAINDER of the ride back to my salon, I had figured out how I would run the Syd play. Since I had already told Abuelita that Dré and I had broken up, I wanted to stick with that. For one, it was one less lie I'd have to keep up with but two, I had a feeling Sydney would find some sort of joy in the fact that Dré and I had finally split which would make the rest of the play fall right into place. She had never expressed directly that she didn't really fuck with him but just like Dré said during our visit, I knew Syd like the back of my hand and energy has never been hard for me to read. Anyway, essentially, Syd was going to feel like she was helping me find a new nigga. You know just like I know, that when your girl breaks up with the nigga you hated for her, you can't wait to help her find a replacement and that's the energy I wanted Sydney to have. At the same time though, I had no intention of tolerating any slander surrounding Dré's name and or character because whether Syd knew or not, he was still very much my man.

Once my driver pulled up to my salon, I scanned the

block before exiting and then thanked him for getting me to my destination safely. In my mind, I was also grateful that he had gotten me there quietly, too. There's nothing worse than a driver who can't read the fucking room enough to identify that a passenger has no desire to converse. Based on my quick scan of the block, everything appeared to be business as usual but in an effort to avoid making any more small mistakes, I pretended to be adjusting my boots while I waited for the driver to pull off before I unlocked the salon door. There was literally no reason for me to assume he cared which business I'd be walking into but there was also no reason for me to assume he didn't care. No time for complacency or the chaos it creates.

On top of my mind scrambling to figure out how I was going to run the play, as Dré put it, I also had to maintain the trucking company, get my salon off the ground, go to Cosmetology school, be fake best friends with my actual best friend, keep up with every lie I'd already told Abuelita and mourn the five year loss of my man without displaying emotions because I didn't have time for that. Shit was chaotic enough.

As I entered my salon, I quickly locked the door behind me and my heart began to race. It was the first moment I felt like I could release even a small fraction of the weight I felt on my shoulders. Again, it was starting to feel like it was almost too much to bear. I stood at the front door contemplating whether or not I would allow myself to feed into the pain I was feeling on the inside and then my mind traveled back to one of many mornings after my mother suffered abuse at the hands of my father. She was taking me to school and randomly gave me a lesson on how important it was for me as a woman of color to feel my feelings.

"Lexington, you should be proud of who you are." She said out of nowhere.

"You're Black and Puerto Rican. You carry your fathers name and his dark skin, but you carry my strength. Do you know that?" She asked.

I had no clue where she was going with her speech or how it pertained to anything at all, but I said, "I know, Ma." I knew better than to respond any other way.

She continued, "Good. You keep that strength, my love. But do not allow it to weigh you down. The world expects women of color to weather every storm without getting wet. The world expects us to carry every burden without growing tired. But you're a living, breathing, feeling, human. If you allow the world to ignore that, then you will too ignore it. You must protect yourself in the storm, release the burden when it becomes too heavy, rest when you are tired and feel everything that you feel. You have to feel it, my love. Or else it kills you. Do you understand?"

I remember looking over at her from the passenger seat that morning so that I could sort of gauge where she was coming from. I knew what happened the night before because I heard her cries but I didn't understand how it played a part in what she was saying to me at that moment. Even still, I said, "I got it, Ma. I got it."

It didn't make sense to me on the way to school that morning, but it made all of the sense in the world as I stood at the front door of my salon. My mother's message to me was a message to herself. It was her way of pleading with herself to save herself. My mother wanted to be free the same way I wanted to be free. The freedom I wanted was different, though. I just wanted my man to come home. There was no such thing as freedom from pain for me but the closest I could get to that was Dré. And with that thought, I decided that my mother's story was different from mine and I didn't have time to feel everything that I felt. The sound of my phone notifying me of a text message confirmed my thoughts.

The text was from Syd and my heart sank. I was nervous because her reply would show me just how much I'd have to finesse her for my play to work. Before I mustered up the courage to open the text, I walked over to my soon-to-be workstation, took off my boots and sat down. To my surprise Syd's text read: *well well well*. That was typical Syd shit, which meant there wasn't going to be any instances of awkwardness in us reuniting. Luckily.

Oddly, reading the text gave me confidence and from that moment on, I knew that the next five years weren't going to be as much of a challenge as I thought they would be.

My first thought was like, damn, Dré was right; ain't shit changed. I was just hoping he was right about there not being shit to finessing niggas out of money. Dré was very clear when he said I couldn't give his pussy away and as much as I had no desire to have sex, I struggled with the idea of it actually working because as far as I knew, niggas weren't investing in women without a return on that investment. The return on the investment? PUSSY.

After reading Sydney's text message, I replied with: *Oh, nothing. Just getting some work done at my salon.*

That was my way of telling her that I missed her and that we had lots of catching up to do. I know that she hadn't exactly given me the energy I wanted when I first mentioned the salon to her, but she was a pawn at that point. Not my best friend.

Syd and I had been friends for practically our entire lives, I knew that she would understand that message and just like clockwork, she called me. We talked on the phone for about an hour as I poured out lie after lie. Honestly, I didn't even know I was capable of telling so many fuking lies but there I was, successfully lying through my fucking teeth. By the end of our phone call, Syd was under the impression that Dré and I had amicably broken up because he moved out-of-state and I didn't want to leave Abuelita alone. Ain't that some shit? Anyway, I told her that it had been about two months since the break up and I was ready to get back outside and find me a new nigga. It didn't make sense to me until much later, and I will tell you that story soon, but just as I expected, she was happy to hear that Dré and I had broken up. So happy that before we got off the phone, she suggested that we get fine and go to a rooftop dinner that same night.

That phone call, much like everything else in my life at that point, put me in an interesting space internally. One part of me couldn't wait to hear from Dré so that I could tell him how easy it was for me to get the ball rolling but the other part of me was genuinely excited to spend time with Syd. Underneath the unspoken, underlying drama that we had, she really was my best friend. She was the only other person besides my abuelita who really witnessed the excruciating pain I went through when my mother went to jail and my father died. Besides Syd and Abuelita, no one saw that pain first hand. No one knew how it destroyed me. I mean, yes, everyone can imagine what it had done to me, but no one had been there through the worst parts of it like Abuelita and Syd had been. Not even Dré.

I placed my phone down on the counter and looked at myself in the mirror. "No time for emotions, Lux." I said out loud.

For the next few hours, I stayed at the salon and got as much work done as I could. I made sure the truck drivers were on task with their deliveries, sent in the application I had filled out for the Cosmetology school I was going to attend, and did a little more research on braiding hair vendors. I knew that the sooner I found my hair vendor, I would be able to start selling the hair and begin taking braiding clients again. My plan was to bring awareness to the salon as soon as possible, even if I wasn't prepared to fully open. Social media had never really been my thing so I planned on hiring someone to run my page for me so that I didn't have to spend time learning the ropes. The goal was to maximize my visibility and profitability, not overwork myself. If I never learned anything from watching Dré run businesses and run plays, I definitely learned the power of delegation.

Before leaving the salon, I realized that I was proud of what I had accomplished that day. I was proud of myself for pocketing my emotions and weathering every storm that hovered over and within me. I was proud of myself for getting so much done when really all I wanted to do was curl up in a ball and cry my eyes out. And by the time I was done with that day, I felt like Lux Lex was there to stay. I felt like with Dré's playbook and my billion dollar brain, I was capable of holding shit down just like I said I would.

When it was time for me to leave the salon, I turned out all of the lights, locked up, and went straight home. My spirits were high and it felt good. I mean, yes, there was definitely a lot going on in my brain, but I was on my way home to see Abuelita, who always provided some form of peace in my life and then I was going to see Syd, which, if nothing else, was going to be a much needed girls night out.

As soon as I got home, I showed Abuelita some love and then took a hot shower. Afterwards, we talked about her day and the meeting I lied about and then I told her that Syd and I were going to get together. She was super excited to hear that. Even though she hadn't asked about Syd since I had moved back, it was clear that we weren't on speaking terms. I'm sure Abuelita noticed that Syd hadn't been to the house in a while.

Anyway, the time had finally come for me to get dressed. Black was my go to color at the time because it made me feel empowered. Syd and I were going to be meeting at a rooftop bar, so I kept my outfit cute and casual: black crop top, black jeans and a pair of black *Gisuppe's.* The amount of stress I had been under had caused my hair to shed pretty excessively, so I kept it simple with a low bun and big hoop earrings and made a mental note that I needed to find someone that could give me a cute bob cut.

My nerves began to kick in once I left the house. It was like getting dressed and knowing the real reason I was meeting up with Syd was starting to hit me. Plus, I had been in a relationship for so long that I wasn't even sure I knew how to flirt with men. My heart and pussy still belonged to Dré and even though what I was getting ready to do was at his command, it still felt disloyal to me. In order to psyche myself out, I told myself that more than likely, I wasn't even going to meet any niggas worth finessing at the bar, but it would be a good start at getting my feet wet and figuring out what my angle would be when I did come across a nigga I could finesse.

Syd and I decided to meet at the bar instead of riding together and we ended up pulling up to the valet line at the same time. When we handed our keys over to the valet drivers, we both squealed like little girls and swayed back and forth as we hugged one another. Seeing her was just like old times and it killed any nervousness I felt.

We took the elevator to the rooftop and I immediately fell in love with the view. You could see the entire city and it literally looked like something out of a movie. The first thing I did was have Syd take a photo of me with the city lights as my backdrop because I wanted to send it to Dré as soon as I could. If Syd knew that, she would've lost her shit. After that, we hopped in the photo together and got a cute usie in.

After our photo, Syd said, "Let's sit at the bar. That'll let these niggas know they can form a line 'cus we fine."

We both laughed.

"Syd. What does that even mean?!" I asked through laughter.

"That means if we sit at a table, they'll think they can't come talk to us. But if we sit at the bar, they'll be lined up to buy our drinks." She said in a very matter of fact tone.

She was right though, because as soon as we made it to the bar, a man on the other side of the bar smiled and made eye contact with me. He looked to be about thirty years old in the face but his hairline was easily fifty years old. The buss down on his wrist and the chain on his neck told me two things: one, he had a little money but two, he wasn't doing it for his family, he was doing it for the bitches. That math, math'd enough for me to smile back at him. And I guess a smile was all he needed because he began to walk over to my side of the bar as a man in all black followed close behind him and another led the way.

"Ok, Syd. I see you. We just got to the bar and niggas are already flocking our way. Your stupid line theory was right." I whispered jokingly.

Syd didn't have time to reply before the man approached me. He was only about five foot nine and he was a little heavier than I expected him to be, but none of that really mattered. I knew he wasn't actually my type of nigga as soon as I saw him from across the bar with all of his jewelry buss'd down. On the flip side, he was exactly the type of man Dré wanted me to finesse.

"What y'all drinkin'?" He asked as he leaned forward onto the bar.

"Oh. You don't say hello, first?" I said as I looked past him and at the two men that stood nearby him in all black.

He smiled and shifted his body so that he could shake my hand. "My bad, baby. How you doin'? I'm Romeo. Can I buy you and your friend a drink or two?" He asked.

"Romeo, huh? How fitting." I smiled. "Hi, Romeo. I'm Lux. Who are your friends?" I asked without shaking his hand and keeping my eye on the two men wearing black.

Romeo smiled. "That's Tank and Bull. They cool. They with me." He replied.

Shaking my head in agreement I replied, "They better be. Cus this is my shooter, Syd. She don't miss." I seductively bit the corner of my bottom lip.

Romeo glanced at Syd and smiled at her. She glared at him as if we both believed we were actually intimidating and then I smiled.

"Ok. Lux. Shooter. I like that." Romeo said as he looked at both of us.

I placed my forearms onto the bar counter and said, "Red wine. Shiraz if they have it. Cabernet if not." I looked over at him. "A double shot of tequila for my shooter, please. Top shelf only." I said.

"Oh and she has class? Ok, Lux." Romeo replied with a smile as he summoned the bartender.

Before I knew it, I was four glasses of wine in while Syd was on her second double shot of tequila. I'm not even sure how it happened, but by that time, I knew that Romeo had two children by two different women. They were both strippers but one of them was a bum bitch and the other was a boss bitch. Based on what he told me, he took care of both of them so that their money could be their own because he didn't believe women should have to spend their own money on fundamentals. Hell of a conversation for my first day back in the field, right? It was music to my fucking ears though becasue I knew that it meant I was going to be able to finesse him for at least ten racks over the next few months. Anyway, Sydney was mingling with different people around the bar while Romeo and I stayed put the entire night. His men in black, who I later learned were his bodyguards, didn't leave his side.

I'm not sure how much Romeo drank prior to me meeting him, but I could tell that he was starting to reach his limit. He wasn't belligerent or anything, but the trajectory of his conversation began to change. He went from telling me his life story and how much he valued women to implying that he wanted me to go home with him. That play might have worked for him in the past but I wasn't a simple minded bitch. I had watched Dré finesse too many niggas the same way a nigga would finesse a bitch, far too many times to fall for the okiedoke. I felt like I had done exactly what Dré told me to do; I penetrated Romeo's mind. Instead of playing into the bedroom conversation, I put my number in his phone and told him to text me when he was ready to take me on a proper date. As far as I was concerned, I had him right where I wanted him – he wanted me, so I wasn't going to hold his drunk conversation against him. After that, I told Sydney that it was time for us to go home.

Sydney and I left the bar and ended up stopping to get Coney Island on the way home. There is nothing in the world like Coney Island after a night of drinking. Granted, I had drank wine all night, but I was feeling good. Everything was going according to plan and for the first time in what felt like years, I didn't feel like I was under too much pressure. The wine could have been the reason I didn't feel pressured up but it didn't matter, I was enjoying the freedom. Even if only temporary. Anyway, for about two hours, Syd and I chilled in my car while we ate tacos and caught up on each other's lives. She tried to pull more info out of me about the salon and my fake break up with Dré but I kept avoiding those topics. Overall, it was good to see her. It felt like old times and I didn't feel any underlying shade from her, which was also nice.

By the time I made it home, Romeo had called me saying that he enjoyed my company and wanted to take me out to dinner the next night. Of course I agreed to dinner and told him that his little bodyguards were not welcome on our date. Honestly, it didn't matter to me that he walked around with security, it mattered to me that it felt disloyal for me to walk around with his security. If Dré and Blanco were around, I'd have my own security so it wasn't something I had considered when I went through my mental playbook. It was uncharted territory and I wasn't really willing or ready to step into it before I ran it by Dré.

I knew that Romeo liked me and I could tell that he was a simp and a trick but he wasn't an idiot so he was clearly not going to risk his safety for a bitch he met at a bar. Instead, he compromised with me. He told me that they absolutely had to show up with him but he would have them stay outside of the restaurant. That was fine with me. It wasn't like I was actually trying to get to know the man — I just needed to see if I could really finesse him.

Before we ended our phone call, he countered my 'no bodyguards' request with a request of his own. "Wear something upscale and sexy." He politely demanded.

I smiled a sinister smile before I replied. "I'll see what I can do." And then I hung up without waiting for his reply.

The next day, Syd came over to Abuelita's house and spent time with us. I braided her hair, Abuelita made us lunch and we just enjoyed each other's company like old times. You know Abuelita loved her some Syd, loved having company and loved when I stayed home, so she was living her best life. It was the first time since Dré had gotten locked up that I hadn't done any type of work for the entire day. It was the weekend though and after bagging the first nigga I could finesse as quickly as I did, I deserved a day off. Plus, the way I saw it, going to dinner with Romeo would technically be considered work.

Syd hung out at Abuelita's for the entire day. She helped me pick out my outfit for the date and all. We ended up agreeing on a long sleeve black dress that had a mixture of velvety material and mesh. It was a little shorter than I was comfortable with, but it was both classy and sexy. It gave enough skin to leave Romeo's mind wandering but enough class to remind him that I wasn't to be played with. It was giving penetrate his mind and break his pockets. Both Abuelita and Sydney thought I looked beautiful. Being that they both thought I was single, they were both excited that I was starting to date again. Abuelita swore I was too beautiful to be single and Syd just didn't like Dré. Anyway, Syd and I left Abuelita's house at the same time. She went home and I was off to meet up with Romeo.

As I was leaving the house, Romeo sent me a text telling me to call him as soon as I pulled up to valet. Being that it was a restaurant that I had never been to before, I was glad that I wouldn't have to search for parking and since Romeo walked around with security, I knew that his reasoning for it was for safety. I respected it. I guess I appreciated it, too.

When I pulled up, the valet line was full of all types of foreign whips. Now, Dré had me around some luxurious shit, but nothing as luxurious as that. I'm not even going to front, I was impressed but I would never admit that to Romeo or anyone else for that matter.

"I'm here." I said when Romeo answered the phone.

"Bet. Where are you? What kind of car are you in?" He replied.

"Parked behind a blacked out *Wraith*. I'm in a black *Rover*." I said nonchalantly.

Romeo said, "Yup." And then hung up.

The next thing I knew, the doors of the *Wraith* opened and two men wearing all black hopped out. Romeo followed. They all moved very strategically. I watched both men in black scan the block as Romeo greeted the valet workers. If nothing else, I was intrigued by the power Romeo and his security exuded and the way in which they moved so gracefully. It was almost like a scene out of a movie; very uniform and rehearsed. It was very different from what I remembered seeing at the bar the night before. It even had me confused as to why he was even at that bar – it was obviously the ghetto compared to what he was used to.

"Oh, no shooter?" Romeo said as he opened my door and looked over at the empty passenger seat.

Both of his bodyguards posted up at the front of my car. One at the front driver side with his back toward me, the other at the front passenger side standing in the opposite direction of his partner. I mean, you would think Romeo was the fucking President.

I shifted my eyes from guard to guard and then looked over at Romeo. "Well, I knew the Secret Service would be here, so." I shrugged.

Romeo laughed. "You don't miss a beat. I like that. Come on, let's go." He motioned for a valet worker to come over.

As the valet worker climbed into my car, Romeo handed him a one hundred dollar bill and grabbed my hand simultaneously. It felt weird holding another man's hand. For a moment, my heart sank and my throat became dry. For a moment, I wanted to cry because I missed Dré so much.

Romeo interrupted my quick lapse in emotion. "You

look good as fuck." He said as he released my hand and placed his arm around my waist.

His touch gave me chills. Not because I liked it, but because I didn't want to be there anymore. I had to remind myself that there was no time for emotions. I told Dré that I was going to hold shit down and that's exactly what I needed to do. I didn't reply to Romeo's compliment because we had approached the entrance of the restaurant and I was amazed by how beautiful it was inside.

Apparently Romeo was a big deal around that restaurant because as soon as we walked inside, there was a hostess prepared to walk us to our table.

"Ok, Romeo. A little class, I see." I whispered to him as we followed the hostess.

Romeo's laugh carried confidence. "Oh. This is nothing, baby girl."

Ok, listen, in my mind, I was spending all of that man's money but I kept my composure because I didn't want him to think that I was too impressed by a nice restaurant and a *Wraith*. I mean, I definitely was, but he didn't need to know that.

The hostess led us to a private room where one wall was a floor to ceiling fish tank. Some shit I had never seen before. The hostess pulled my chair out and told us that our server would be with us shortly.

Before Romeo could even get comfortable in his chair I asked, "You bring all your bitches here, or am I special?" I smiled.

"Nah, just the ones that complain about security." Romeo said with a straight face.

I bursted into laughter.

"Why you so mean?" He asked.

"Been through a lot. And I'll be damned if I get *finessed*

out my panties by a nigga named Romeo." I leaned into the table, gave him sex eyes and smiled.

He quickly said, "You can't get finessed, baby. I already know that."

I hate to say it, but I enjoyed being in Romeo's company.

"What gave it away?" I asked.

"Well, for starters, you still haven't asked me what I do for a living and that's usually the first question that comes out of a woman's mouth." He answered.

I shrugged my shoulders. "Well, for starters, your money doesn't mean anything to me unless you're putting it into my business. But I respect hustle regardless of what it is. Your Secret Service out there seem to care enough about your life to move like soldiers. I met you at a bar, which was a nice bar but definitely not the same caliber of where we're sitting right now. So between that and your ghetto ass jewelry, I'm willing to guess that you came from the trenches and hustled your way out. That's all I need to know." I was very matter of fact in my observation and covered my lap with my napkin.

That response was a play right out of Dré's book. I had watched him negotiate business deals and drug deals by using weird compliments, expressing things that he had observed and telling a man that he didn't care about his life all at the same time. And somehow, it worked every single time.

Our server had finally arrived and Romeo ordered our food without even asking me what I wanted. It didn't bother me, but I had definitely taken note of it.

"Oh, you got me all figured out, huh?" He didn't wait for a response. "So what's your story? Where you from? What have you been through?"

Without hesitating I said, "My mom's in jail. My dad is dead."

Our server arrived with red wine. Romeo never took his eyes off of me as the server poured each of us a glass of wine. I think he was trying to decide whether or not I was full of shit or dead ass serious but neither of us said a word until the server left the room.

"Why are you looking at me like that?" I laughed.

"I wasn't expecting that. I'm sorry to hear that. I can't imagine." He was serious.

I took a sip of my wine before I said, "You told me your life story yesterday, so I figured it was only fair that I told you mine." I smiled as I placed my glass back onto the table.

"Fair enough. Ok. Well, you don't care about what I do for a living, but I'm curious to hear about your business. I mean, what if I want my money to mean something to you?" His tone was sarcastic, but I knew he was serious.

"Dang. You're nosey." I laughed. "No, I'm kidding. I braid hair. I was recently gifted a salon. I start school soon to get all of my licensing squared away. And I'm searching for braiding hair vendors because I will also curate my own line of braiding hair to sell in addition to the salon services."

Romeo was all ears. "Dope. What services will you offer?" He asked.

I was surprised that he didn't ask about the salon being given to me but I didn't make mention of it. "I'll rent out three stations to other stylists and then rent out the suite in the back to a brow and lash girl. Eventually I'd like to have an entire line of products centered around braiding hair but I want to start with the hair first."

"Pretty and smart. That's rare." Romeo shook his head in fascination.

I laughed. "Is it? That's unfortunate."

The rest of the night was honestly a breath of fresh air.

We talked about my salon for a little while longer and I ended up telling him where it was located which felt like I was making a big mistake. It only felt that way because it wasn't like me to share personal business like that with a man but I knew that he was intrigued and I knew that if I was going to get in his pockets, I was going to have to step out of my comfort zone. It was a small step forward in accomplishing my goal and the quicker I finessed him, the quicker I could move on to the next. Anyway, at the end of the night, he was a gentleman. I was worried that he'd try to get me to go home with him like he had done the night before but honestly, he was almost a completely different man from the bar to the restaurant. I'm willing to bet that he thought I was a different type of woman when he met me at the bar, so I chalked it up to a nigga being a nigga. They will always test your boundaries to see if you really stand on them or not.

The next morning, I knew there was no way I could go another day without going to the salon to get some work done. For one, I wanted to start determining what furniture items I needed for the soon-to-be-suite room. And two, as usual, I needed to check in with my trucking dispatchers to make sure everything was running smoothly. Before I left the house that morning, I made sure to sit with Abuelita a bit. She and I had a cup of tea together while we briefly discussed how happy she was to see Syd and then we quickly gossiped about my date with Romeo. After that, I packed my laptop, my notebook, the gun I had taken from the hideaway house and a few snacks and made my way to the salon.

On my way there, Romeo *FaceTimed* me. He was being

driven around in the *Wraith*, handling whatever errands one handles from a *Wraith*. He told me how much he enjoyed our date and said that he wanted to take me out again but I played the busy card and told him I'd be at the salon all day because I was focused on getting things moving as quickly as I could. From one hustler to another, he understood and I was grateful for that because I wasn't really prepared mentally or emotionally to see another man three days in a row when I couldn't even see my own man three days in a week.

The first thing I did when I made it to the salon was check my emails. My heart was racing as I skimmed through the first few subject lines, hoping to see anything that resembled a congratulatory message from the Cosmetology school I had applied to. Just as I began to give up hope, my laptop notified me of a new message and low and fucking behold, it was from the school. Before opening the email, I took a deep breath in my nose and out of my mouth, wiped my clammy palms onto my sweats and then double clicked the message. I was hype after reading the first two lines that stated I was accepted. The rest of the email included details on my start date, tuition payment options and a few other minor details.

My joy was only short lived because the first thing I wanted to do was tell my best friend that I had gotten into my dream school but I couldn't tell him because he was in jail. A single tear rolled down my cheek and I wiped it away as quickly as I could because I knew that if I succumbed to my emotions, it'd be entirely too hard for me to bounce back. I reminded myself how well things were going. Told myself that I just needed to get through five years without Dré and pumped myself up to believe that phone calls and visits would keep me sane until then. It was almost becoming too challenging to psych myself out until my phone rang.

I knew it'd be Dré, so I scrambled around for a second trying to pull myself together so that he wouldn't sense my energy or emotions when I answered.

I allowed the automated recording to do its thing and then I said, "Hi, baby!" before Dré could even let me know he was on the line.

"What's up, mama. What you doin'?" Dré said from the other side of the phone.

I screamed. "I just got accepted into Cosmetology school!"

"Good shit, baby. Damn. I called just in time then, huh?" I could hear the joy in his voice.

"You're always on time." I replied as my energy shifted back into sadness.

I know Dré felt the shift. "I miss you. How's everything going? You talk to Syd?"

Hearing Dré ask me if I had spoken to Syd made me super nervous because I knew that it was time to tell him about my night.

"I did, actually. We hung out a couple of nights ago and I met this guy named Romeo." I hesitated.

I could tell Dré felt uneasy. "Oh. Ok. So how did that go?" He chose his words carefully.

"I mean it was cool. We went to dinner last night. He pulled up in a *Wraith*. We had a private room. Seems like it'll be easy to get in his pockets. But I'm not sure. We'll see." It felt awkward saying any of that.

"Not we'll see, Lux. You're not doing this shit for nice dinners. You're doing it so that we can be up." He tried to mask his frustration and maybe even jealousy.

"Dré. Nobody is going to just give me thousands of

dollars the first night I meet them unless I'm fucking. So nice dinners come with the territory." I explained.

He took a deep breath. "Ok, Lux. I told you not to give my pussy away. Don't play with me."

I wanted to shift the energy. "If I give it away, will you break out of jail to come and put me in my place?" I asked jokingly.

There was silence on the other end of the phone.

"I'm joking, baby. Relax. I know the rules of the game. It's yours. You know that." I reassured him.

It was crazy to see how the tables had slightly turned for a moment. I was reassuring Dré instead of him reassuring me. The same way I was keeping us afloat instead of him sailing the boat.

"Yeah, ok." He changed the topic. "When are you going to the salon? I got somebody ready to come up there with product for you to check out. You know, perm shit and blonde dye."

I could only assume that *perm shit* was code for percs and *blonde dye* was code for cocaine. "I'm here now. I'll be here all day."

"Ok. It'll just be samples. Just to see if it's quality like they say it is. If it is, you can stock the salon up. If not, tell him we'll find new vendors." Dré was in hustle mode.

"Alright. Bet" I tried to match his energy.

Shortly after that, it was time for our call to end. Even though Dré had mentioned a new plug when we spoke during his visit, I thought there would be a little more time before that actually happened. Some part of me was happy that it was happening sooner than I had expected because I knew that it meant money would start coming in much quicker than it had been.

About twenty minutes after my call with Dré ended, a delivery man with what looked like two dozen red roses walked into my salon. My heart melted because I assumed Dré had somehow arranged for them to arrive after our phone conversation. I signed off on the delivery, thanked the man who delivered them and then pulled the card out of the middle of the bouquet. The card read: *A nigga named Romeo*.

It was a cute gesture but mildly overwhelming for me. It was easy to reassure Dré that I had everything under control but the truth was that I was dying on the inside. I hated that I connected with Romeo so easily. I hated that I felt as though I was being disloyal to my man even though he was the one that called the play. It was just a lot. Too much. And to add to it, Romeo walked into my salon almost immediately after I read the card.

Seeing him scared me because I wasn't expecting it. I screamed. Not a loud scream, but definitely a scream.

"What the hell are you doing here?" I said through laughter. I was trying my best to mask how scared I actually was.

Romeo was thoroughly amused. "Oooo. You scary without ya shooter. You want me to call my niggas in here? I know they'll protect you." He laughed.

"Shut up!" I was still laughing. "Thank you. They're beautiful."

He walked toward me and I did the same.

"I thought you had errands to run." I said as I reached for a hug.

"I do. This was one of them." He said as he gripped my body with his arms.

"Excuse me? I'm not an errand, I'm an experience." I joked as I pushed away from him.

"My bad. You right. You right. Nah, for real. I wanted to come check your spot out." He said.

I smiled back at him. I was shamefully flattered but I

didn't hesitate to give him a full tour explaining my vision to him every step of the way. We ended our tour at the front counter where I explained I'd have my grandmother holding things down up front.

Romeo seemed to be completely enamored with my vision. I stood behind the counter to maintain some sort of distance between us as he leaned against the front side of the counter.

"Alright, so look. I guess I'm too late to gift you an entire salon." He rolled his eyes sarcastically as he waved his hands back and forth and then from side to side. "But I'm a real nigga. I respect hustle just like you. So, this is my way of saying congrats." He started playing with the back pocket on his jeans.

Truthfully, I had no idea where that conversation was going and then he pulled out a stack of money wrapped in a rubber band.

I didn't say a word but my face showed every bit of confusion that I felt.

Romeo smiled. "Look. That's ten bands. Start selling your hair while you get your license."

"Romeo." I said in disbelief.

"Look, I know yo mean ass don't care about my money but I fuck with you. I like how you move. I like how you think. I like how you look. I even like your smart ass mouth. I'll make this back in three hours. It don't mean shit to me the same way it don't mean shit to you. So run it up." He sat the stack of money onto the counter.

"You're trying to finesse me out of my panties, huh?" I laughed as I walked around the counter, closing the distance between us.

"Man, I'll buy you some new panties. Shut up." He laughed.

"Well, thank you, Nigga Named Romeo. For the flowers and for cashing me out." I began to hug him.

He wrapped his arms around me and said, "It's all good. Now that I got this errand out of the way, I need to go handle some business so I can get it all back."

I laughed. "Errand." I said sarcastically. "Yeah. Ok."

And just like that, Romeo walked out of my salon. My mind was completely blown. I couldn't believe what had just happened or how quickly it happened. Romeo was probably in the salon for all of ten minutes before he just casually placed ten bands on the counter and walked out like he was a fucking delivery man. Life went from me telling my man that I wouldn't be able to get thousands of dollars from a man I just met unless I fucked him, to me getting thousands of dollars from a man I had just met without me even kissing him.

I almost didn't want to but I picked up the stack of money and thumbed through it. I was in complete shock. Part of me was afraid to tell Dré because I wasn't sure he'd believe that I didn't fuck for it. The other part of me couldn't wait until he called again so that I could tell him that I had successfully run the first play. I wasn't sure if I had actually finessed Romeo or if he had finessed me. I wasn't sure what I was supposed to do next or what it meant for him and I. The only thing I knew for sure was that I didn't want to have sex with him. Some part of me felt a sense of bitterness toward Dré for putting me in that predicament. It was a passing emotion, but one that hit hard.

You know, I hate that everything in my life always seemed to move so fucking quickly. Like, it was always one thing after the next. There was never time to process anything including getting ten bands from a nigga I had just met. What I did process though, was that I needed to put the money somewhere safe and thank God I did. As soon as I placed the money in my bag and hid it by placing my laptop inside of the bag as well, a man that I had never seen before, walked into the salon and stood at the front counter.

"Yo. You Lux?" He called out without hesitation.

I met his confidence with my own confidence. "Why? Who are you?" I threw back at him.

He didn't move from the counter. "Taboo. Dré sent me."

Dré hadn't told me the name of whoever the fuck was supposed to be pulling up on me at the salon, so I had no choice but to believe that the man that was standing at my front counter, was the new plug Dré was referring to when I spoke to him. My heart began to race because there was still a slight chance that Taboo was full of shit. He was a young hispanic looking man who stood at about five feet eleven inches tall, wearing all black with an iced out pinky ring and cuban link necklace. Despite the full arm sleeve of tattoos and another one that covered the entire back side of his hand, Taboo didn't look like he was a street nigga, but at the same time, neither did Dré and for that reason, I had to go off of my gut feeling. My gut feeling was telling me that he really was the new plug.

"Sent you for what?" I asked to reassure myself.

"Look, Ma. I don't got all day. You wanna play these fucking mind games or you wanna talk numbers?" Taboo was frustrated.

I grabbed my phone and began to type in my passcode and for about five seconds, I pretended to be completely unbothered and uninterested in what Taboo had to say. In real life, I was scared as fuck, but in the world I was living in at the moment, I knew that anything over five seconds would create chaos and I wasn't willing to take it that far.

I placed my phone into my pocket. "Lock the door." I said.

As I walked toward the back room, Taboo did exactly as I told him to without saying a word. When he was done, he made his way toward the back room, too. Instead of going inside, I leaned against the edge of the doorway and nodded my head toward the inside of the room, signaling for Taboo to enter the room. I had no problem with him going into the room but I refused to put myself in a corner with a man that called himself Taboo. Regardless of my fear, I did my best to keep the boss bitch energy I had been giving off from the moment he walked into my salon. Don't forget that Daddy always taught me not to let a nigga see that he got me pressured up. It was no different than Dré telling me to *play chess or get check'd*. The sentiment was the same: stay on your shit, period.

With my arms crossed in front of me as I leaned against the wall, I picked at my nails and said, "Ok, Taboo." I said his name with sarcasm in my tone. "Show me why Dré sent you."

Another thing Dré had always taught us was not to fall into any traps that resulted in telling on yourself. I know why the fuck Dré sent Taboo, but I wasn't going to stand there and say *hey, buddy, show me the cocaine*. Ain't no way in hell. So, I simply told him to show me because if he wanted to get fake and act like he didn't know what time it was, then I could prepare my mind to navigate the situation differently than I had planned.

Anyway, Taboo knew what time it was. After I demanded that he show me the reason he pulled up, he stuffed his hand in his pocket and pulled out a small plastic bag with what appeared to be cocaine but no percocets.

"Line it up on that table right there." I said from outside of the room.

Taboo pulled a pocket knife out of his pocket and my heart sank. He flicked the blade out of its fold and gracefully sliced a corner of the plastic bag. As the white powder slowly funneled through the bag and onto the counter, Taboo wiped the tip of the knife off on the inside of his shirt before folding it back into place. I felt like such a little bitch for getting scared when I saw the knife at first, but once he placed it back into his pocket, I realized that a knife was the perfect pocket protection for me. Yeah, walking around with a gun was fine I guess, but I felt like there was too much room for error. When I saw that pocket knife, I knew it was what I needed.

I kept my thoughts to myself as I looked Taboo dead in his eyes and said, "Alright, run it."

Confused, he looked at the small pile of coke he had just put on the counter and said, "Run what?"

With a smirk on my face, I tilted my head and said, "Oh, sweetheart, I don't play with my nose. If ya shit is pure, then you shouldn't have a problem proving that to me." I raised my eyebrows and widened my eyes to imply that I was dead ass serious.

Taken aback, Taboo laughed through a gust of air out of his nose. "Oh and you think I play with mine?"

I stood up straight. "Listen, I don't have time for bull-shit ass games. Show me the product or don't. But if you're not, then get the fuck out so that I can tell Dré that you're too much of a pussy to be the plug."

Man, listen. I was proud of myself. I had run so many plays with Dré and watched him handle so much business that I channeled him when I spoke to Taboo. Dré used to always tell me that the streets were dirty like politics and if we were going to survive the streets, we had to find a way to play the dirty game and keep our souls clean. That meant that we had to find a way to stay true to ourselves no matter what games we played. He always stayed true to that. He always stayed true to himself and his morals, but there was something different about him whenever he was taking care of street business. There was an extra layer of grit and grime to him. One that I only witnessed in the streets because he never brought that part of him home. But somehow, I was able to channel that same grit and grime in that moment despite all of the internal battles I was experiencing. I was feeling like Big Lux – unfuckwithable, unbothered, and unstoppable.

Taboo stood quietly for a moment and then placed a small amount of powder on the flat of the back of his hand. Whether it was because he wasn't sure about his product or he didn't typically use his product, it was obvious that he was nervous as fuck. After about three seconds of contemplation, he snorted the powder off of his hand and quickly wiped his nose. I could almost see the drugs enter his system as his eyes became glossed over and he stretched his neck from side to side.

"Alright, so you fuck with it or not? I ain't got all day." Taboo was frustrated.

I took a few steps into the room toward the counter and pinched a small amount of the powder between my thumb and index finger.

As I rubbed my fingers together I said, "Yeah, I fuck with it. Wait for Dré to hit you. Don't come back here until then." And then I walked out of the room.

Taboo didn't say a word to me as he walked toward the front door in a hurry. I waited a few seconds after the door closed behind him and damn near sprinted to the door so that I could lock it. My breathing was heavy as if I had just run a marathon but the only thing that had been running was my mind. I needed to pivot.

AFTER THE FUCKING unbelievable series of events that happened at the salon, I decided that the cash Romeo had given me needed to be stashed somewhere safe. At first, I was going to hide it in my bedroom at Abuelita's house but something about that didn't feel right. Abuelita's house was my home. It was the only place I had that didn't feel like chaos and I didn't want to start making it a habit to bring the chaos of my life home with me. Now, ten bands is far from chaotic but I knew that there was more where it came from. I was also pretty sure it was just as dirty as the money that purchased my salon and there was no telling what other bullshit would follow. With that being said, it only made sense for me to take the cash to the hideaway house until I was able to figure out how I would tell Dré.

Before leaving the salon to head to the hideaway house, I made sure any trace of Taboo was washed away and then I locked everything up. Scanning the block had a whole new level of pressure added onto it because I felt like I had no fucking clue what was going on in my life so what the fuck was I even scanning for, you know? Since my car was parked right in front, it wasn't like I had to walk far but knowing that Blanco wasn't parked somewhere nearby with the burner on his lap while both Taboo and Romeo knew where my salon was, made me feel like a target.

Something as simple as getting into my car without being approached by a fucking delivery man, somebodies pregnant girlfriend or a nigga I just met, felt like a huge accomplishment. And I wanted to stay in the lead so I didn't wait around for any more surprises, I drove off almost immediately. As an extra precaution, I also took a different route to the hideaway house, which probably wasn't necessary but you know paranoia had me in a chokehold.

On my way there I called Sydney, just to see what she was up to. It felt good to finally have a regular conversation that didn't have anything to do with my livelihood. We only stayed on the phone for about ten minutes before I told her that I had to take Romeo's phone call. He wasn't actually calling me, but I wanted to focus on the road as I got closer to the hideaway house so that I didn't make any amateur mistakes. Syd was happy to hear that Romeo was calling but also suggested we go back to the bar so that I could add to my roster. She felt like I should have a full roster so that I didn't focus too much on Romeo. In her opinion, it was probably too soon for me to take anyone seriously but it was the perfect time for me to play with as many hearts as I wanted to. I laughed to myself because she had no fucking idea that one of those hearts was hers..

Anyway, I didn't spend much time at the hideaway house. I didn't feel like dealing with the emotions that being there brought me. Plus, I wanted to get home and be in Abuelita's presence. I knew that without her even knowing, she would help me decompress. And Sydney wasn't going to let me flake on going back to the bar with her, so there wasn't really time for me to do anything besides hide the money in the same spot I found the gun, lock everything up and get out of there.

Dropping the money off took some of the weight off of my shoulders but it also gave me motivation. Not even six months into our five year bid, and Dré and I were already up ten bands because of me. That shit was lit. I was very quickly learning that I was going to have to celebrate the small victories so on my way home, I picked up a bottle of Abuelita's favorite wine and some flowers. She wasn't going to know that we were celebrating, but I was and that was good enough for me.

When I made it home, Abuelita and I had girl talk over a glass of wine. Even though she never really did anything exciting other than some house chores and maybe switching the location of a family photo, I enjoyed listening to her talk about her day as much as she enjoyed telling me about it. Abuelita loved life differently than I did and for that, I loved her even more. I mean, like I've said before, we both obviously carried the pain of my mother being taken away from us and she carried some of my heartache from losing Daddy, but somehow, Abuelita found a way to carry her pain on her sleeve in a way that allowed her to exude love and freedom. Me on the other hand, well, you know. I was in some sort of fucking identity crisis.

Abuelita and I chilled for about an hour before Romeo called me. As soon as he called, anxiety rushed through my body as if I had done something wrong. I told Abuelita I'd watch a movie with her after the phone call, and left the kitchen to answer the phone in my bedroom.

"Romeo, oh, Romeo." I said sarcastically as I answered the phone.

He laughed. "Hey, Beautiful. What you doin'?"

"Oh, I'm at my grandmother's house right now. Spending a little time with her." Not technically a lie.

"A little family time. I like that. How was your day?" He asked as if he hadn't just given me ten thousand dollars earlier in the day.

I laughed hysterically. "I mean, you know." I stopped laughing. "It was cool. Some nigga named Romeo dropped ten bands off while I was at the salon. So you know. Lightwork or whatever." I said sarcastically.

Romeo met my sarcasm. "Damn, that nigga named Romeo sounds like a real ass nigga. Don't fumble."

"Oh I never fumble. This shit too easy." I said with confidence.

"Yeah, aiight." He shot back. "What you got goin' tonight?" He asked.

"Tonight is ladies night. Me and my shooter are going to go out for some drinks, girl talk, people watching. You know, the usual." I said with a smile.

"I fuck with you, Lux. You keep shit simple and you keep shit real. Don't switch up." Romeo said.

"Hm. It sounds like you're getting a little sentimental here." I said with a very proper tone. "Keep that shit gangsta with me." I deliberately switched my tone.

Romeo laughed, obviously catching the pun intended. "You're a character. Alright, Ma. Enjoy your family time and then hit me after girls night if you're not too lit. Or get too lit and hit me. Either way is cool."

"Yeah. Yeah. Yeah. Ok. I'll talk to you later." I said softly.

When I hung up the phone, I noticed that I had a text message from Syd. She was letting me know that she had gotten a hotel room for the night and suggested we take an *Uber* to the bar so that we could really turn up. After the day I had, I wasn't mad at that idea. She had also decided on a different bar than the one we had previously gone to because it was a little closer to the hotel room she had booked for us. I didn't mind that either because the new bar she had chosen was a little more casual than the bar we had been to already which meant that I could ditch the heels and be comfortable all night. After a quick shower, I threw on a gray long sleeve jumpsuit and a pair of white patent leather boots.

Once I was dressed I ran the flat iron through my hair to smooth it out a bit and then I sat with Abuelita for about thirty minutes and watched a courtroom drama show with her. For some reason, she loved watching those shows and coming up with her own ruling before the judge would grant an official ridiculous ruling over a petty case that never should have gone to court, or TV for that matter, in the first place. I guess when you're in the house all day the way Abuelita was, you've got to find ways to entertain yourself, so you better believe I was right there with her coming up with my own ruling, too! I was looking forward to seeing her make more memories with Dré. I was looking forward to them getting to know each other better. Sitting on the couch with her that night made me realize that I was going to have to put in more of an effort to get her out of the house more often so before I left, I made a mental note that I'd take her out to dinner at least once a month. It was way less than what Dré could have done, but it was more than I had ever done and I was sure Abuelita would appreciate it.

When I was growing up, I never liked sleepovers like the other girls my age did. Maybe it was because they had to do sleepovers in order to live the lives they wanted to live and I didn't because Ma trusted that I would make the right decisions but it was just never my thing. If I wasn't sleeping in my own bed, I would be sleeping in my bed at Abuelita's house. And then after that, it was Dré's house until I completely moved in with him. Therefore, I didn't bother packing an overnight bag for the hotel Sydney had booked for us because I had planned on Ubering back to my car as soon as I sobered up enough to drive from her house to mine. That's the other thing, I was a lightweight. I drank wine more than I did hard liquor for as long as I could remember because Abuelita had always let me have a glass with her even when I wasn't of age. But after the day I had paired with the fact that we weren't driving and had a room, I was ready to turn the fuck up.

Sydney was happy to see me when I got to her house. As soon as I pulled up and rolled my window down to greet her, she hugged me through the window. We laughed about the fact that she was holding two mini bottles of tequila in her hand as if we weren't getting ready to go to the bar. She said that we needed to pregame in case there weren't any men at the bar to pay for our drinks. Which wasn't a bad idea whether somebody was paying for our drinks or not. One thing about Syd was that she was always going to find a way to save some money.

Anyway, she requested the *Uber* and we sat in my car and listened to music while we drank the mini bottles of tequila she had for us. We briefly talked about Romeo but I didn't tell her that he cashed me out. As far as I knew, she hated Dré because of his lifestyle and I was pretty sure Romeo lived that same lifestyle so beyond it just not making sense to tell her something that would create distance between us – based on what Dré said, I couldn't tell her, so I didn't. We didn't have time for her to tell me the tea on her life because our *Uber* driver pulled up. Syd quickly hopped out of my car and into the backseat of the *Uber* while I pretended to fix my lip gloss. Really, I was scanning the block. I had chosen to drive my car to Syd's house instead of having the Uber pick me up from my house because just like when I went to go visit Dré, I didn't want an *Uber* driver knowing where I lived. Gotta play chess.

By the time I was done scanning the block and had a pretty good idea of the cars that were parked, I double clicked the lock button on my keyfob and hopped into the *Uber* with Syd.

"Get me lit!" I yelled as the *Uber* driver drove away.

Syd laughed.

~

The bar was actually a super dope spot. It had all types of oversized games like *Jenga*, *Connect 4* and *TicTacToe*. The crowd was a bit younger than I was used to but everyone seemed to be having a good time. Well, when I say younger I just mean that everyone seemed to be around my age, twenty-one. Besides Sydney and Blanco, I hadn't really spent any real time with anyone under the age of like twenty-seven. And Blanco didn't really count because he was an old soul like me. Being that the crowd was younger, I was glad that Syd had us pregame beforehand because as I looked around the bar, I knew that we were going to have a good time but I also knew that it was going to be on our own dime. It wasn't like I was broke, so it was fine that I'd have to pay for my own drinks, it just wasn't something I was used to. I knew it was only going to take me all of two shots and maybe one more cocktail to get super turnt, so I wasn't pressed about using my own money.

The first hour of the night consisted of us playing different games with different groups of people and babysitting our drinks in an effort to pace ourselves. The night was still young and we knew that the hypest part of the night wouldn't begin until much later when more people started to show up. We were living our best lives though. Honestly, I hadn't done something like that since high school so I felt like a kid in a fucking candy store. It was nostalgic, you know? Like I got to enjoy the things I had missed out on or would have done had I not ended up with Dré. Now, don't get me wrong, I one thousand percent preferred the lifestyle Dré and I had created for ourselves over the young bar scene, but that doesn't negate the fact that I was having fun. Syd was having fun, too. Funny enough, that bar was just her speed. Those were the types of things she enjoyed doing on a regular basis with people her age and tax bracket.

After babysitting our drinks for about an hour, I told Syd that we needed to finish them and take a shot and she was excited to start spicing things up a bit. We both sucked our drinks down in about thirty seconds and then laughed hysterically at how childish it was to have a brain freeze before we walked over to the bar.

The entire front of the bar was all glass. The way the bar was set up was so that you could right inside from the street and clean out of the bar from inside. It was definitely different, but it made sense for what the vibe was. Anyway, as Syd and I were walking to the bar, I noticed that a black *Lamb* truck pulled up to the front of the bar and a tall White boy got out of the driver seat. From the passenger side, a handsome Black guy got out. Both of them had pretty athletic builds but they looked real young in the face. The *Lamb* truck was nice but both of them looked way too young for my liking and they didn't strike me as the type of men who would be coming into the bar we were in, so I continued to mind my business while we waited for the bartender to pour our shots.

By this time, it was starting to become pretty crowded inside so it took the bartender a few minutes before she was able to take our order. When she finally made it over to us, I placed an order for myself and for Syd.

"Let me get two double shots of tequila, please. Whatever your top shelf is." I basically yelled so that she could hear me.

"Make that four doubles. Please." A male voice said from behind me.

I looked over my shoulder to see the cute White boy that drove the *Lamb* truck. He flashed a *Colgate* smile, threw his hands up and shrugged his shoulders.

Without saying a word to him, I turned back to the bartender and said, "Put all four of 'em on his tab. Please." And then I turned back to him and gave him the same *Colgate* smile and a shrug.

Sydney was standing right next to me. "We found our sponsor for the night." I said to her under my breath.

She laughed and squeezed my hand in excitement.

"You got here just in time!" I smiled at the White boy.

"I don't ever miss." He said.

I was a little shocked because he sounded like he had a little flavor to him. I had never found a White boy attractive before, but something about him had my attention. At first, I thought it was the *Lamb* truck, but when he spoke, I was even more attracted.

"Jake." He put his hand out for me to shake it.

His friend introduced himself as well. "Brandon." He said as we shook hands.

Syd introduced herself as she shook hands with both of the men.

"You look like a baby, Jake. How'd you get in here?" I said with a smile.

"Oh, nothing about me gives baby, trust me." He snapped back. "What's your name beautiful?"

"Lux." I replied with sex eyes.

"What's that short for?" He asked as if he knew that it was short for something.

With attitude I said, "Luxurious."

"Ok. Pop yo shit!" He laughed.

The bartender had finally poured our shots and topped each of them off with a lemon. Jake handed her his card, told her to keep the tab open and the four of us tapped glasses and took our shots. From there, we found a table and played *Jenga*. Jake ordered two more rounds of double shots and I was starting to feel it but I was having so much fun that I didn't care. As the tequila started to settle into our systems, Jake started opening up a little more.

He started off by telling me that he and Brandon were childhood best friends. They grew up in a predominantly Black neighborhood and he didn't say it, but based on the descriptions, I knew that they both came from wealthy families. That explained the *Lamborghini* truck. Just like I had assumed, both Jake and Brandon were pretty young; twenty one, like me. Apparently Jake was a social media influencer turned model. Being that I had only recently created a social media page for my brand, I had no idea what it really meant to be a social media influencer, but he stood at about six foot one and seemed to have a nice body so the 'turned model' part was obviously fitting. Between social media money, modeling money and the unmentioned Daddy money, Jake invested into stock and cryptocurrency and was making a pretty good life for himself. It was clear that he was a playboy, living a fast life with legal money. I couldn't even knock his hustle. Hell, I wanted to learn it.

More and more people started to pull up to the bar as the night carried on and it actually made it even more poppin'. Sydney and I were enjoying each other's company while we got to know Jake and Brandon a little better. Like, as much as you can get to know somebody in a bar.

The music was good, Jake kept the drinks flowing and then I was starting to feel more turnt than I had ever been before. I was super touchy-feely with Jake and Syd knew that meant I had to have been super fucked up because it wasn't in my character to be touchy-feely like that, especially with someone I had just met. At one point, Jake was kissing on my neck and I was letting him! It was fine then but when I think back on it, I'm like who the fuck was I?!

Anyway, eventually, I had to sit down to gather myself and I chose to sit on Syd's lap. And just like drunk girls do, my drunken mind started to speak my sober heart.

"Syd, I missed you so much, bitch!" I slurred my words.

"I missed you, too! I'm so happy you're all mine now." She yelled back over the loud music.

I was sitting on her lap, but my body was twisted to face her. "No. You don't understand. You've literally been through everything with me. You are my best fucking friend. Like, you've been holding shit down for so long. I can't even imagine what I would do if I didn't have you with me through this part of my life too."

Sydney didn't say anything in response. Instead, she gently removed the strands of my hair that were attached to my lips by my lip gloss.

"See!" I said and then Jake handed me another drink.

"You always take care of me, Syd. You been making sure I'm good since we were kids!" I continued before taking a sip of my drink.

The next thing I knew, Sydney had her hand tangled in my hair as she pulled my face to hers. We started kissing like we were a whole ass couple. I had never kissed a girl in my entire life and never had the desire to but I guess I was just that drunk.

When I realized what I was doing, I stood up from Syd's lap real quick. She stood up and attempted to apologize and Jake quickly stepped in to intervene. He stood in between us with one hand in front of her and one in front of Sydney. I don't think he was sure how either of us were about to react and quite frankly, neither was I.

Brandon stood in front of Syd but watched over his shoulder to ensure that Jake had a good hold on me. Sydney struggled to find her balance as she sat down in the chair that we had been sitting in together. I could tell she was mortified. But what the fuck? She should've been. We were never the girls that kissed their friends in the mouth and even if we were, we for damn sure wouldn't have been kissing each other the way she kissed me.

My heart was racing and I kept toggling back and forth between the feeling of rapid soberness and the inability to stand on my own but I kept my eye on Sydney as Jake stood in front of me. I was drunk and confused as fuck. Syd moved Jake out of the way and stepped closer to me.

"You good?" She asked.

"Yeah. Leave it." I replied.

Jake and Brandon made their way over to us just to make sure we were both good and then a waitress showed up with two more shots.

"Nah. I'm good." I said as I put my hand up to reject the shot.

Syd did the same. "Yeah. I think it's time for us to dip." She said, grabbing my wrist.

"Nah." Jake said as he attempted to prevent me and Syd from walking away. "Y'all can't drive like this. Chill."

"We Uber'd – YOU chill!." I pressed.

"Bet. I'll take you home. You don't need to be in an *Uber* like this either. Shit ain't sweet just because it's an *Uber* driver." Jake was still making it hard to remember that he was a White boy and even harder to remember that he was my age.

I looked up at him and rolled my eyes. "We aren't going home. We're going to our hotel room. I don't care how we get there but we're leaving now. Move." I pushed him to the side.

Jake moved out of my way without protesting. "B, Let's go. Grab her." He motioned for Brandon to grab Sydney.

Sydney was way more turnt than I was. She looked a mess and needed Brandon's support to stand up and walk out of the bar. She and Brandon followed close behind Jake and I as we maneuvered through all of the drunk people in the bar. When we made it outside, Jake's truck was still in front where he parked it and I was grateful for that because walking was starting to make me nauseous.

Brandon and Jake stood in between Sydney and I as we waited for the valet driver to hand Jake his keys so that we could leave. When he got the keys, Jake unlocked the car doors and opened the passenger door for me while Brandon and Syd climbed into the back seat. Syd was so drunk that she was barely able to lift her leg into the car which meant that the chances that she would remember the kiss, were going to be slim to none. Once everyone was settled into their seats, I told Jake what hotel to take us to and then involuntarily fell asleep.

The sound of Jake's voice woke me up when he pulled up in the front of the hotel. I was feeling even more nauseous than before. The kind of nausea that has you bargaining with God to make you sober and promising that you'll never drink again. Even through my nausea, I was coherent enough to hold Syd's hand while we both tried to conquer the walk into the hotel.

Anyway, Jake and Brandon insisted on walking us up

to our room but I had enough sense not to allow that. Especially because Sydney was so twisted. She and I had our moment at the bar, but it was always us against the world if it ever came down to it. Jake and Brandon were nice to us the entire night and hadn't really displayed any creepy characteristics but you just never know. Since I refused to allow them to walk us inside, Jake insisted that we exchange numbers so that I could let him know that we were safe.

As soon as we entered the hotel room, I began to help Syd take off her clothes so that she could sleep comfortably. I knew after years of friendship that she didn't like to sleep in too many layers because she gets too hot. Instead of calling Jake, I sent him a text that simply said: *made it, thanks.* It wasn't much, but it was enough to let him know that I appreciated his effort, and respected his request. Nothing more, nothing less. And right after hitting send on Jake's message, Sydney grabbed the back of my head and pulled me into her.

She started to kiss my neck and I guess for a second, I liked it. The more she kissed me, the more I started to lean into her body as she caressed mine. She started kissing my lips and I was kissing her too while I gently placed my hand into the front of her panties. Apparently I'm gay when I'm drunk. Anyway, she bit my bottom lip and I slipped my finger between the lips of her vagina and started to massage her clit while she took my shirt off of me. When my shirt was off, she pulled my hair while she stuck her tongue down my throat. I started to finger her and then she pushed me onto the hotel bed and pulled my pants off. I must have taken my shoes off on my own because I don't remember her doing it. Next thing I knew, Syd was on her knees eating me out. Her tongue touched every part of my vagina, and when she finally got to the clit, she started to finger me at the same time. I was letting her eat me for about thirty seconds before I suddenly sobered up and realized what the fuck was going on.

"Syd. No. What are we doing?" I panicked. I pressed her head away from my vagina and she stumbled backward.

"Lex. It's fine. No one is going to know. This is long overdue. You know it." She said as she tried to prevent me from putting my clothes back on.

"Syd? What the fuck? No." I yelled as I stormed into the bathroom with my clothes.

Luckily, my phone was in the back pocket of my jeans still, so I immediately called Romeo.

"Yo." I said as soon as he picked up the phone. "I need you to come get me, but I don't want to have sex with you." I could hear Syd calling my name in the background.

In my right mind, I knew it was a bad idea for me to call Romeo. There really are men in the world that can give a woman ten bands off the strength of wanting to see her win but more likely than not, it's a down payment. Real niggas know that pussy isn't free. Never has been. Never will be. The price isn't always monetary, but there is always a price. To that same effect, money isn't free either. I wasn't sure yet if the ten bands Romeo had given me was off the strength or if it was a down payment so I shouldn't have drunk dialed him. But for my sanity, I needed to get away from Syd. I didn't have time to deal with whatever the fuck had just happened.

"Oh. You turnt. Drop a pin. I'm on my way." Romeo said.

I couldn't tell if he was concerned or being thirsty.

"My car isn't at the salon, though. It's at Sydney's house. That's where I need to go." I replied dryly.

"How are you going to drive, Mama? You can stay in

the guest room and I'll take you back to your car as soon as the sun comes up." Romeo said.

I agreed to the guest room sleeping arrangement and told him that he wasn't allowed into my room for any reason and he laughed and agreed. The fact that I told a grown man that he couldn't come into a room in his own house is outlandish but I felt the need to draw a line somewhere; even if it was in the sand.

About twenty-five minutes later, Romeo called me to let me know that he was parked in front of the hotel. I'm embarrassed to say, but I literally stayed in the bathroom until that moment. I couldn't face Syd and luckily, she was already asleep by the time Romeo pulled up.

When I got downstairs, I expected to see the *Wraith* and Romeo's bodyguards waiting for me but he was alone in a blacked out *Maybach*. His way of laying low I guess.

"Here, drink this." He handed me a water bottle as soon as I sat in the passenger seat.

"Thanks, Dad." I said sarcastically.

Romeo laughed. "Don't Dad me. You the lightweight. Learn ya limits, kid.

I gave him the finger and started downing the water bottle he had given me. He laughed and then turned *Future* up as he pulled out of the hotel parking lot.

It had to be at least thirty minutes into the drive that I started to realize that we had been driving for a while.

Trying not to sound too paranoid, I yelled over the music, "Why is it taking so long to get to your house?"

With a smile on his face while he turned the volume of the music down he replied, "I'm taking you to the crib for real." He replied

"As opposed to the crib for fake? Got it. Thanks." I said sarcastically.

"Damn. You even got a smart mouth when you drunk, too? I ain't never gone get a break, huh?" He laughed.

"Nah, I'm just saying. I don't have my shooter with me and you didn't bring the Secret Service with you so it's giving kidnapping." I said with a straight face.

"It's giving kidnapping." He mimicked me. "No, fool. I'm taking you to my house in Bloomfield Hills. So you can be comfortable. It's niggas at the penthouse. You don't need to be there." He said.

He didn't wait for me to reply, he turned the music back up to its highest volume and placed his elbow on the center console with his fist toward me so that I could dap him up. I tapped his fist with mine acknowledging that what was understood, simply didn't need to be explained. But I had no clue how I was going to explain any of it to Dré.

A few minutes later, Romeo pulled up to a three car garage that prefaced a house that basically looked like it belonged in a *Disney* storybook; it had everything but a moat. By that time, I had already started sobering up just a little, so I was trying my best to take in how fucking beautiful the house was. I knew that Romeo had money, obviously, but I had no clue that he had it like that. My guess was that the house was easily worth upward of three million dollars and I couldn't wrap my head around how dirty money afforded him a whole ass castle.

"Alright, I'm sober now. You can take me back to Syd's." I joked as Romeo reversed into the middle garage door.

He slowly hit the break and looked over at me with a smirk on his face and disbelief in his eyes.

"My nigga. You waited 'til we were damn near half way here to tell me we were going to Bloomfield Hills. You knew I would be sober by the time we got here." I laughed. "You played ya self." I deepened my voice.

"Girl. Take your ass in the house and take a nap. You'll be fine here. No one is here but us." He continued to reverse into the garage.

As the garage door closed I asked, "Why do you have this big ass house if you live here alone?"

"Solitude. Ownership. Both of them are priceless. Somewhere safe for my kids to play. Everybody that runs with me is taken care of. I got spots all over the D. But this one is for me and my kids. No matter what you do in life, you need a person and a place of sanctuary. A place where you can reset. A place where you find solitude no matter what is going on in your life. One day I'll have a wife and I'll share this with her too. But there are some things in life that are reserved for the family." Romeo shut the car off.

"You don't consider your crew family?" I asked.

Romeo laughed a little and then he stopped and looked at me with a bit of confusion in his eyes. "No, Baby Girl. We from the streets. The streets don't love nobody." He said nonchalantly.

Romeo opened his car door and then reached over my lap to open my door for me as well. "Come on, Princess. Let me show you to your quarters." He laughed.

That was the moment I knew how much Romeo and Dré differed. Dré loved our crew like they were his own flesh and blood. Romeo obviously kept his crew at a distance. His statement was short, but it held a power that I didn't understand.

We entered the house through the garage and walked through a hallway that automatically lit up like the frozen section in a grocery store.

As we walked into the kitchen, Romeo said, "Alright, you got two options. First floor guest room, or second. Which do you prefer, Your Highness?"

I smiled, placed the back of my hands flat underneath

my chin and posed. "The first floor. Thank you."

Romeo shook his head at me in both amusement and disbelief. "You gone be a problem. I already know." He walked toward the refrigerator. "Are you hungry? Or do you want to go right to bed?"

Just then, my phone buzzed. It was Syd.

I answered on the first ring. "Yo."

"Lex? Where are you?" She asked.

I was sort of irritated with her question. "With Romeo. Why? What's up?"

Sydney immediately became hostile. "So you left me in the hotel to go be with a nigga you just met?" She was obviously pissed.

"Syd, I'm not trying to deal with this right now." I replied as calmly as I could, trying not to agitate her more.

"If you don't do nothing else, you always gone be up under a nigga." Syd said with a sarcastic giggle.

"Syd. You're drunk. Go to sleep. I'll pick my car up in the morning." I said before hanging up on her.

She had me fucked up but I didn't have the energy to deal with it. I didn't have the energy to deal with anything but it had finally dawned on me why she hated Dré and apparently Romeo too. It was because she wanted me. It blew my fucking mind but I genuinely didn't have the capacity to even think about what it meant for our friendship or her as a pawn in my game.

I rolled my eyes and then looked at Romeo. "Right to sleep for five hundred, please."

Romeo laughed, showed me to my room and made sure that I had everything I needed. Honestly, he was more of a gentleman than I had expected for him to be. He told me that I could just call him in the morning when I was ready to go home and we could head out immediately. It didn't take me long to climb in bed and start to doze off and then

Sydney called me back crying hysterically. I barely got a word out because she was on a whole rant telling me how I always chose men over my friendship with her and she didn't appreciate it. She told me that instead of chasing men, I needed to heal from all of the childhood trauma I had experienced.

My first issue was that her rant was uncalled for. My second issue was that growing up, Syd and I chased boys together. If I had a nigga, she had one too. Shit, nine times out of ten they were from the same crew. When my daddy died and they took my mom, Dré was the only man I had been with so I don't know where the fuck she got off saying I had chosen men over her. But my third issue was the one that trumped everything. Syd knew how much childhood trauma I had experienced because she was there through almost all of it. Even though we had grown apart a bit as adults, I know she knew how much I had healed and grown since we were kids so as far as I was concerned, she was dead ass wrong for throwing that shit in my face.

Ultimately, I told her about herself. I told her that I was happy that she was being blunt for once instead of trying to sneak diss me like she usually did. And thenI told her she was a bitch for trying to throw my pain in my face by masking it as some deep advice that nobody even asked her for. Before I hung up in her face for a second time, I didn't say shit about our little lesbian sneaky link but I told her she could consider me dead to her.

I didn't have a desire to continue a friendship with her after that. Part of me struggled with it because Dré said that I needed to use her as a pawn but I was laying in the guest bedroom of a three million dollar house that belonged to a man that had given me ten thousand dollars after one date. I was confident that I didn't need Sydney as a friend or a pawn and Dré would have to understand.

seventeen
blanco.

THE NEXT MORNING I was woken up by the sound of my phone vibrating on the side table.

"Hello?" I answered without even really opening my eyes.

The automated message to let me know that an inmate was waiting to speak to me played on the other end of the phone and my heart sank. There was no way in hell I could tell Dré that I was sleeping in another man's house but I also hadn't figured out how I was going to tell him about the money or the fact that Syd and I were done being friends for good because I gave her, his pussy. Regardless, I accepted the charges and waited for Dré to come on the line.

"What up doe?" He said.

"Hi, baby. I miss you." I answered.

"I miss you, too. Just five years, remember?" He tried to reassure me.

I laughed softly into the phone.

"Did dude pull up on you yesterday?" He jumped right into business.

To be honest, with everything that had occurred in such a short period of time, I guess I forgot all about Taboo.

"Yeah. He came. He said the blonde dye was supposed to be a one-step process. Completely pure. He asked me to test it on my own hair but I had him test it on his instead. It's good." I spoke in code.

"Ok. Ok. Check baby out. I'm proud of you. So, I'll have him send a full shipment next week then." Dré was mildly excited.

"School is going to be from six to ten Monday through Thursday night so just make sure it's delivered during the day. The earlier, the better." I replied.

"Bet. What about the nigga in the *Wraith*. What's up with that?" He followed up.

My heart dropped and I immediately transitioned from laying down to sitting up.

"It's cool. It's going to take time but I'm supposed to have breakfast with him before I head into the salon today." I lied.

I have no idea why I lied. Dré literally wanted me to finesse niggas for money and that's exactly what I had done. He *finessed* me or I *finessed* him. I don't know. But either way, I had the money. But for some reason, I wasn't ready to tell Dré just yet.

Before Dré could respond, I continued, "I met some White boy last night. Young nigga. Got a lil' bag though. He was born into money though, so I don't know." I hoped I switched Dré's focus.

"He was fuckin' with you though?" Dré asked. Seemingly intrigued.

"I mean, yeah. He was buying me and Syd drinks all night and then took us back to the hotel." I said, immediately wishing I hadn't.

"Hotel?" Dré tried to keep himself contained.

"Oh. Yeah. Syd had gotten a room last night because she didn't want to go back to her house super faded. I didn't stay though. Just got dropped off and made sure she was good. Uber'd back home this morning." I lied.

"Complacency creates chaos, Lux. Come on." Dré pleaded.

"Babe. I'm fine. I'm not complacent. I'm on my shit more now than ever before because I'm out here dolo. I'm TTG, remember?" I reassured him.

Dré said, "You won't be dolo for long. Blanc is on his way back. Just sit tight." He sounded like he was focused on something else.

We didn't even have time to discuss his statement about Blanco before I heard alarms sounding in the background.

"Fuck. Five years, Lux. I love you." Dré said before hanging up the phone.

I could only assume that the sound of the alarms meant that there was some sort of drill or riot happening in the jail that forced Dré to rush off the phone the way that he did. I felt sick to my stomach because I didn't know if that meant I wouldn't be speaking to him for a while or what. But on top of that, I had lied to him. I can't think of any other time in my life that I had lied to Dré for any reason at all. I literally felt like shit. Between that, lying to Abuelita, basically being pimped out by Dré and sleeping in Romeo's guest room, I didn't know who I was becoming. And there was no time to figure it out.

After giving myself a few minutes to find a new place to hide all of the pain I was experiencing, I went into the bathroom attached to the guest room to wash up using the toothbrush and washcloth that Romeo had given me the night before and then I called him to let him know that I was awake and ready to be taken back to my car.

Romeo didn't play any games when I told him I was

ready to go home and I really appreciated that. We stopped at a cute little mom and pop restaurant for breakfast on the way back to the D. We were only there for about forty-five minutes to an hour and the entire time, Romeo just wanted to hear more about my plans for the salon. Some part of me felt uncomfortable sharing my ideas with him but the other part of me felt refreshed. The salon meant so much to me so obviously getting to talk about it with someone made me happy.

We had only known each other for a short time but I felt safe in Romeo's presence. Oddly enough, I felt safer when it was just him and I than I did when he had his boys with him. His energy felt familiar to me but it wasn't a familiarity I could identify other than a feeling of comfort. I didn't know much about him and he didn't know much about me, but being around him made me feel like we had known each other for years. Sometimes, that's a dangerous feeling because it leaves room for complacency and you already know what that means – chaos.

Ok, I hate to say it, but I liked Romeo. I liked that he was mysterious. I liked that he was curious about me. I liked that he was sort of a gentleman. I'm saying sort of because I won't forget about his shenanigans at the bar when we first met and with the amount of money that I could see he had, I knew that there had to be some serious flaws waiting to come out and play. But, that was another thing I liked: his money. It was interesting because Daddy's theory about a man's jewelry showing you if he does the street shit for his family or the bitches didn't really prove to be valid with Romeo. All his shit was icey but he also, as far as I knew, owned a whole ass mansion that he didn't share with his crew. And I wasn't comparing him to Daddy or Dré but facts are facts and they were both doing the street shit for their families and neither of them had it like Romeo appeared to have it. There was also something to note in the fact that Romeo didn't consider his crew, his family. Him telling me that the streets don't love nobody insinuated to me that he didn't trust his crew the way that Dré trusted ours and at the time, I couldn't figure out if that was weird or wise.

After a Belgian waffle topped with strawberries and whipped cream, hash browns, turkey bacon and freshly squeezed orange juice, I greatly considered telling Romeo to take me back to his house so that I could take a nap but that felt too much like complacency. Plus, while Romeo and I were at breakfast, Jake sent a text that simply read: *lunch?* To which I replied: *Busy day. Dinner.* So I wanted to get back to my car so that I could check on Abuelita, take a quick shower and change clothes before I went to the salon to handle all of my business for the day. Now, Jake didn't really seem like the type I would be able to finesse in a way that made much sense to my life but I didn't want to rule him out before a thorough investigation.

So, anyway, Romeo and I were just enjoying each other's company as *Future* blasted through the speakers on our drive from Bloomfield Hills when it dawned on me: *why did he feel comfortable taking me to his house if he doesn't even let his crew go to his house?*

I reached toward the center console and turned the music down to about half the volume and then leaned back into my seat and crossed my arms for dramatic effect. "Romeo, oh, Romeo." I teased. "So, if the fucking castle that we just left is just for you, your kids and your future wife – why did you take me there? You don't know me, nigga." I was trying my best to hold back laughter.

Romeo took his eyes off the road to glance over at me and said, "I don't know, Lux. Somethin' about you." He smiled.

"What if I was like a killer or something? Now I know where you live." I was being facetious.

Romeo laughed. "Lux." He almost couldn't control his laughter. "Your shooter damn near drank more than me the night we met. You not like that." He tapped my thigh. "Sorry, Baby Girl." He said sarcastically.

I couldn't do anything but laugh so I leaned forward and turned the music back up.

My mind was occupied with the thought of Dré racing to get off of our phone call when those alarms sounded. There wasn't a thing I could do to protect him but I was worried. I kept thinking about how I had lied to him and if something had happened to him after that phone call, I wouldn't be able to live with myself. And then I kept thinking about Blanco. As much as I missed my boy, I knew that random nights like the one I had just had would have to be cut to a minimum if at all. Dinners and shit like that? Cool. Sleepovers? Absofuckinglutely not. I knew Dré wasn't going for that shit and I knew Blanco wasn't going for it on behalf of Dré so that meant I was going to have to figure out how to tighten up before Blanco came home, without knowing when that would be.

We had finally arrived back on my side of town and as we got closer to Syd's house, I was praying that I wouldn't run into her when I got there. I was also praying she wasn't dumb enough to damage my car out of some emotional hungover rage. I was also thinking about how stupid I was to allow that shit to happen.

Romeo turned the music down as we started to drive through more residential neighborhoods.

"Thank you for picking me up last night. And bringing me back."I tried to be sweet.

"It's nothin', Baby Girl. You wouldn't have been able to drive home last night. I'm glad I was still on this side of town." He replied as he turned onto Sydney's block.

"Well, you're appreciated." I said.

Romeo parked, blocking Sydney's driveway.

"Likewise." He replied.

I laughed. "Oh, please. I haven't even done anything for you to appreciate. I'm damn near a liability at this point." I said.

"Definitely not that. You special. I can tell. Your authenticity is appreciated." He smiled.

If I didn't know any better, I'd say he was trying to finesse me but I still couldn't figure out how.

"Alright, well. I have a busy day ahead of me but I'll call you tonight or something." I said as I opened the car door.

"Or something? Damn. Not even for sure?" He shook his head in disbelief.

"Oh. A nigga named Romeo in his feelings? That's cute." I said as I quickly got out of the car and closed the door behind me.

Romeo and I kept eye contact as I walked around the front of his car to the driver side. I could tell that he wanted to laugh just as badly as I did but we were having some sort of competition.

I opened his car door. "What? No hug?" I said with a smile while I rolled my eyes.

Romeo looked up at me and laughed. He was shocked that I was willing to hug him. It was the least I could do after he had given me ten bands and let me sleep in his guest room. I still didn't know if his behavior was off the strength of our connection or if it was a down payment for what he really wanted but I knew that I would have to contribute something if I wanted more from him. My issue was that not only did I not know if I was willing to contribute anything to receive more, but I was also unsure just how much I was allowed to contribute based on Dré's playbook.

Luckily I didn't run into Syd while Romeo and I said bye to each other. But on my drive home, I finally had time to process everything. I made sense of the conclusion I had come to after I spoke to her on the phone when I was at Romeo's spot. The fact that Sydney had a crush on me and seeing me with men, ate her up inside was really something I never saw coming. I can't imagine Dré saw it coming either. And I know for a fact he would have never thought her eating my pussy would've been a thing. Bitch, I didn't even know it could have ever been a thing.

Anyway, the rest of the day pretty much went exactly as planned. Well, except for dinner with Jake, I guess. Although I didn't have any specific expectations, it was underwhelming to say the least. I mean, I knew he didn't stand a chance with me but I didn't think his mind was as underdeveloped as it was. He didn't come off that way at the bar at all. Then again, I was super turnt that night so I could have very well completely overlooked it. I think having dinner with him was the first time I learned that you can be a blistering fool and still be rich. It was actually frustrating to listen to him talk about absolutely nothing because it felt like I had wasted time that I could have been spending with Abuelita, or even Romeo. It was almost insulting to know that the amount of work, research and brainstorming I do in one day was nowhere near what Jake even held the capacity to do in his entire lifetime. Yet he had the bag to fund my wildest dreams. Truth be told, if I played the game right, I probably would have been able to finesse him but he was so fucking stupid that I couldn't find the value in it and I wasn't willing to waste any more of my time with him.

However, Dré always taught me to take something valuable from every experience no matter how worthless it may seem. Seeing as though Jake had Mini Influencer on his resumé, I was able to get him to give me some game on how to grow my business with social media. One of the main things he really stressed was how important branding is. He said that content was going to play a major role in branding my business properly. Apparently, it was going to be the key to turning the followers I gained into loyal customers. The way he explained it was that on social media, if people like who you are, they will purchase whatever you sell. Which meant that ultimately, I was building two brands — one for myself and one for *Luxurious Cabello*. He explained to me that as long as I chose a specific market to target and got them to like me for me, they would be ready to purchase from any business I was associated with whether it was *Luxurious Cabello* or a damn foot scrub. And you know what, for somebody that was otherwise an idiot, he was fluent in social media branding and that alone made the dinner worth my time. I mean, I had already planned on never speaking to him again but I was glad that speaking to him at all didn't end up being in vain.

For the next month, my main focus was on Cosmetology school. There were a lot of things I had taught myself about hair but there were also a lot of things I didn't know at all so as time progressed, I was even more hopeful of the earning potential *Luxurious Cabello* had. And low key, it released some of the stress I felt from having to run the trucking business, finesse niggas and run plays too. The things I was learning in just the first month of school had me feeling like I was about to be the best braider Detroit had ever seen while selling the best hair products they had ever used. I had so many ideas for content that I would spend some nights just writing my ideas out rather than doing my homework. That habit was short-lived though because I knew that if I didn't do the homework, my grades would slip and I couldn't have that. See, more than anything, I wanted to be certified and able to say and prove that I had done shit the right way because nothing else in my life was being done the right way.

Dré and I would speak almost every day over the course of that month and he never asked about school one time. I know he was going through a lot being in jail and all, but my feelings were a little hurt. Part of that could have been because Romeo made it a point to ask me how class went every night and the only thing Dré ever wanted to talk about was how many fucking bottles of "blonde dye" Taboo had sent over, how much more time I thought I needed in order to successfully finesse Romeo and whether or not I was actively trying to meet other men that could be *finessed*. And I get it. Dré's main focus was making sure that I did what needed to be done for us to live a good life together when he came home but I had a lot going on too and I still made sure to ask Dré how he was holding up each day. I still made sure to put money on his books and I still made sure I sent him letters and photos every week so that he had something to look forward to. Therefore, I didn't think that wanting my man to ask me how Cosmetology school was going, was too much to ask.

Of course I never expressed that to anyone because who could I express it to? Was I supposed to sit at one of the private candlelit dinners Romeo and I had and tell him how bothered I was that my nigga was in jail forgetting to ask me how my day went? Was I supposed to tell Abuelita that Dré and I hadn't actually broken up and I was hurt that he wasn't being attentive enough from jail? Nope. To all of the above. I had no one to share my frustrations with and I didn't want to add more to Dré's plate by bringing it up to him so I just kept that shit to myself. There was no time for emotions, remember?

Speaking of emotions, Romeo and I started to get closer. He respected my time and my space and made sure that we spent time together at least one a week. I still hadn't told Dré about the money Romeo gave me, because I felt guilty. I wasn't supposed to catch feelings for anyone. I was supposed to finesse niggas for what I could and move on to the next one. I wasn't even supposed to give Dré's pussy away and I had already fucked that up too. With a girl at that. I was in over my head. I was way off book. Romeo hadn't done anything else as drastic as giving me large lump sums of money but he was making sure that I had all of the resources I needed to have the best braiding hair vendor I could have. To me, that was worth just as much as cashing me out and it was making me like him even more. I hadn't had sex with Romeo yet but I knew that it was only a matter of time.

I don't know if you remember this, but prior to Dré surprising me with the salon as a gift, I genuinely wanted to make it happen on my own. At first it was because I wanted something of my own that no one could take away from me no matter what. Obviously I suffered very deeply from some form of PTSD due to losing my parents at the same time which was the main reason I wanted the salon to be my own. I mean, I know that Ma was in jail and not dead like Daddy, but it all felt pretty much the same to me. Anyway, I knew that regardless of how I got the salon, Dré and I would use it to clean some of the money we got from the streets. It was in the plan as one of the ways we would go legit. You know, multiple streams and shit. But Dré getting locked up changed that. Unfortunately, Romeo helping me find hair vendors and being genuinely interested in my growth made me feel like I was getting shit done without Dré.

In other news, on top of everything else, I was damn near becoming a king pin. There were plenty of situations in the past where I was the one that connected with the plug instead of Dré and it was fine. Nobody ever tried to finesse me because they knew who I ran with. Plus, Blanco was always posted up somewhere nearby in case shit went bad. With Dré being locked down, not only was I the person that had to link with Taboo but we were damn near running a drug cartel out of the back of my salon and that wasn't anywhere in my playbook – ever. Cleaning money through the salon would have been one thing but actually running business out of it was some whole other shit. I was starting to despise Dré for making it so that my salon was the drop spot, the stash spot and the fucking headquarters because it gave my power away. It created a space where both me and my salon were susceptible to being taken away.

Taboo and I would link on Saturday mornings like clock work. He would pull up with boxes packaged with what appeared to be hair dye and I would carefully store them in the backroom that I had been transforming into a suite. On this particular Saturday morning, I pulled up to the salon and started to transfer the few hair dye boxes that remained in the backroom onto a three row shelf I had set up behind the front counter. My backroom suite had almost every-thing it needed for me to start the hiring process for a lash tech and I wanted to get that done as soon as I could so that I could start getting traffic into the salon and bringing in money that I earned from actual salon services and not trap shit.

Normally, I'd keep the front door locked until I saw Taboo standing there but this day, I was running late and I wanted to get the boxes transferred before he got there. It's stupid but I wanted to keep him out of the backroom because it was starting to look completely different than it did when he and I first met so it felt new. It felt like it was mine. Anyway, I was in the backroom, reaching for the last two boxes and I heard the front door toggle open.

I was irritated that I hadn't finished transferring the boxes. "Yo!" I yelled and rolled my eyes. "I'm back here." I said in order to let Taboo know that he could walk to the back of the salon as usual.

I could hear his footsteps as he got closer to the backroom.

As soon as his footsteps stopped, I heard, "Complacency creates chaos, Lux. You lookin' real complacent right now."

My heart dropped. The voice I heard didn't belong to Taboo. Shit, that man hardly ever spoke more than three words at a time so I'm not even sure I really knew what his voice sounded like. The voice I heard belonged to Blanco. I'm not going to lie, for a second, I thought I was trippin'. It had been more than a month since Dré told me that Blanco was coming home and I hadn't heard a word about it since that day.

Without turning my body around, I turned my head to put a face to the voice I had just heard.

"Blanc!! Oh my gosh!" I screamed and ran toward him.

"What up doe?" Blanco said through laughter as he met me for a hug.

"Oh my gosh!" Was all I could say.

We hugged for a moment longer and then I screamed again.

"How you doin, sis? The spot looks dope." He said as he looked around the salon.

"Man. I'm better now. I'm so happy to see you!" I smiled.

"Here." I said as I walked back into the suite. "Put these on the shelf behind the front counter." I said as I handed him the last two boxes of dye.

"Oh, you not wasting no time, huh? Right back to business." He said as he grabbed the boxes from me.

I laughed. "Sorry, bro. Taboo is about to pull up any second now and I don't want him coming in this room anymore." I said.

Blanco went into protection mode, stopped dead in his tracks and turned around to look at me. He gave me a look that I knew very well. Dré always told me that I was TTG but Blanco was the real savage. He was always ready for whatever, whenever, especially when it came to me. I mean, I had never seen him kill anyone and I doubt he ever did but I did see him rock a couple niggas before, so I knew.

"Slow down, turbo." I smiled as I made my way out of the suite. "I just got it poppin' in there and I'm getting ready to rent it out. That's all." I reassured him.

Just as I said that, Taboo opened the door of the salon and Blanco quickly turned around and reached behind his back into his waistband with the hand that wasn't holding the boxes of dye.

"Yo." I said to Taboo as I gently placed my hand onto Blanco's in an effort to let him know that everything was fine.

My heart was racing because Blanc had always been on top of his shit but I had never seen him actively reach for his gun before.

Taboo stopped in his tracks and Blanco kept his hand in place with mine over top of his.

"Taboo, this is Dré's right hand, Blanco. Blanco, this is Taboo. Tab – from now on, if it's not me, it's Blanc. Got it?" I ordered.

The best way for me to handle that situation was to be proactive and assertive. I couldn't leave room for any type of miscommunication because shit could have gone bad, fast.

Taboo looked unamused as Blanco kept his focus on him. "Yeah. I got you." He stared Blanco in his eyes. "Where do you want these?" He motioned toward the box carrying the dye.

Without saying a word, Blanco had finally taken his hand off of the handle of his gun and walked toward Taboo to pick up the box. Taboo didn't move any closer and didn't offer Blanco any help in unloading the box. I reached behind the counter and handed Taboo an envelope, he took a quick peek inside, thumbed through the money, tapped the envelope on the counter, gave Blanco one last look and walked out of the salon.

That was the moment I knew that things were getting ready to change. Blanco was home and he was more protective than he had ever been. As he loaded the shelf with the dummy boxes of hair dye, he checked each box as if he was making sure they really contained what they were supposed to. Something I hadn't even considered that morning.

I couldn't blame Blanc for being on high alert when Taboo pulled up to the salon because that's what he was trained to do. Let's not forget he was conditioned to believe that my life was worth more than his and on top of that, there was no telling what he experienced while he was on lock down for those months. But while I watched him load the boxes onto the shelf, I couldn't help but think about how hard it was going to be to explain the whole Romeo situation to him. Dré hadn't really discussed much of anything with me as it pertained to Blanc so I didn't know what he knew or didn't know. Ultimately, I decided that the best way to tell him about Romeo, was to just spit it out.

"Dré told you the play?" I asked from across the salon.

"Nah, run it." He said, still focused on the boxes.

I silently took a deep breath. "Well, basically, I'm supposed to finesse niggas out they pockets for the next five. Obviously keep running these plays with Taboo, but finesse niggas so that I can stack it up as much as possible." I said reluctantly.

I decided to leave out the part about our trucking company and the money Romeo had given me. Blanco would never have pressed me to tell him anything more than I voluntarily shared, so I wasn't too worried about any follow up questions.

To my surprise, Blanco asked, "What does finesse niggas out they pockets mean?"

I masked my nervousness as I said, "Meet them, finesse them and have them cash me out."

Blanco stopped stocking the shelf and turned to look at me. Confusion was written all over his face.

"Bro told you to do that?" He asked.

"Yup." I said with a sarcastic smirk on my face.

"You've been doing that by yourself?" He asked for clarity.

"Yup." I answered, with the same sarcastic smirk.

"Bet." Blanco looked away quickly and started stocking the shelf again.

I'm pretty sure neither of us ever questioned Dré's leadership in the past and we both made it a point not to do so at that moment but we knew that it felt weird. It was just so left field for Dré to say some shit like that. Especially with how big he was on loyalty. I knew that Blanco didn't like it but I also knew that he wasn't going to question it. Instead, he was going to do his part to keep me safe. His reaction was actually sort of comforting because I knew then that he wouldn't think twice about the time I was spending with Romeo because I was basically given an order to do so. From that moment, I decided that I would only tell Blanco certain things as it felt necessary. I didn't want him getting all worked up over nothing and I didn't want him telling Dré anything I needed to tell him first.

lexington rae williams.

WHEN BLANCO CAME HOME, my life started to move even faster than it had already been moving and to be honest, I felt really good about it. For the next six months, we were able to run the bag up double what I was doing on my own which gave me the ability to really get things moving in the salon. Even though I was still working on my certification, I hired two stylists and a lash tech which motivated me even more. It really felt like going legit was closer than planned.

I would visit Dré once a month, send him mail once a week and by that time, talk to him over the phone just a few times a week. I finally grew the balls to tell him that Romeo had given me some money but I downplayed it a lot. Instead of telling him the entire truth , I completely left out the fact that I was letting Romeo blow my back out and I made up two separate instances of where he supposedly gave me five bands. Dré was hype because in his mind, I was making progress and doing exactly what he had coached me to do.

The truth was that I was becoming resentful toward

Dré and falling for Romeo. So much so that Romeo and I started to plan to move out of state together. He wanted to take me and his kids to Atlanta and I didn't think it was such a bad idea. Honestly, I was tired. I was tired of living a double life. I was tired of being a fucking trap queen. I was tired of taking orders from and reporting back to Dré, too. The same way that I knew that our crew could do without him back in the day was the same way I was starting to see that I could do without him and it had only been just shy of a year since he had been gone. Having Romeo helped a lot, of course because he was finally funding everything I needed for *Luxurious Cabello* without even mentioning a return on his investment. He wanted every dollar I earned from the salon to be mine to do with as I pleased.

Romeo was the type of man that believed the streets were not the place for a woman but that's what I was used to. I was used to running plays with my man because that's what Dré taught me. I remember the first time I told Romeo that I felt like he was excluding me from his life by not introducing me to the crew or letting me run plays with him, he damn near lost his mind. Now, I had some fucking nerve even fixing my double life living ass mouth to tell him that he was excluding me from anything but I was on my shit enough to say it with confidence. He wasn't trying to hear it though.

"The streets is for bitches that can't hold a family down. Not for women like you. Shit, the streets don't deserve you. And if the streets get me, my legacy lives through my kids and the kids I'ma put in you. If the streets want me, all they have to do is get you. I'm willing to die about you. You're the reason I got my shit together so that we can leave all this shit alone. The streets don't deserve you, Lexy. And because of you, I know that they don't deserve me either." He told me.

Part of me allowed that to go in one ear and out the other because Dré was supposed to be getting out of the game too and we saw where he ended up. Part of me allowed it to go in one ear and out the other because I still loved Dré. I still felt like I had to be strong for him and loyal to him. If it weren't for him, I don't know when *Luxurious Cabello* would have come to life. Even deeper than that, if it weren't for Dré I don't know how I would have survived losing my parents. Dré saved my life. He changed my life. So the idea of falling in love with the nigga I was supposed to finesse on behalf of my future life with Dré, didn't feel right. On top of that, even though Romeo knew nothing about Blanco, he was a huge extension of me. His livelihood, and that of his newborn son, depended on the decisions I made. He was my family and I couldn't fold on him. And then there was Abuelita, of course. Her health was pretty stable but she was only getting older and there was no telling what type of stress it would put on her if I left her. Besides a daily phone call with Ma, I was all she had. Hell, I wouldn't even sleep at Romeo's house for more than a night at a time because it was too far from Abuelita. As a matter of fact, he ended up getting a two-story penthouse closer to the city so that I could spend more nights with him but Abuelita was still home no matter what.

Outside of the obvious, another reason Abuelita always had to be home was because it was the only way I was able to keep Blanco from peeping that Romeo was more than a nigga I was finessing. The way I saw it was that unless or until I made a definite decision to move to Atlanta with Romeo, I had to stick to the playbook to the best of my ability. I was deep in that shit and I knew that I had four years or less to either fall off the face of the Earth, or completely end things with Romeo.

Now that I think about it, everybody attached to me

was being finessed by me in one way or another. And I don't want to say that it was easy, because it was far from that, but I was running a tight ship. With Blanco being a new dad, I made it so that the only time he needed to be away from his girl and his child was when we were running plays and during the hours I was at the salon. When I wasn't at the salon, I was with Romeo or Abuelita. Even though Blanc was under the impression that my situation with Romeo was very basic, he insisted on not becoming complacent; which was why he would still post up outside of our date nights. Besides that, I gave him the address to the penthouse Romeo had gotten for us. Whenever I would spend a few nights at the penthouse, I would share my location with Blanco and he would check in on me a few times throughout the day. Blanco knew my schedule like he knew his own, so he'd call me every morning around the time I should have been on my way to where I was headed so that he could make sure I was solid. Whenever I would talk to or see Dré, I'd make sure he felt secure in the fact that I had my feelings in check. I had to make him feel as though it made more sense for me to finesse one nigga with a bag than it did for me to spread myself thin trying to finesse multiple. With Blanco as his eyes on the outside, Dré was under the impression that shit was going smooth. And to be honest, I thought it was.

It wasn't until I had a pregnancy scare that I started to experience a little turbulence in my life. One night Romeo and I had gotten super turnt because the samples of my braiding hair and packaging had been delivered to the salon and I couldn't have been happier with the quality of the hair or the design of the packaging. Romeo was genuinely happy just off the strength of my happiness. It's funny because I remember spending six hours putting Bohemian style twists in my hair using *Luxurious Cabello* hair and then driving up to the rooftop of our penthouse in the same black dress that I had worn on my first date with Romeo, to take photos for social media. Jake's advice to be a walking billboard was never lost on me but I wanted to wait until it made the most sense for me to pop out. With school graduation being around the corner and the hair samples and packaging being perfect, I was ready to turn shit up.

That same night during our celebratory turn up at the penthouse, Romeo fucked me in that little black dress. You would have thought he had never seen it before the way he was gassing me up all night. It must have been the new hairstyle because he was all over me, congratulating me, telling me how beautiful I was and how much I meant to him and shit. He was more turnt than usual because we were in the house – safe. Any other night, his pull out game was strong but that night he just couldn't do it.

Now, Romeo had already planned to spend the rest of his life with me but like I just mentioned, I was still very much unsure if that's what I wanted. With that being said, I was pressured the fuck up when my period was late. I couldn't focus for shit and Blanco noticed that I was unfocused.

He kept saying, "Tighten up, Lux. Chess is a long game."

For about a week, I had no desire to do anything. One day I almost missed a meeting at the salon with Taboo but Blanc pulled up to Abuelita's house and practically bullied me into hopping into his car so that we could handle our business. It wasn't like him to be that assertive but he had no idea what I was going through and times were way different so I didn't even think anything of it beyond my brother wanting to make sure I stayed on top of my shit. Needless to say, I wasn't pregnant. Thank God.

Anyway, that pregnancy scare was what finally slowed

me down enough to make time to go visit Daddy. Blanc and I had actually gotten into a small argument because he insisted on escorting me to Daddy's grave and I insisted on doing it alone. I had to remind him that I had been doing shit on my own before he came home and if nothing else, I was going to sit face to stone with my daddy alone. Period. Blanco wasn't thrilled about it but he had no choice. Honestly, the thought that I might have been pregnant had me shook and I needed to be alone. It put everything into perspective for me and I knew that it was time for me to make some very serious life changes and hard choices.

At Daddy's grave, there was one single blue rose left from the last time I had visited him. Somehow, even though it was wilted, the rose managed to maintain its color over all of those months. When I sat down, I picked the rose up and smelled it, just to see if it still held the scent of a rose.

Before even speaking to Daddy, I closed my eyes and tears started to stream down my cheeks. It was the first time in months I had made time for emotions. While my eyes were closed, it was like I started dreaming, but I was awake. The same glass chess board from before, the one with the clear and frosted pieces had made its way back to me. I could see the pieces clearly as if they were right there in front of me. The board was spinning around in circles as if it was on some sort of turntable and the king piece had fallen. Between every spin, I could see myself holding the blue rose as I walked up a spiraled staircase that I had never seen before. I was wearing all black – the same exact outfit I wore when I visited Dré in jail for the first time. Out of nowhere, the chess board stopped spinning and even though I couldn't see myself, I knew that it was my hand that knocked over the remaining pieces. As soon as the pieces fell in the dream or vision or whatever the fuck it was, I gasped for air as if my breath had been taken away and my eyes opened.

When I opened my eyes, I looked around me just as a reflex but I was the only one at the cemetery. For so many years, I had always had somebody watching me so I know what it felt like to have eyes on me from a distance and that's what it felt like that day. Like somebody was watching me. Blanco insisted that I shared my location with him since I wouldn't let him post up, so I checked his location and he was nowhere near the cemetery, so I thought I was just losing my fucking mind.

I laughed to myself and then said, "I'm losing my mind, Daddy."

I sat there in silence for a second, waiting for Daddy's energy to find me.

And then I said, "You think Ma was scared when she found out she was pregnant?" Obviously I knew that I wouldn't get an answer to that question but it was the only thing on my mind.

I took a deep breath. "I thought I was pregnant. I'm not. But I thought I was. It made me think about Ma though. Like… what it must have been like for her, you know? She was lucky to have you. I mean, for the most part. You left her. You left us. But you came back. You did your time and then you came back for us." I was thinking out loud.

My thoughts were all over the place. "Why'd you do it? Huh? Why'd you put your hands on Mommy?"

I had never once spoken to Daddy about the abuse he had put my mother through. Ever.

I continued. "She loved you, you know? I bet she still does. She's rotting away in a cell, but she probably still loves you. It's funny isn't it? How love and loyalty work. Mommy suffered at your hands on a regular basis but she still gave you all of her. She still put on a smile and gave me the very best version of her no matter what. She weathered every storm you put her through, just to keep our family together. She loved you so much." I started to cry again. "She loved you so much that she allowed you to destroy her."

I allowed myself to cry for a little bit longer and then I completely shifted gears.

I took a deep breath. "Anyway, the salon is doing well. I got two girls in there doing hair and another one doing lashes. Pretty soon I'm going to have Abuelita pull up everyday to hold the front desk down. I'm going to start selling braiding hair, too. That's where the real bag is at. My shipment will be here in like two weeks and I'ma run it up. From the streets to the salon." I laughed. "A real life success story. I wish you and Ma were here to see it."

For the next hour, I just sat in my own company. My thoughts went back and forth between whether or not I should've kept playing Dré's game or started a new life with Romeo. The idea of leaving everything and everyone behind and completely starting over in New York or some other city too big to find me in also crossed my mind. Somehow, my thoughts took me back to the days that I would sit in the corner of my bedroom with the headphones Ma had given me to block out the sound of her cries. And then my mind went blank again. Everything felt wrong. The weird vision or dream that happened when I first sat down paired with the lasting feeling that I was being watched, felt wrong too. I finally understood why Dré always pressed the issue of not making time for emotions. My emotions were feeling like a black hole. There was no more time for emotions.

After telling Daddy that I loved him, I told him that I'd do my best to visit him more often but I needed to take some time. The things I said to him shocked me. They were questions that I deserved answers to but they were also questions I didn't even know I had.

"I'm sorry I didn't bring you any flowers. You still deserve 'em." I said as I walked away.

Before leaving the cemetery, I sent Blanco a text to let him know that I was heading to Abuelita's house but he insisted that we link at the salon instead. He was getting on my last fucking nerve that day but I knew that if he insisted on an in-person link, it had to be about business. Business always came first, so I told him I'd be at the salon in fifteen minutes.

I hadn't spoken to Romeo for a few hours that day, so I called him on my way to the salon. Linking up with Blanco was unplanned and to completely avoid complacency, I wanted to make sure that I didn't put myself in a position where Romeo popped up unannounced just because he hadn't heard from me all day. Granted, Blanco would have been able to come up with something off the top of his head as to who he was and why he was at the salon with me, but I didn't like the odds. Not with the way I was feeling that day.

When I pulled up to the salon, I let Romeo know that I'd call him when my day was over and then we hung up the phone. You know that I used to feel so calm and collected after I visited Daddy but that day, I was still feeling extra paranoid so I sat in my car longer than I usually would so that I could scan the block a little longer. Everything looked fine. There was nothing out of place or unusual, I figured I was just on edge.

Anyway, the salon was closed by that time. The girls had gone home for the day and locked everything up just like they were supposed to. I knew Blanco would be pulling up soon so I finally decided to go inside. To my surprise, he was already inside. You can imagine that my soul jumped out of my fucking body considering the fact that I was already on edge.

"Oh, shit. You scared me. My nigga, why are you just sitting in here like this? Why didn't you tell me you were already here?" I was genuinely confused and bothered.

"My bad, Lux." Blanco's energy was off.

"All good. What's up. Why did we need to link?" I asked as I placed my purse down onto the front counter.

"I have a family now, Lux." Blanco said. His gaze was blank.

He wasn't looking me in the eyes when he started speaking, so I thought he was getting ready to give me the *I quit* speech.

"I know, Blanc. I'm doing my best. How much you need?" I insisted.

Everybody can be bought. It doesn't matter if you're a man or a woman, you have a price. There's a payment that can and will convince you to stay a little longer, do a little more, or give something up. Whatever it is, there's a price. Even if that means a price to entertain the idea of accepting the payment. Whether that payment is monetary or not, is up to you. But there's a price. Everybody can be bought. Blanco didn't just come from the streets. He came from the trenches. I told you before that he never really spoke much about his past, but I knew it was the reason Dré took him in. I knew it was the reason he hustled so hard and stayed so loyal. I didn't even know if I wanted to stay but I knew that whatever his price was, I was willing to pay it until I figured my shit out.

Blanco's face had confusion all over it. "Nah, Lux. It ain't even like that. You my family. But shit is different now.

I need to be here for my son. I need to be a better father than my pops was. I need to be a better man for my girl. I need to give my son a chance, Lux." His eyes started to gloss over as if he was going to cry.

Before I could even find the words to say, a team of police officers swarmed out of the back room and another team through the front door.

"Put your hands where I can see them! Now!" An officer yelled with a gun pointed at me.

My ears rang and my vision became blurry. The officers threw me to the ground and placed my hands behind my back. As I laid face down on the floor of my salon, *Back Door by Pop Smoke* played in my head for a moment and then I must have blacked out because the next thing I remember was being on my feet with my hands cuffed behind my back. The officers were all huddled around me as a female officer searched me. So much confusion filled my mind and then I remembered that Blanco had been at the salon with me so I tilted my head to look beyond all of the officers just to see that Blanco was still sitting in the same chair he was sitting in before the raid. He sat there hopeless and helpless and tears rolled down his cheeks. There wasn't a single officer around him and that was when I knew that he insisted we link because he set me up. Blanco. My brother. My family. Dré's right hand man, set me up.

I knew better than to say a word so I just stood there burning a hole through Blanco with my eyes. I was waiting for him to look at me. I wanted him to see me. I wanted him to see what he had done. I wanted him to see that I knew exactly what went down but he didn't even have the balls to look at me. When the officer finished searching me, she told the other officers that I was good to go.

A male officer placed his hands in the middle of my handcuffs and said, "Lexington Williams, you're under arrest for drug trafficking, possession of a controlled substance, possession with intent to sell and money laundering. Anything you say can and will be used against you in a court of law. You have the right to have an attorney present…"

My ears went deaf as the officer finished reading me my rights and escorted me out of my salon. As he placed his hand on the back of my head as if he cared whether or not it was protected to place me in the back of the squad car, it started to make sense why Blanco had gotten out of jail dumb early. They bought him. His price was his freedom and their price was mine. After everything we had been through together, Blanco *finessed* me. He *finessed* Dré. I laughed to myself as the police car drove away from my salon because I was so caught up finessing everybody around me that I became complacent. Complacency creates chaos and I hadn't known a chaos like the chaos of losing my own freedom.

Once we finally got to the jail, booking me took the jailers hours and the only thing I could think of was Abuelita. It didn't matter that Blanco had set me up. It didn't matter that Romeo would have no idea what had happened to me or that I would have to explain so much to him if or when I finally spoke to him. The only thing that mattered was that I let down the one person who had never left me. The only form of consistency I had ever known was Abuelita. The only person I had left that knew the purest form of me, was Abuelita. I was all she had left the same way she was all I had and I let her down. My heart ached for her. When I got my phone call, I could hear the pain in her voice when we were connected. I could feel the joy leave her heart and the peace leave her spirit. I was the last thing holding my abuelita together and I left her.

Believe it or not, I ended up being transported to the

exact same jail my mother was at. Like mother, like daughter, right? Imagine her surprise when I walked past her cell to be placed in mine. God has a funny way of sitting you down to heal. I spent so much time avoiding the thoughts and feelings associated with my mother just to end up in the same place she was. I spent so much time being angry with her for her decisions and convincing myself that my decisions were so much different than hers, just for me to end up right where she was.

I was sentenced to five years in prison. Here I am with four years to go and now I understand what my mother meant by not allowing my strength to weigh me down. Now I understand what she meant by protecting myself in the storm. Now I understand what she meant by releasing the burden when it becomes too heavy to bear. For so many years, I refused to make time for emotions only to have nothing but time for them. For so many years I refused to face my past because it was too painful, only for my past to become my destiny.

Abuelita died. Alone, because of me. She died about six months after they got me. I'll never be able to forgive myself for it. I'll be out of here before I'm thirty, free to start over and create a new life for myself but knowing that my angel spent her last days alone makes me feel like I don't even deserve that freedom.

On the other hand, my mother and I have started the process of mending our relationship. Today, our conversations come from a space of love and healing as opposed to heartache and resentment. Jail is one hell of a place to start that journey but I guess I'm still finding the value in things no matter how worthless they seem, just like Dré taught me to do.

It's unfortunate that both me and Ma ended up in jail for the same reason. A man. We were surrounded by other women that were in jail for that reason too. So many women on our block were inside for doing something to, for or behind a man and that really pisses me off. I've listened to everyone's story at least twice since I've been here. Every story shares one thing: a woman who didn't leave a man that was no good for her. The idea that as women, as nurturers, we've all allowed a man's feelings, safety or livelihood to trump our own, doesn't make sense to me. I don't understand why they allowed it and I don't understand why I allowed it either.

It's funny because I realize now that had I given my mother a chance – if I had just spent the time it took to hear her out, I probably wouldn't be in here with her. She tried to tell me that Dré was no different than Daddy and I wasn't trying to hear it. She tried to tell me that I was following in her footsteps and I just wasn't trying to hear it. Instead, I was sitting at Daddy's grave telling him how much Dré reminded me of him like it was a good thing. I refused to listen to what my mother had to say to me because of all the pain and resentment I had toward her. I was so angry with her for leaving me that I refused to heal myself. I refused to forgive her. I refused to listen to Lexington; the child version of myself who just wanted to be free. I knew better but every ounce of pain that I harbored from my childhood prevented me from making better decisions as an adult and now I'm paying for it. Romeo was right. The streets don't love nobody.

get lock'd in.

Hi, Friend!

I can't wait to hear from you! Get lock'd in from your favorite social. Don't forget to visit my website and subscribe to my email list so that you can stay up to date on all the Kee Notes + get exclusives & discount codes!

cute & chaotic here .. @ _ _ _ lowkee | **IG**
hardly here .. @authorbae_ | Twitter
it's complicated .. @keenotepublishing| **FB**
the safe .. www.keenotepub.com | Subscribe

also by lowkee

Looking for a spicy trilogy? I got you!

Sideb!tch: A Twisted Love Story

Exies: The Final Act of Love

Toxic: We're No Good For Each Other

www.keenotepub.com

also available on amazon.